The Rage

By

Shelley Crowley

PART I – The Discovery

Chapter 1

Gabriel crossed his legs at his ankles and sighed in bliss, lifting the mug of blood to his lips whilst catching up on the new BBC drama he had been finding rather compelling. Although he did think the story only needed three episodes, there was no need to drag it out for six.

"I bet he's a dirty cop."

Gabriel glowered at the TV. He'd forgotten he had company.

"Yes, he's obviously a dirty cop," he replied.

"I don't know how you sit and watch these things. The *twists* are obvious from the start."

"If you're just going to sit there and complain, you know where the door is." He finally turned and shot a pointed look at Ezra, sitting in the corner playing on his phone.

Ezra let out an overdramatic sigh. "I'm *bored.*"

"My job is boring. You were the one that wanted to come with me-"

They both looked to the wall when they heard fitful groans from the next room. They were loud. Ezra's eyebrows quirked up. "What's going on in there?"

Gabriel turned back to the TV. "He has pretty bad night terrors. Wakes up thinking there's a demon living in his house trying to suck out his soul."

"Is said demon lounging in his recliner watching shitty police dramas by any chance?"

Gabriel smirked over the rim of his mug.

When a crash followed the groans, Gabriel picked himself up and went to check on the old man. As soon as he was on his feet, Ezra dropped himself into the vacated chair. His hand went for the mug of blood but he was prevented by a thwack of a walking stick on his knuckles. He yelped and glared at Gabriel.

Gabriel pointed the walking stick at him. "You said you came here for my company. Hands off the goods."

Ezra pulled a face. "Bet it's all thin and mealy anyway."

Not trusting Ezra one bit, Gabriel took his mug into Julian's bedroom with him. The old man was hanging half off the bed, his clock on the floor behind the door. He was gasping for air, his full head of snowy white hair plastered to his scalp with sweat like a swimming cap. Gabriel placed his mug on the cabinet and helped the old man back upright.

"Oh, Gabriel," Julian gasped. "He was here again. Scratching me with his huge claws!"

"Everything's okay, Julian, I'm here." *And I get a bi-weekly manicure, thank you very much.* "Sit up for me now. There you go. Let me get you some water."

He filled up a mug in the kitchen and returned. The old man took it in his feeble hands but Gabriel had to help him bring the mug to his lips. They seemed to be a shade whiter. Gabriel wondered how long this stash would last. A couple of weeks at the most. Although Julian McGowen was a fighter. He'd already outlasted his neighbour, Mrs. Buttersfield, and she had been ten years younger than him. She did have kidney failure, though. It gave her blood an acidic quality. Not the best.

When a noise came from the kitchen, Julian nearly choked on his water. His pebbly eyes, yellowed with cataract, flew to Gabriel, fear alight in them.

"It's okay. I brought a friend over. Everything's okay."

"A friend?" the old man asked. "You don't usually bring friends over."

Gabriel inwardly seethed. "No, no I don't." *It wasn't my choice, trust me.*

"Becca says she sees you with a lovely lady. Is it her?"

Gabriel laughed lightly. "No, it's not her. Now, let's get you more comfortable so you can go back to sleep, okay?" He took the mug from the old man and helped him slide further down the bed so his head rested on the pillow. "Comfy? Okay, great. I'll just be in the living room if you need me."

"What are you even doing?" Gabriel dropped both mugs in the sink.

Ezra closed one of the kitchen cupboards with a shrug. "Just being nosey. The guy's got a whole drawer full of shortbread."

"Well, you've outstayed your welcome. Julian is skitty enough as it is without having a stranger in his house."

"Oh, so what does that make you? A friend?"

"Leave, Ezra. I mean it."

"You're not as subtle as you think you are, you know? There's been more deaths here since we've moved in. People are starting to notice."

"Yeah, and all those deaths have been people already about to croak."

Ezra gazed out of the window into the back garden, clearly trying to look wise and distant. "I'm telling you. This is a small village. People are gonna get suspicious."

"If anything, I'm helping this place. Old people are such a burden. What do they provide for this community? Nothing. I'm giving them painless deaths and ridding their families of their responsibilities."

Ezra just looked at him and headed to the back door. "Whatever helps you sleep better," he said before leaving. Gabriel rolled his eyes. That expression didn't even make sense for a vampire. *We sleep when the suns up no matter what.*

It wasn't until 7.00am when Gabriel was disturbed again. From his seat in front of the TV, he heard Becca heading up the driveway. He went to the sink to double check he had washed his mug and hung around looking busy until she came in. His throat automatically grew tight when the glass panelled door to the kitchen swooped open and their eyes locked.

"Anything to report?" she said in her usual chirpy manner.

Gabriel leaned back against the counter trying to look casual. "Nope. Just the usual. All night medication is done."

She smiled and his jaw clenched. She didn't smile at him like she used to. She smiled at him like the help. Being polite to keep up appearances.

"Is he awake?"

"I don't think so. But I'll help you get him to his chair."

She smiled that smile again. When she turned around to put her bags on the dining table, Gabriel squeezed his eyes shut and rubbed them. The silence that rang between them was stifling, but filling it with mindless chatter was just as bad.

Becca came back into the kitchen, now stripped of her big winter coat.

Underneath she was wearing a flowery dress, and wool tights. He couldn't help but find her dedication to summer dresses endearing. It was 6 degrees outside.

"I'll go check on him and call you in."

Gabriel nodded and she left.

He waited, staring out the window, listening into their conversation.

"Another nightmare? Perhaps it's your medication. Did you sleep through the night?" her voice was so soft when she spoke to her grandfather.

"Oh, it was terrible, Becca. So clear! I swear it's like it was right here. Gabriel heard me and gave me some water. He had a friend over. Not the lady, I asked. I think he's still single."

"*Gran*dad."

"You know, I don't think he's dated anyone since you."

"Stop it now. We're not talking about this."

"I think he still likes you."

Gabriel's gut twisted.

"It's better this way. I need a man who shows up. And things would have just gotten complicated anyway. He's your care nurse. I want you to be his top priority."

"But I'm just an old man. And you do so much for me. You're nearly thirty. You're beautiful. You deserve a life of your own, Becks. A lovely man to take you on romantic getaways so you can stop worrying about silly old me."

"I will never stop worrying about you. And I hope you're not talking to Gabriel like this. I don't need you to be my matchmaker."

"Of course not. I wouldn't embarrass you like that."

Becca laughed. "Oh, I have some tales to tell to prove you wrong. Gabriel and I will bring you into the living room for breakfast, okay?"

Hearing his cue, Gabriel started heading down the hallway. Becca popped her head around the bedroom door.

"Oh." Her eyes brightened when she saw him ready. "Perfect timing." Her cheeks flushed.

Ezra lay in bed, listening to Gabriel making his way to his bedroom. He'd been cutting it fine. The sun was going to be up in less than half an hour. But he wasn't going to say anything because he wouldn't listen. He also wasn't going to say anything about the sinking feeling he'd been having in his gut the past few nights. There was something in the air. He couldn't quite put his finger on it but he just felt like this was a calm before the storm. There was going to be a shift of some sort. Perhaps it was because this was the longest the three of them had stayed in the same location. Perhaps he was just not used to 'settling down'. They had all made roots here in the past five years. Maybe Ezra felt content? A feeling he wasn't used to.

Whatever the odd sensation was, it was forgotten about as soon as the sun came up and he surrendered to his comatose state of slumber.

7

Ezra rolled out of bed with just enough time to shower and dress before his shift at the pub started. He crossed paths with Gabriel in the hallway.

"Fridge is looking low," Gabriel said, flattening down the collar of his navy, wax jacket.

"I'm going to the city tomorrow. Should I get extra for you?"

Gabriel gave him an exhausted look. "I've got mine covered."

Ezra mirrored his expression. He was fighting a losing battle, he knew it. But he was basically an ancient. At first it had been a blessing to have stopped aging at twenty, to be fresh-faced and youthful forever had its perks. But when it came down to trying to be taken seriously by Gabriel, Ezra was sure the bird-boned, boy body packaging that his knowledge and experience was wrapped up in was why he struggled so much.

"Anyway." Gabriel sat on the stairs and shoved on his soft-soled care nurse trainers. "I'd better get going. Claudia gets pissy if I'm not there at shift change."

"Alright, have a good night." And just like that, it was like there had never been an altercation. Ezra and Gabriel had been dancing the same dance since they'd been brought together back in the late 1960s. Big festivals were the perfect hunting ground for their kind. Because drugs didn't have an effect on them, the only way to get high was by drinking from someone under the influence. And with everyone hopped up on hallucinogens at those kinds of functions, stealth was no longer required. There was something so tantalizing about the 60s. The hedonistic lifestyle meant that everyone was free to be who they wanted to be, even those like Ezra and Gabriel.

They had met out there among the field of writhing bodies, the music of the bands mixing in with the intoxicating rhythms of erratic heartbeats.

Back then there had been others, but, like with any friendship group, they had drifted apart. Some joined Nests. Some moved countries. Some died. Ezra and Gabriel entered the 80s with only each other. Gone were the recreational drug fuelled parties under the moonlight with strangers, replaced with moving from place to place, never staying long enough to form attachments to anyone else, all the while shame eating in the back of dark, dank alleys.

The two of them had been through a lot together and even though Gabriel liked to give him attitude every now and again, Ezra knew he wouldn't still be living with him if he didn't actually want to.

Ezra strolled into the kitchen and opened the fridge. Three milk bottles of blood rattled in the door. There was very little on the shelves. A couple of peppers, some butter, and two packs of eggs. If it hadn't been for his progeny's incessant need to cook, even if she couldn't eat the food herself, there wouldn't be anything else in there at all.

He filled a saucepan with one of the bottles of blood, drank down a mug and filled his thermos with the rest. He chucked the thermos into his backpack and headed to the door.

"Later, Lillian!" he called up the stairs. It was more of a routine than anything. He knew she was a heavy sleeper; the new ones always were.

The kid was on his phone again. Did he actually think standing behind the bar smiling down at his crotch didn't look suspicious? But, no matter how unprofessional it looked, it wasn't Ezra's place to say anything. He wasn't the manager. He could have been in charge of this place if he wanted to be. He had more than enough experience. But it always got confusing when he was asked to elaborate on said experience. How could a twenty-year-old have worked in hospitality for over fifteen years? It was just best to keep a low profile.

He wiped down the tables and brought the empty glasses back behind the bar. There he could clearly see Mitch scrolling through a news article. The News? Usually he was liking some Instagram model's half naked pictures.

Mitch caught Ezra looking and instead of putting his phone away, he saw Ezra's interest as permission to lean against the bar with his phone now on full display.

"You see this yesterday?"

Ezra shook his head.

"About the club that got raided?"

Ezra looked about the bar warily.

Mitch laughed. "Relax. It's dead in here." He waggled his phone and Ezra gave in. He came up beside him and leaned his forearms on the bar top to get a better look at the screen. As he read, he felt his legs start to go numb. His throat went dry. The backs of his eyes burned when he saw the picture of the club cordoned off with police tape. The club he had been planning to go to tomorrow night to pick up his next supply.

"Can you believe that shit?" Mitch let out a wild laugh. He was the type of guy that found the humour in everything. It made him a decent guy to work with – despite his lack of front of house etiquette. But this was no laughing matter. Ezra felt dizzy with this new information. He straightened and ran his hands through his tousled hair.

Mitch watched him and quirked an eyebrow. "You don't actually think it's real do you?" He looked back at his screen and kept scrolling. "I'm telling you. Just read the comments. It's a load of bullshit. I'm sure it's just some weird cult or something. Satanists. They exist, right? They do a load of dodgy shit like sacrificing chickens and whatnot."

Ezra leaned back against the bar. His eyes were trained on the minifridge of beers but he felt like the ground was tilting.

"Whenever there's blood involved, it's cult shit. I mean, they were down in the club *basement.* And did you read how those guys were dressed? All in black leather and latex? Latex… huh. Actually, maybe it's some sex thing."

"I'm going on my break," Ezra said and quickly headed into the back. He opened the fire door and looked up at the night sky.

He knew there had been a weird feeling in the air these past few nights. He'd sensed something was going to happen. Something that was going to completely upturn life as he knew it.

He took his phone out of his pocket and paused, taking a deep, calming breath, before typing the one word that now seemed to be on everyone's lips.

VAMPIRE.

Chapter 2

Ezra held his phone to his ear, feeling more and more panicked the longer the ringing continued. When it went to voice-mail, he sent a text instead.

'*Just heard about the raid. Is everyone okay? What's happened?'*

Staring down at his phone screen, he searched within himself for his bond. Not his bond to Lillian, but the bond to his own Maker. It was still there, faint due to distance, but there. Ezra closed his eyes with relief. At least his Maker wasn't dead.

For the remainder of his break, he sat on the doorstep staring at the screen, chewing the inside of his cheek as he awaited a response.

"Dude, it's suddenly got super rammed. Gonna need you back," said Mitch, slapping the doorjamb. When Ezra turned to look at him, he furrowed his brows. "You okay?"

"Yeah, yeah." Ezra got to his feet.

"You sure? You look spooked."

Ezra walked past him. "Yeah, I'm fine. We've got customers waiting."

Ezra felt like he was on autopilot for the rest of his shift; he barely remembered serving anyone. He spent the next four hours either checking the clock or his phone. *Now who's being unprofessional?*

When it finally got to 2am, he handed the keys to Mitch to lock up and headed home to grab the car. He usually vampire-sprinted his way to the city but with what the News was covering at the moment, he felt it was best to be extra cautious, even if it did mean the journey would take twice as long.

The blue Audi station wagon had been Lillian's car when she had been human and married to her boring accountant husband, Derek. He had bought the car for her as a way to apologise for being a workaholic. Now the three of them shared the vehicle. It wasn't to Gabriel's and Ezra's tastes but it saved them from clogging up their narrow street with three separate cars.

It was just coming up to 4am when Ezra drove by *Moonlight*. The windows were bordered up and the police tape was still there. Usually at this time, the club would still be heaving, with groups out in the smoking area making new friends and girls trying to chat up the security guards.

Ezra kept driving until he found the other club he frequented. *Black Velvet* was still in business. He found a parking space a few streets away and headed inside, not without being stopped by the bouncer at the door. Ezra showed him his fake driver's license and popped out his fangs. The bouncer nodded and stepped aside.

Black Velvet was much more lowkey than *Moonlight*. It was a simply decorated club with low ceilings and high stools – velvet, of course. For a Thursday night, it was pretty empty. There were a few groups in the booths and a couple of people lingering around the bar, but there was a melancholy feeling in the air.

The music was slow and sensual. The red strip lighting beneath the bar and booths that pulsed to the rhythm of the song added to the sexy feeling. Ezra spotted his friend behind the bar and crossed the dancefloor.

"Dalia," Ezra said in greeting, showing the bartender an easy smile.

"Thought you'd stopped doing business with us," replied Dalia with a smile of her own. The woman had thick black hair pulled up in a messy ponytail. Her skin was almost just as dark, making her smile a striking flash of light. She was dressed in her signature black corset and leather trousers.

"You know it's nothing personal." Ezra eased onto a bar stool.

"I know. You can't stand the heat." She winked.

The truth was, *Black Velvet* attracted the kinds of vampires out to find an extra body or two to join them in the bedroom, and so were very much *not* Ezra's sort of people.

"I tried calling Silas but I'm not getting through. What the hell happened?"

"You not watched the News?"

"I read an article but I couldn't get my head around it. Seemed like they were holding a lot of story."

Dalia shook her head and sighed. "It was a drug bust."

"What?"

"Humans were claiming they went there for nights out and forgot what happened. It's been going on a while and I guess they just brushed it off as people getting too drunk. But then it just kept happening so police probably thought it was some spiking situation. Of course, we know it was rookie vampires not compelling right." Dalia looked tired of the whole thing. "So yeah, police raided the place and found a bunch of vamps drinking from humans down in the basement." She leaned back against the back counter, folded her arms over her chest and let out a bitter laugh. "And now we're all in the shit, aren't we?"

Ezra was silent for a moment as he processed what she'd just said. The News had said nothing about drugs – just that the club was raided for reasons that were not being disclosed. He had been to *Moonlight* at least twice a month for the past five years and, of course, he knew that they bled humans there. It was where he got his stash from. But he'd had no idea that they had vampires actually *drinking from the vein* hiding in the basement.

Dalia was smirking at him. "And you thought this place was too seedy for you."

"But… how could they be so *stupid?*" Ezra could feel anger, hot and acidic, boiling in his chest.

"Apparently vamps pay good money to drink from the vein in a comfortable and *safe* environment."

Ezra shook his head, disappointed with his species. "What's gonna happen to this place? You had police here?"

"Nah." Dalia looked down at the floor. Ezra could tell that she was trying to act cool and casual for the sake of saving face. This raid was a big deal, they both knew it. Being the owner of a vampire bar was not a good situation to be in right now. "We're good. But if you need new supplies, you'd better get them now because I'm gonna have to cut people off, at least 'til this blows over."

By the way she was watching her boots and hugging herself tightly, it was clear she didn't want to discuss this matter any further.

"I'll take twenty bottles of 0 negative, if you've got it."

"Sure." Dalia pushed herself off the counter. "But you're gonna have to buy a regular drink too, club policy."

"A pint of your cheapest beer, please."

She smiled and poured his drink. It was obvious she needed a distraction, so Ezra was going to sit and nurse his disgusting human drink and keep her company until that smile looked real.

Ezra returned home at just past 6am, with about an hour to spare until sun-up. He sensed that Gabriel was home even before hearing his TV on in his bedroom. He also sensed Lillian in her room, asleep but not alone. His jaw clenched. He'd deal with her at sundown.

In bed, Ezra lay in the dark, staring at the ceiling. He had a dilemma. Should he tell them about what was happening? If they hadn't heard it already. Perhaps it was best to hear things from him? Gabriel would dismiss the whole thing – tell them that there was nothing to worry about. But Lillian would panic. She'd only been a vampire for twenty years. She wasn't ready to deal with something of this magnitude.

In truth, was he?

It was 6pm when Ezra awoke and headed downstairs. It was his night off but he really wished it wasn't. With nothing to do, his mind was playing his conversation with Dalia on a loop. He had been right in thinking that she had needed company last night. They had reminisced about the past. About how they had both moved around throughout their lives. Dalia had lived in almost every European country in the past seventy years and was considering moving again. Ezra hadn't asked, but he knew why. But if the government started sniffing around for vampires here in England, how long would it take the rest of the world to follow?

"Good evening."

Ezra looked up from the table to his company. Lillian strolled into the kitchen in her fluffy pink nightgown and matching slippers. Ezra's smile fell when she was closely followed by Ben.

"So, he's staying over now?" Ezra arched his eyebrow at Ben over his steaming mug of blood.

Ben audibly gulped and his wide eyes found Lillian like a frightened child.

"Be nice." Lillian swatted Ezra playfully on the shoulder. "Want me to make you some eggs?"

Ben smiled enthusiastically but then caught Ezra's death glare. "Actually, I'd bet get going."

"You sure, hun?"

Ezra watched him. "Yeah, you sure, hun?"

"Stop that." Lillian swatted him again, this time with an oven mitt.

Ezra put down his mug. "But seriously. What do you do all day when she's out cold, huh?"

Ben shrugged, pulling at the hem of his checked shirt awkwardly. "I dunno… play on my phone. Watch Youtube videos."

"While she's just lying there like a corpse next to you? Please don't tell me you cuddle her."

"Well-" He looked to Lillian for help.

Ezra's lip curled up with disgust. "That's creepy, dude." He shook his head. "So creepy."

A beat of silence followed.

"So." Lillian clapped her hands together. "Eggs?"

"No, really, I'd really better get going." Ben dropped a quick peck on Lillian's cheek, very clearly avoiding Ezra's gaze, before swiftly exiting the room. "I'll see you later!"

When they heard the front door shut, Ezra was whacked again. He smiled.

"Why do you have to be like that?" Lillian scolded. Even though she had left that housewife life behind her two decades ago, she still hadn't lost that shrill mumsy voice of hers. Her blonde, 70s shoulder-length hairdo that was all kinks and flicks also added to the misinformed image that she was a tired mother in her forties chastising her son for being mean to his new toy-boy stepdad.

"Because he's *human*, Lillian. It's weird," he complained. "And also, *very* dangerous."
Especially with what's been going on lately.

Lillian sank down into the chair opposite him at the small, square table. "But he's also very sweet and he cares about me."

"Your relationship started with you biting him and not being able to compel him right so that he forgot but *hey*, turns out he's totally fine with you drinking his blood anyway. It's weird."

"So, you're saying it's weird for someone to love me?"

Ezra sighed. "You know that's not what I'm saying. What I am saying is are you really doomed to make the same mistake over and over again?"

"And what mistake is that?" A defensive edge crept into her tone. She folded her arms on the tabletop challengingly.

"Picking the wrong guy. C'mon. You had an affair and ran off with a vampire barman when you were human."

"I had an affair with *you*."

"Yeah." He gestured to himself. "A vampire barman."

She smiled despite herself. "You weren't a mistake, Ezra. I've loved every moment of being your progeny. I asked for this life, remember?"

"Is that what this whole thing is with Ben, then? Are you planning on Turning him?"

She scoffed. "God, no. Sure, I missed out on being a mother with Derek but now I'm a vampire, I feel like a kid again. I don't want that responsibility."

Ezra looked over to the pack of eggs waiting on the side, then at the loaf of bread by the toaster. He smirked. "Are you dating a human so you get to cook for someone?"

She smiled coyly. Lillian had the wonderful ability to look like a stern mother one moment, and a giddy teenager the next. Her agelessness was what had first attracted him way back when. "Maybe that might have a *little* something to do with it."

Ezra laughed and took another sip of his blood. Lillian got up and opened the fridge.

"I'm not going to stop teasing him. The boy's gotta man up."

"And might that have a little something to do with how Gabe isn't scared of you?" Lillian peered at him.

Ezra's smile fell and he shuffled about in his chair. He thought for a moment then shook his head and glared at her, "Shut up."

Gabriel dressed into his jeans and a long-sleeved t-shirt, throwing his nurses tunic on over the top as he left his bedroom. The smell of freshly baked scones was slowly consuming their quaint terrace house.

Lillian was in the kitchen, wrist deep in a bowl of some sort of baking mix. Ezra was at the table, his eyes stuck to his phone screen.

"You got in late this morning," said Gabriel with a smirk. Ezra was always the first to call him out on playing fast and loose with sunrise – and in turn, a brutal death.

"Yeah," Ezra replied casually, not even taking his eyes off his phone.

Gabriel frowned. He rather liked a little confrontation to start the night. And Ezra usually never disappointed. *Weird.*

"Hey, Gabe." Lillian smiled over her shoulder and nodded over to the stack of sultana and raisin scones on the side. "I made Julian's favourite."

Gabriel laughed. "You know he can't eat that many. His stomach is like the size of an apple."

"Well, then pass them around. I know Becca would appreciate the kind gesture." She wiggled her eyebrows suggestively.

Ezra's phone buzzed and he was on his feet in an instant. "I gotta go."

Gabriel watched as he left the room, not even acknowledging him as he passed.

"I'm taking the car!" he called back before the front door shut behind him.

17

"What's up with him?" Gabriel looked back to Lillian.

She was now kneading what he assumed was bread dough, her back to him. "Dunno. He was just sat there for like an hour. Fridge is fully stocked. Way more than usual. Didn't think he was going to the city 'til tonight."

Gabriel opened the fridge and indeed, there were four times as many blood bottles than his usual pick-up. He shrugged and filled his thermos.

Gabriel entered Julian's living room to find Becca sat in his chair. There were dark rings around her eyes and her hair had that frayed quality around her temples that seemed to happen when people were tired, stressed, overworked – or all of the above.

"Hi," she said but it came out as more of a sigh.

"Where's Claudia?" he asked. It was usually Julian's daytime care nurse who would be sat waiting for him. With a scowl set on her face most of the time. It did make Gabriel wonder how people with very unwelcoming and unapproachable demeanours were able to become care workers. Not that Gabriel was the jolliest of people, but he also didn't have a frown line so deep you could rest a pencil across his forehead.

Becca slouched back into the chair. "Claudia's kid got sick. School called her and she had to leave."

"What time was that?"

Becca rubbed her eyes. "Just after midday."

"And you've been here all day? You okay? I know he can be difficult." Gabriel crossed the room to see her better and rested his shoulder against the wall.

She shrugged. "He's been fine. He's only difficult with Claudia. He's alright with you, right?"

Gabriel smiled. "He's a saint."

She got to her feet. She was wearing a blouse, and pencil skirt. She must have had to leave work to come here. "Good. Because I have a feeling he'll be up tonight. He's been napping a lot today. Before I got here, Claudia tried to wake him up and he called her a fat cow."

Gabriel chewed his bottom lip to refrain from laughing. Becca noticed and also tried to hold back a smile. She looked down at the plastic bag in his grasp. He'd almost forgotten about it.

"Scones." He stuck out his hand, and then clenched his jaw at how stupid he sounded. *I'd been doing so well.* Her big green eyes shone at him expectantly and she politely took the bag. "They're Lillian's. I mean, Lillian made them. For Julian. Or you. If you want them."

"Awh, that's so lovely of her." She headed into the kitchen and Gabriel followed. "I know my grandad shouldn't eat anything at night but if he does wake, I'm sure he'll love to have a natter with you over a plate of these."

"That would be lovely." *And worth the throwing up that will undoubtably follow on my end.*

She smiled that tight smile again. They were heading back into niceties territory.

"Well," she let out another exhausted sigh and ran her hand through her hair before looking at her watch. "Eight o'clock. Right. I'd better go and leave you to it."

"And you go and get an early night." *Shit. Did that make it seem like I think she looks tired? I mean, she does look tired. But not in a bad way. No. She just has a lot on her plate.*

But if Becca took offence, she didn't show it. Instead, she sighed wistfully. "A bath and bed does sound very appealing."

And now Gabriel was thinking about her in the bath. His eyes widened and he looked out the window. She stroked his arm as she brushed past him and headed down the hallway. "I'll see you in the morning. Hope he's not too much trouble."

Gabriel opened his mouth several times before spluttering about a garbled, "Yeah, see you then."

After making sure Becca had definitely left the bungalow, Gabriel sighed and stared at his reflection in the kitchen window.

"You're pathetic," he chastised himself. But then he looked down to his left sleeve where she had *casually* caressed him. Ever since the two of them had stopped dating, they had both, very obviously, tried their best *not* to touch each other. Which made things very awkward when they both helped Julian move about the house. But that touch had been so deliberate. And was putting the image of her naked body all lathered up in bubbles also deliberate? What kind of game was she playing?

19

Was this all because of the scones?

Why did Gabriel suddenly feel like a pizza man in a porno?

He shook his head, laughing to himself. *You're in your own head far too much, buddy.*

Chapter 3

Noises came from Julian's room at around 10pm. This time they weren't screams of terror, just a lot of incessant shuffling and annoyed grumblings. Gabriel got up from his chair in front of the TV and went to check on him.

He knocked on the door that was always left slightly ajar. "You okay in there, Julian?"

"Gabriel, is-is that you?" the old man replied, sounding disorientated.

"Who else would it be?"

"What time is it?"

"I'm coming in."

The light from the hallway took over the room, lighting up Julian sitting upright in the middle of his double bed. A smile played on Gabriel's lips. There was just something he always found amusing about the way that huge bed seemed to swallow up the old man. He looked so small and delicate within the bulk of fluffy duck egg blue bedding.

Julian's white hair was sticking out at all angles. He looked from Gabriel, to the closed curtains, then back to Gabriel.

"What time is it?"

"Quarter past ten."

Julian blinked. "Then what are you still doing here?"

"No. At night. Ten at night."

He frowned. "That bitch shouldn't have let me sleep. She knows I shouldn't nap! Now I don't know where I am!" He folded his arms over his chest. Without his dentures in, his pout was magnificent.

"Now, now, Julian, that's no way to talk about your only grandchild."

Julian's jaw dropped and his eyes grew huge, looking completely mortified. His mouth open and closed several times but only flummoxed expels of air left him. Gabriel bit his lip to hide his smile.

"Not Becca!" Now the old man was shuffling about under his covers all flustered. "It's that other bloody nurse. She's the bloody swine! Not Becca. Never Becca! She's an absolute angel, that one. Wouldn't be here without her. Couldn't do enough for me."

"Relax, relax." Gabriel was laughing now as he patted at the lump under the covers that was Julian's leg. "I'm just teasing."

Julian stopped thrashing about and gave Gabriel a sharp look before his lips curved into a smile. "You're a bloody swine an'all."

"But you wouldn't have me any other way." He switched the light on. "But since you're awake, Becca said I'm allowed to get you up if you want. Got some freshly baked scones in the kitchen, if you're interested?"

The old man blinked up at Gabriel like he'd just told him he could have the key to the universe. "Scones, you say?"

"With sultanas and raisins."

"The ones that lady of yours makes?"

Gabriel sighed, shaking his head. "Yes, Lillian made them and no, she's not *my lady*. I've already told you this. I know you've got dementia but keep up."

Julian held his palms up. "You're the one who ruined things with my darling Becca so don't be telling me I'm the one with the mind full of marbles."

Gabriel rubbed his forehead, torn between wanting to talk about Becca and desperately needing to change the subject.

"And here you come into my home prancing around with another lady's scones," Julian tutted.

Gabriel ran his tongue over his top teeth. *Man, this old man's a character.*

"Do you want the scones or not?"

He was already shuffling about the bed, smacking his lips together as his feet tried to find the edge. "Oh, yes please."

Gabriel helped the old man to his chair by linking his arm and keeping him steady as he made slow, shuffling steps. Julian would rest almost all of his bodyweight onto Gabriel but he had to remind the old man he was just there to guide him and catch him if he stumbled, not to support him. The sooner Julian gave up on using his own leg muscles, the sooner he would become immobile. For seventy-six years of age, Julian's body was in good shape, he just enjoyed everyone else doing things for him.

Gabriel placed one of the big scones on a plate and opened the kitchen drawer for a knife. He smiled down at the packet of bourbons stuffed into the cutlery holder. The old man had biscuits hidden everywhere. He cut the scone in half and added jam and butter before returning to the living room. He placed the plate onto the side table beside Julian's chair and looked over to the wooden chair by his little dining table. With a frown he grabbed it and set it down beside the old man.

"Oh, you have the comfy chair, Julian, don't mind me," he said as he sat down.

The old man chuckled, and then noticed the scone beside him. His eyes grew twice their size.

"Better get your choppers." Gabriel left to grab the old man's dentures from his bedroom and returned to see him with half the scone already in his hand. He passed him his teeth and he slid them in, the addition making his thin cheeks look less sunken.

23

As Julian ate, Gabriel turned on the TV and searched in the recordings for anything entertaining. He wasn't going to put any of the dramas on. He didn't want Julian talking over it and making him lose focus. Instead, he put on a film he'd seen a million times before. By the time the intro started, Julian had already eaten half the scone and was smacking his lips together.

"Be a good lad and make us a brew, would you?" he asked.

"Sure." Gabriel got up and headed to the kitchen.

In the kitchen, Gabriel made the cup of tea just how Julian liked it. Milky with two sugars. He returned with the mug and his own thermos. Julian lifted the plate that now held nothing but a smattering of crumbs.

"And another scone."

Gabriel set the mug down on the table, his thermos on the carpet by his chair, and grabbed the plate.

"I might be able to enjoy the film at some point."

"Ah, what am I paying you for?"

Gabriel laughed and went to butter another scone.

Thankfully, Julian was so greedy when it came to freshly baked goods that he hadn't even seemed to notice that Gabriel wasn't participating in the night-time snacking. The two of them sat in silence as they watched TV, Gabriel making sure to drink from his thermos only when he started becoming acutely aware of the old man's pulse so he wasn't too keenly aware of the strange smell.

"We never should have told them about that swimming pool," Julian tutted. "Bunch of lowlifes, they were. That was *our* thing. They trusted *us*."

Gabriel could see the old man's forehead wrinkle with contempt and had to suppress a smile.

On the TV, the retirement home residents were jumping around and splashing in the pool. "Disgraceful behaviour," said Gabriel.

Julian nodded, his wispy white eyebrows at his hairline. "They broke one, you know? One of those things? I told 'em. I did. I told 'em to be careful. Bunch of thugs."

Gabriel held in his laugh as the old man told him that he was, indeed, in the film *Cocoon*.

A mind full of marbles.

Losing interest in the film, Gabriel grabbed the newspaper from the table and read it with ease in the dim lamplight. His insides grew cold at the image at the bottom of the front page and quickly turned to the page with the story.

Oh no. Oh no. Oh no. Shitshitshitshit.

Moonlight had been raided. A vampire bar… had been raided. Vampires had undoubtedly been taken. There was no possible way that could end well.

Gabriel felt sick. He was even more thankful now that he hadn't ate a scone out of politeness. He would have most definitely painted Julian's gaudy flowery carpet with it.

The film was nearly over. Gabriel cleared his throat.

"Julian, what do you think happened to the aliens they left behind? Do you think they were found?"

Julian sighed. "I'm not sure."

"But what do you think would have happened to them, if humans – if we – if we found them?"

The old man looked solemn as he watched the boat sail away. "Oh, nothing good."

Gabriel gulped. "Nothing good?"

He shook his head and sighed, "They shouldn't have trusted us."

After the film ended, Gabriel helped Julian back to bed and he fell asleep almost instantly, leaving Gabriel sat staring at the blank TV screen, his leg doing that twitchy thing it did when he was restless. He had sat in Julian's chair scrolling through social media, the knot in his stomach tightening more and more as he read. People were saying outright that the people in the basement were vampires. Sure, there were comments telling these people to stop being delusional. But there were just enough 'delusional' people to make noise. And when humans shouted about something loud and passionately enough, they were heard.

When Becca came over in the morning, looking well rested and smelling like vanilla. Gabriel had recounted the events of the night and had left promptly. Becca had seemed confused by the quick exit and Gabriel fought back his annoyance at his own behaviour, especially after she had stroked his arm which may or may not have been her extending an olive branch. But his mind was preoccupied. He had sat there in that chair the remainder of the night, panic sitting like a lead ball in the centre of his chest. He'd wanted to scream, to break something, to tear something apart. He had messaged Ezra to ask him if he knew anything about the raid, to which he had replied with 'I'll tell you when you get home' and had sent Gabriel spiralling even more.

Gabriel kicked off his shoes in the hallway and stormed into the living room, throwing the newspaper on Ezra's lap in an angry flourish.

"Explain."

Ezra was sitting alone on one of the sofas and had barely reacted to Gabriel's sudden ambush. He picked up the newspaper and looked at the front page. Gabriel dropped onto the other sofa, elbows on his knees.

"I met up with Silas tonight," said Ezra, sounding defeated. Gabriel's stomach knotted. "He says he wasn't at Moonlight when it happened and most of their workers are off the books, money under the table kinda thing. But the ones they caught…"

A heavy silence filled the room as Ezra stared down at newspaper. Gabriel clenched his jaw.

"What happened?"

Ezra blinked slowly and his jaw jutted out, something he did when he was trying to suppress his emotions.

"They're dead, Gabriel." His voice came out hoarse. "The ones that were picked up. None of them survived."

Ezra's eyes flickered to him. Red rimmed them. He looked so young in that moment, like all his vampire years had been stripped away and he was just a lost twenty-year-old burdened with far too much.

Gabriel hadn't been to a vampire bar in years and so had no connection to any of the staff. That was not the case for Ezra. Gabriel was going to end the conversation there because, even though they had been together for several decades, the two of them weren't great when it came to talking about their emotions; but it was clear that Ezra had a lot to get off his chest.

"The younger vampires… they were taken to hospital in the morning when they started throwing up blood in the police station. Some just kept throwing up until they…" He shuddered. Blood tears escaped his eyes. He smeared them across his temples with the back of his hand. "And the older ones who weren't affected by the day sickness as badly… the sun got them in the station anyway."

Gabriel could picture it. Vampires screaming in pain as their insides turned to mush. Blood pouring from every orifice as human doctors and nurses tried to pin them down on hospital beds, not understanding what was happening. Vampires setting on fire in the police station when they passed by a window.

"How do you know all this?" Gabriel asked, own voice thick with emotion.

"Silas." Ezra looked down. The sound of his blood tears hitting the newspaper was so loud in the silence. "He knows a doctor. He sneaks blood bags out for him from donors. He witnessed the whole thing."

"Fuck." Gabriel ran his hand through his hair and dropped back against the back of the sofa.

They both sat there, looking everywhere but at each other as they processed the information. Anger suddenly burned deep inside Gabriel's chest. He clenched his jaw, folded his arms, and expelled a heavy breath through his nose.

"So this is it, isn't it?" he hissed, knowing full well his anger was just a coating for his real absolute terror. "It's over. We're done for. They know."

Their eyes found each other. Ezra's face was now streaked with blood, emphasising the helplessness in his huge, brown doe eyes. His mouth worked before it formed the words.

"We're not a secret anymore."

Chapter 4

Ezra rapped his knuckles on Lillian's bedroom door. "House meeting."

"What? What for?" she called back.

"Well, if you come down and join us, you'll find out."

Gabriel was already on one of the sofas, his fingers interlaced between his knees and chewing on his bottom lip. Ezra sank onto the opposite sofa, feeling equal parts drained and anxious. Even though vampires were forced to slumber in the daytime, there was still a grogginess in his head like he hadn't had the right amount of time knocked unconscious.

The two of them had stayed awake close to sun up, just sat there in silence while Ezra swatted at his tears and Gabriel stared blankly into some dark abyss. They had both agreed that Lillian needed to be brought up to speed. She was going to find out eventually through the News or social media so it was best it came from people who loved her first.

A few moments later Lillian entered the living room. Ezra frowned when he spotted Ben lingering in the hallway.

"House meeting," he reiterated.

Lillian looked from stern Ezra to helpless Gabriel and her natural smile fell away. "What's going on?"

"Get him out of here and take a seat."

By the look in her eyes, Ezra could tell she felt his fear and adrenaline through their sire bond. She gulped hard and pushed Ben towards the door. "I'll call you later."

After he left, she perched beside Gabriel, tying the cord of her fluffy dressing gown tighter around her waist.

"First things first," Ezra started and jerked a thumb in the direction of the front door. "Is he gonna be staying here every day?"

Lillian gave him a tired look.

"Vampire and human relationships don't work. Gabriel can attest to that."

Gabriel's head jerked up and he pulled a face. "Why you bringing me into this?"

Ezra shrugged. "I'm just saying. What do you see in that guy anyway?"

Lillian lowered her eyes.

"It is nice to build relationships and connections outside the three of us," Gabriel answered for her, to which she nodded and arched her eyebrow at Ezra.

"But why him? He's so… beige. And to go from *me* to *him*? It's insulting."

Lillian laughed. "Oh, so that's why you're so against me having a relationship?"

"Maybe it's the beard. Y'know girls like a man with some nicely maintained facial hair," added Gabriel, his eyes trained on Ezra's smooth baby-face. Just because Gabriel was Turned in his mid-thirties and had already grown into his big shoulders, had an appealing sun-kissed complexion thanks to his Greek heritage and had a constant five o-clock shadow despite shaving most nights, it didn't make him any more of a man than Ezra.

"Okay." Ezra held up his palms. "First of all, it'd be a crime to cover up this jawline, and second of all, this isn't why we're here."

"You brought it up," Gabriel grumbled. He was clearly pissed that Ezra brought up Becca.

Lillian looked at them both. "This isn't about Ben?"

They both shook their heads. She seemed to sink further into the sofa.

Ezra cleared his throat and rested his elbows on his knees, closing the distance between himself and his progeny.

"Have you seen any weird stuff on social media the past couple of nights?"

Lillian shook her head. "You know I don't do any of that stuff." Fear had crept into her voice. "Why? What's happened?"

When Ezra paused, she looked to Gabriel. He avoided her eyes. Ezra could feel her unease like a wave between them.

Gabriel shook his head and gritted his teeth. "Something happened-"

"We're gonna be found out," Ezra interjected quickly, needing to be the one to break the news. She was his progeny. It was his job to look after her.

"What?" Her brows furrowed.

Gabriel closed his mouth and leaned back, a move to show he was exiting the conversation. Ezra reached out and held Lillian's hand. She remained silent as Ezra explained everything to her. About the raid. About the vampires being found. About them dying in front of many, many, *many* humans.

"Now more than ever, we need to be careful," he said. "I know I give you a hard time about Ben but can you look me in the eyes now and tell me that you trust him not to tell anyone about what we are?"

Her eyes found his, her irises so blue and terrified. Ezra searched them, felt for their bond and knew he could believe her when she said, "I trust him with my life." She looked to Gabriel, who had been so silent and still throughout their conversation that Ezra had almost forgotten he was there. "I trust him completely. I would have never brought him here, never introduced him to you guys, if I thought he would be a problem. You know that, right?"

Gabriel sat up and placed his hand on her shoulder. "We know. This is just something none of us expected to happen. We need to be a strong unit. A family."

Ezra watched Gabriel console Lillian, bringing a sad sort of smile to her face. He smiled a little too, because it seemed that, for once, he and Gabriel were on the same side.

"What about the church party this weekend?" Lillian asked in a small voice. "I was so looking forward to it. Are we still going? We always go."

Shit. Ezra had forgotten about that. Living in a small village did come with its perks. The three of them weren't big fans of vampire culture, with their sucking on necks and only wearing leather and latex, and places like Hicklesbury didn't attract vampires looking for the raunchy nightlife. But a downside to being a part of a small community meant that gossip spread like wildfire and if the three of them suddenly stopped going to church gatherings? Well, that would cause quite the stir.

"We're still going," Ezra said.

Gabriel looked sceptical. "We are?"

Ezra nodded. "It'll be a good opportunity for us to scope out how everyone is reacting to the story. If they believe what people are saying on the internet."

"We do *not* want to get on the wrong side of these people. Village folk are the *worst*," Gabriel pulled a sour face.

"I've always found our neighbours quite lovely," said Lillian.

"That's because you bake them bread and cakes. Trust me, once they've figure out were outsiders, we're dead. Remember all the looks I got for the first couple of months we moved here just because my skin is a slightly different colour?"

"Yeah, imagine how they'll take the news that you're feasting on their elderly," said Ezra dryly.

Gabriel cut him a look. "I've stopped doing that." Ezra blinked, surprised. He'd actually gotten through to him? "I mean, with Julian. Olive who I care for when her son's away is a different story. She's a racist. Doesn't count."

Ezra sighed and rolled his eyes. *So close.*

"So, we're going on Saturday?" Lillian asked, clearly steering the conversation away from the inevitable argument that followed this topic.

Ezra nodded.

"I'll bake a pie." Lillian beamed like her pie had the power to solve all of their problems.

The bar top was already clean but Ezra kept running the damp cloth over the shiny wooden surface. His eyes were downcast but his hearing was tuned into a group of twenty-somethings in a booth at the back of the room.

"Mate, it's his own fucking fault. What did he think would happen?" said one of them.

"The guy's dead, Adam," replied the other.

Ezra's hand froze on the bar top mid-wipe.

"And like I said, it's his own fault. After everything that's been going on? What does he expect to happen? He was feeding the crazy. Might as well have covered himself in chum and thrown himself into shark infested waters."

As much as Ezra hated seeing Mitch on his phone in work hours, he wished he could check his now and look up what these guys were talking about. He knew it was about the raid. Even though the News were keeping hush about the *exploding people*, social media was rife with speculations – most of which was leaning towards the truth.

He could feel his throat tightening. His heart, cold and dead, felt heavy in his chest.

"Pint of Carling, please, mate."

Ezra blinked and looked up at the man before him. He gave him a nod, his throat too dry to attempt to speak.

"The kid was only twenty-two. Probably around your age, right?" continued the man, his smoker's breath invading Ezra's nose as he poured his drink. Ezra gulped and cleared his throat, ready to ask him to elaborate, but the man was clearly a talker and didn't need the prompt.

"That kid that was beaten? Only about an hour's drive from 'ere'. Did you see it on the News? Dressed like a vampire for a fancy-dress party." The man tutted. "That's the problem with kids these days. Think everything's a joke."

Ezra slid the pint to him and took a measure breath before asking, "How did he die?"

The man blinked at him. "You didn't see the story? Beat him to a bloody pulp." The man sucked in a breath through his teeth at Ezra's wide-eyed reaction. "Yeah, I know. Right there in the street. He died from his injuries in hospital."

"Did they get the people who attacked him?"

The man nodded. "They said they were protecting their town. They thought he was actually one of them." He huffed a sad laugh. "This story is gonna be a breeding ground for those kinds of people. Y'know, the conspiracy theorists? Those who just desperately want something interesting to be going on they just jump on whatever fad they can."

"You think that's all this is? The vampire thing? A fad?"

The man shrugged and stuck his hand in his pocket. "Seems a bit far-fetched to me but I haven't left this village in twenty years, I'm not exactly well up on what is or isn't out there. What do I owe you?"

"Three fifty."

The man paid him and took his drink. "I think we'll be safe here. We stick together." He winked and left to take a seat on a table alone.

Ezra placed his palms on the bar, bent his head down and tried to calm the erratic energy that coursed through him. His heart didn't beat, his breath didn't quicken – the tell-tale signs of a human having a panic attack. No, for vampires, it was their energy that altered. Like static zapping in his veins. He felt restless.

We stick together, the man's voice rattled in his brain. *Yes, that's what I'm afraid of.*

On his break, Ezra sat with Mitch in the back while the bar was being manned by Stewart, a stocky man in his late thirties who thought himself too good to socialise with the 'youths' he worked with.

"What kind of injuries did the guy have?" asked Ezra, searching through his phone for the article.

"Why do you wanna know, sicko?" laughed Mitch, spitting bits of his chicken wrap onto his lap.

Ezra cut him a look. "I mean, he died in hospital so the beating must have been pretty bad, right?"

"Hell yeah. Fractured skull, busted lung. The guy was bleeding internally."

"All because he was just *dressed* like a vampire?"

"Well, I mean, that's what the story says. They obviously want the people who jumped him to look like monsters. But I bet the guy antagonised them. Who in their right mind would dress in a cloak and fangs right now? And you know what? I think this is gonna be the first of many. You seen this?"

Mitch showed Ezra his phone screen; on it was a meme. The first picture was of a group of lads on a bar crawl with their shirts off, fists pumping the air and that mad look in their eyes that came with intoxication. The caption read 'Me and the Boys on Nights Out Then,'. The next picture was of a group of medieval knights, kitted out in complete suits of armour, helmet visors down and swords ready, with the caption 'Nights Out Now'. Underneath was the message, 'Vampires, Come at Me'.

Mitch was laughing as Ezra puzzled over the image.

"There's loads of 'em." Mitch scrolled down, revealing more and more memes making light of his death sentence. Pictures of people carving their table legs into stakes. Pictures of Van Helsing with the caption 'When You Get The 2am Munchies and You're Out of Pringles.' "Fucking gold."

Gabriel brought his thermos to his lips and drank, pressing his back hard against the old man's chair so the footrest sprung out. He tried his best to relax, to focus on the five hours' worth of dramas he'd recorded to keep himself occupied throughout his shift, but he couldn't get what Ezra had told him out of his mind. He'd never witnessed a vampire meeting the sun, but he'd seen them get killed. It was not a pretty sight. Back in the early 90's there had been vampire gang wars. There probably still were, in the big cities and places where crazy Nests still occurred. Vampires turned stakes on each other, ripping off limbs, caving in skulls. But at the end of those attacks, there were never any bodies besides a stray arm or leg. Because when vampires died, they became a bloody, pulpy mess.

And those people in the hospital where the vampires had been taken would have seen all of that happening with their own eyes. There would be no mistaking that they had most definitely not been human.

It was 3am when Julian started groaning in his sleep. It was low mumbling at first. Then his breathing started to become erratic. It crackled like his lungs were full of pebbles.

"Not again. No. Be gone, foul beast!" he cried. "Send these foul beasts into the abyss!"

Gabriel smirked as he got to his feet and went to check on Gandalf the White.

The old man was tossing and turning under his duvet, getting more and more tangled within his sheets.

"Julian," said Gabriel. Still the old man grumbled. His white hair was stuck to his forehead with sweat. "Julian."

The old man whimpered. Gabriel went to shake his shoulder but stopped himself. He didn't want the old man jerking awake and hurting himself.

"Julian!"

The old man shuddered awake and screwed his fists into his duvet. His bleary eyes blinked several times before finding Gabriel towering over him. The old man shrieked and spun away from him. "Please, no. No. No."

Gabriel's gut twisted as Julian buried his face into his pillow and cried.

"Julian, it's me," he said softly. "Gabriel, your care nurse. Do you remember?"

Julian sniffled and peaked at him over his thin shoulder like a child wary of being tricked by a parent. He studied him a moment then the lines on his face softened.

"Gabriel?" He blinked hard and turned back over so he was facing him. "You wear your shirts too tight and you don't like ginger biscuits."

Gabriel smiled. "That's me."

The old man looked sad for a moment, his fingers knotting deeper into his duvet. "They were here again."

"I know, I heard. Sounded like you gave them a run for their money, though."

He looked about the dimly lit room as if to check for the monsters.

"Is Becca here?" he asked.

Gabriel shook his head. "Not yet. She'll be here soon."

"And Kathy?"

Gabriel blinked, surprised. He hadn't heard the old man ever say that name.

"No, not Kathy."

Julian looked like he was lost in a pleasant trance. He smiled down at the foot of the bed. "My Kathy. Such a sweet girl."

"Right." Gabriel cleared his throat. "Are you feeling okay to go back to sleep?"

Julian nodded and got himself comfortable. "You'll be here if they come back? The demons?"

"I'm right outside your door. They're not getting past me."

The old man nodded, satisfied, and closed his eyes.

Gabriel jerked up to his feet at the sound of the front door opening and inwardly chastised himself for being so jittery. Thankfully, by the time Becca came into the living room he had collected himself enough to look like he was casually reading a magazine.

"Didn't think you were the green fingered type," she commented.

Gabriel furrowed his brows. She nodded to his lap. It was then he noticed that he was pretending to read a gardening magazine.

"Er, I'm not." He quickly shoved it into the pile with the rest and rose to his feet once again. "How are you?"

She shrugged. "I'm okay. You?"

"Yeah. Good."

He smiled. She smiled. A beat of silence rang between them.

"I'm sorry about the other morning," he rushed when she looked towards her grandfather's room for an escape.

She furrowed her brows at him.

"About leaving so suddenly. I-I had to go deal with something."

"Oh, it's no problem." She placed her canvas bag onto the little dining table and picked out a bottle of pills. "I didn't really notice."

"Oh…" Gabriel deflated. The awkwardness was creeping back into the room like a black fog. "He had his nightmares again," he quickly added.

She looked to him. A worry line creased her freckled forehead. "Really?"

"Yeah. I calmed him down."

"I guess the only thing that keeps them at bay is Lillian's scones."

Gabriel laughed. "Yeah, maybe."

She turned back and started sorting out the pill bottles on the table. Gabriel lingered behind her.

"Are you going to the church function on Saturday?" she asked.

"Yeah, yeah. Are you?"

"Absolutely." Then she sighed. "Weekends are the hardest for my grandad. With you not being there."

Gabriel studied the back of her head. *Is she asking me to pick up an extra shift? Does she not want me at the party?*

"Do you… need me to work the weekend?" he asked cautiously.

She spun around so fast her ponytail nearly whipped him across the face. "No, no. I got Claudia to work Saturday night. It's fine."

Gabriel paused, was he missing something? "Okay…"

She laughed awkwardly and went to tuck her hair behind her ear but there was nothing there. Her eyes scanned the carpet. "I meant that my grandad likes having you here."

Her green eyes found his, carefully, meaningfully. Like they used to.

Gabriel felt that pull towards her. "*Julian* likes me here?" A smile played on his lips. She watched, biting her own.

"*I* like having you here."

They gazed at each other. The silence between them no longer static and awkward. It was now thick with intent.

"Becca?" the old man called from down the corridor. And just like that, the spell was broken.

Becca charged out of the room, instantly switching into caring granddaughter mode.

Gabriel ran his hands through his hair, smiling like an idiot, and went to aid her.

Chapter 5

"I still don't think we should be going," said Lillian, holding the apple pie she'd made tightly like she needed the warmth.

"It'll be suspicious if we don't." Ezra was five steps ahead like he always was when they travelled in a group. His long-legged strides looked cool and casual. His dark hair was styled and shining in the moonlight. He'd never specifically said it, but Gabriel knew he walked ahead because he thought he was their protector. He was sure he had played the classic *if you want them, you've got to go through me* scene in his head a thousand times. And if Lillian's anxious ramblings were anything to go by, this may be the night he got to try to be a hero. Emphasis on 'try'.

"Everything will be fine. You've got me." Ben squeezed Lillian against his side, a reassuring smile on his naïve little face. "They're still your neighbours. Nothing's changed."

Everything had changed. Ezra had told him about the kid that died. An innocent kid playing a stupid prank, thinking he was funny. He had acted like this mass hysteria was a joke and was cruelly proved that it wasn't. But Gabriel knew how humans worked. He'd been around long enough to know that when they're scared, they put on a brave face and laugh about their problems. Even when people died, it was fine because it would 'never happen to them.' If a threat wasn't on their doorstep, it was a meme.

All four of them stopped in front of the door. Lillian and Ben looked to Ezra, eyes wide and shining. Gabriel could feel Ezra's nerves thrumming from him like an electrical charge. But just as Gabriel was about to open his mouth to say something about taking the lead to embarrass him, Ezra pushed the door open and to his surprise, he felt his stomach lurch in protest.

Gabriel expected everyone to stop. For the music to screech to a halt. For everyone to turn and stare. For the world to stand still for a moment.

None of that happened. The four of them entered the party and blended in seamlessly. So seamlessly that Ezra quirked his eyebrow at Gabriel as he crossed the room in an *I told you so* way that had Gabriel clenching his jaw. Not that Gabriel wanted them to be run out of the village like a bunch of monsters, but what drama that would be.

Across the room, Becca stood with her housemate Maeve, wine glasses in hand and caught up in conversation. She was wearing a signature summer dress, and her long, dark hair styled and curled. Gabriel fought the urge to go over and speak to her. He hadn't stopped thinking about their moment in Julian's living room. If the old man hadn't called out for her, what would have happened? Would they have continued flirting? Did he even want them to continue flirting? Sure, he had strong feelings for her but he had ended things for a reason.

 Knowing full well that talking to her right now would only confuse him and end up with him spewing awkward chit chat before he made an excuse to leave; he followed Lillian and Ben over to the food.

"Someone else made a pie." Lillian slid her pie onto the gingham table, her shoulders wilting as she looked at the cherry pie next to hers. This one had pastry crossing the top, exposing little windows of glistening cherries. Lillian's was plain with just a cross detailing the centre. Gabriel had to admit, the cherry pie looked a lot more appealing. Not that he was going to taste either.

"I bet it's not as good as yours though, babes," said Ben.

Lillian was still pouting.

"Try it," she said. "Tell me if it's better."

The colour washed from poor Ben's face. "I'm not that hungry."

"Please." Lillian fluttered her long eyelashes and Gabriel couldn't help envisioning her doing the exact same thing to Ezra twenty years ago. Back when she was human and he was, to her, the enticing young barman that was going to spice up her boring marriage. "For me?"

A dimple cratered in Ben's cheek. "Fine. For you."

She bounced a little and planted a kiss on his jaw.

Gabriel stood there, hands in his trouser pockets, wondering why the hell he hadn't left yet. Ben took the cake knife and cut out a tiny triangle piece of the cherry pie. The first piece. There was always something about being the first person to cut the cake at an event that felt wrong. Although, in the back of Gabriel's mind, he did think that being around Ben while he ate should divert suspicion. He didn't particularly like the way he swooned at everything Lillian ever said or did, but he did help them blend in and he irked Ezra to no end so he was good to have around.

"The pastry is flaky," Ben commented, spitting crumbs. "And I'm not a fan of cherries. Apple pie always wins."

Lillian smiled wide. "Now you've gotta try mine."

And that was Gabriel's cue to leave. He went over to the drinks station and poured himself a glass of cheap red wine to sip as he milled around. Church functions were never the liveliest. They were just a place to talk to the same people you passed in the streets or met in the shops or in the pub every night. But he liked it here in Hicklesbury. It was quaint and quiet and peaceful. It was the type of place British dramas were always based in. Where there was always some sort of juicy scandal. The only scandal that had happened since he moved here was a bunch of teenagers went through a phase of hiding in wheelie bins and jumping out at people. But that stopped after a week when one of them jumped out on the wrong person and ended up with a black eye.

41

As Gabriel casually wandered past his gossiping neighbours, he caught snippets of conversations. Tony's son wanted to study in Birmingham. Carol's fibromyalgia was acting up again. It took her over an hour to get dressed this morning. Bernice had found a new lasagne recipe that you have *got to try.* But it was the conversation between Laura, Ryan and Jacob that made him pause. Gabriel recognised the kids. Ryan was the grandson of one of his first patients. The kid wore trainers to his funeral and everyone did the small village thing where they talked about how disrespectful it was behind his back but never said anything to him or his parents.

"Bet there's some new vampire franchise that they're trying to promote or something. Advertising is taking things way too far these days," said Ryan, scrolling through his phone.

"Really?" Laura sounded sceptical. "They said they found these people in a club basement. They weren't exactly out in public. Pretty shit advertising."

"But it's all over the internet now."

"Nah, I bet it's some kink shit. Drinking blood in the basement of a club? Defo sex club," joined in Jacob, making Laura arch her eyebrow.

"I mean… people are into some weird shit in the bedroom."

Ryan nudged her. "Sounds like something you'd be interested in, aye? Look! She's blushing!"

"Never say never," she said with a comically dramatic wink. That's when she caught Gabriel's eye and flushed beetroot red. Both Ryan and Jacob followed her eyes.

"Sup, Gabe," said Ryan, his voice noticeably dropping an octave.

"Evening." Gabriel lifted his glass in greeting. "What's all this about kink shit?"

Laura pressed her chin into her chest and tried to hide her face behind her cider can.

"You see the story? Some club up north. The police raided it and found a load of people down in the basement chewing on each other's necks. People are making out that they're vampires," said Jacob.

"Really?" Gabriel took a sip of his wine. "No, I haven't heard about it. Don't follow the news much. So, the police are saying they're vampires?"

The boys scoffed.

"Nah, just some tapped people commenting on Facebook. Probably the same people who get their rocks off reading all that vampire romance bullshit," said Ryan, clearly eager to let his voice be heard. He and Gabriel had spent quite a bit of time together when he was looking after his grandfather. The boy wasn't much. He hadn't cared about his grandfather and was very disrespectful to his mother. He liked Gabriel. Well, he always seemed to want to impress him. It was a lost cause. Gabriel had always found him to be a bit of a dick.

"So, what's the real story?"

"Like I said, kink shit," replied Jacob.

"That all? So, we've got nothing to be worried about?" Gabriel masked his real concern with fake concern.

"Why, you scared, Gabe? Think these vamps will come after ya?" Ryan's laugh was loud and obnoxious. If Gabriel hadn't had a rule to drink only from the elderly, he was sure he would rather have this little prick six feet under instead of his veteran grandfather.

"People are a little scared," Laura piped up. Her cheeks had simmered to a rosy glow, but she couldn't hold Gabriel's eyes. She still held the can close to her lips, an insecure reflex. "It's more than just Facebook comments. People have been putting up videos of people's eyes changing colour. There's a video of a woman with fangs. Her eyes are all black and under her eyes are all… like pulsating." She glanced at Gabriel. It was only for a second but he caught not fear in her eyes, but exhilaration.

"Yeah, ever heard of special effects?" Ryan rolled his eyes. "It's just people jumping on the bandwagon. People love to stir shit."

"It's real," she snapped at her friend. "My auntie said it's crazy in the city. That guy that died isn't the only one dressing like a vampire. Apparently, it's like some cult thing. Everyone's doing it. Well, kids are doing it. My auntie said that she's been researching how to protect herself. All the parents have. Just in case, y'know?"

"Yeah? And what's she found out?" asked Gabriel.

This aughta be good. The internet was rife with misinformation about *real* vampires.

43

Laura chewed on her lip, moving the can from her mouth. Clearly, she was getting a lot more confident now that Gabriel was focusing solely on her and was intrigued by what she had to say. "Well, first, they can't go into churches." She gestured to the crucifix with the dying Jesus above her. "Hence, why we're in a church."

"We always have these stupid gatherings here. It's got nothing to do with the vampire stuff," chimed in Jacob.

"Is your mum on the committee?" She sent him a glare. "No? Didn't think so. I know stuff you don't." She looked back at Gabriel and tilted her head, biting her bottom lip to try to look flirtatious. "They don't have reflections. Can't go out in daylight-"

"Then why we having this party in the evening?"

"Because that's when the church is free," she answered Jacob without taking her eyes off Gabriel. Feeling a little uncomfortable by this teenager's lust filled gaze, he turned and spotted Becca still with Maeve by the drinks. As if feeling his eyes on her, she looked up. And smiled. His stomach knotted. "They can't touch silver," Laura continued, a little louder to get his attention. "Burns them."

Silver? They knew about silver? And just like that, he noticed it. Looking around the room at all his neighbours, at the people he had known and grown relationships with, at the community he liked to think he was a part of... most of them were wearing silver.

Earrings. Necklaces. Bracelets. Watches. He'd never seen so much jewellery in Hicklesbury in all the five years of living here.

They believed the stories. They were researching. This was most definitely a problem.

"Excuse me." He headed for the toilets, grabbing Ezra by his shirt sleeve and pulling him away from a riveting conversation about the new Star Wars series.

He pushed Ezra into the toilets and then slammed open the cubicle door to check that they were alone.

"What the hell is wrong with you?" Ezra asked at his back.

Gabriel turned and ran his hands through his hair. "Have you noticed? What they're wearing?"

At this, Ezra's thin shoulders slumped. He turned to the sink, clasped the basin and stared into the plughole. "Silver. Yeah, I saw."

"They believe it. The stories. They think it's real."

"Yeah. Because it is." He looked at Gabriel through the mirror. His dark eyes fixed on him, strong and immovable. It was at moments like this when Ezra's real age showed through his youthful exterior. "Being here. Secluded in this little village. It gave us a bit of time but the internet... news travels fast now. It was only a matter of time."

"Apparently there're videos."

"Yeah." Ezra turned and leaned against the basin. "We're being actively looked for."

"Do you think anyone suspects us?"

"From what I've gathered... no." His jaw clenched. "I know you don't like me telling you how to live but you can't keep killing your patients. Not now. I don't care if they're racist or they don't like your taste in music. They'll be watching our every move."

Gabriel's nostrils flared. "I've got a good thing going here. *We've* got a good thing going here. Do you think we'll have to move?"

"To where? An even more secluded village? Like you said, we've all got a good thing going here. Lillian's all loved up with Ben. As much as I hate it, she's happy. You've got your night-time care nurse thing. I mean, I can be a barman anywhere but this place is our home. We've just got to keep blending in. And be extra cautious." The last comment was accompanied by a very pointed look.

Gabriel huffed. He hated when Ezra was right. "*Fine.* Whatever."

Ezra pushed himself off the sink and slapped Gabriel on the back. "Now, we'd better get out of here before we fuel more gossip. You know Doris Lang thinks we're dating?"

Gabriel pulled a face.

Ezra shrugged. "I mean, why else would you be hanging around with a twenty-year-old you're not related to?"

"Hey, it's Lillian who likes them young. Not me."

"Awh, don't ruin it for her. Doris sounded so excited to be friends with *homo*sexuals."

Gabriel pushed him out of the door.

"Do you know what would stop the rumour? If you actually go talk to Becca at some point tonight."

They were back in the function room at the far end of the church, silver glittering off almost every neck and wrist. Gabriel turned to throw some lie to Ezra about being completely fine with how things were between him and Becca but a messy chime and a gasp sent both of their gazes across the room. Lillian and Ben were by the buffet. Lillian was shaking her hand and then she brought her finger to her mouth and sucked. From where he was standing, Gabriel could hear her wince of pain.

Ezra stormed across the squeaky wooden floor, shoving people out the way without a second thought. Gabriel followed, knowing that the only time Ezra walked with such purpose was when his progeny was in trouble.

"What happened?" Ezra grabbed Lillian's wrist and yanked her fingers from her mouth. They were stained red by her lipstick. The mark under it was already healed but Gabriel could smell it in the air: burnt flesh.

"The cutlery," said Ben, his arm loosely around Lillian's waist. "She just touched it and-"

"They're silver coated," Ezra cut across.

Gabriel looked around, once again expecting everyone to have stopped and to be staring at them. But they weren't that important. Everybody was too caught up in whatever they were doing. Everybody, except for one. She was looking directly at him, of course she was. And, by the look on her face, understood what had just happened.

"Becca," Gabriel breathed.

Her eyes widened when he began heading towards her. She placed her glass on the table, excused herself and started towards the back door at a clipped pace. Gabriel caught up to her outside. The wind whipped her mousey brown hair across her face.

"Becca." He reached out to her but she threw her arms up and backed away. She tucked her wild hair behind her ears, her eyes wide and on him.

"She's one of them, isn't she?" she asked in a rushed whisper.

"I can explain-"

"And you *knew*?" Then she blinked. "You... Ezra... you're all... and Ben, too?"

Gabriel bit down on his tongue. It was time. He couldn't hide any longer. Not from Becca. And he'd be lying if he said he didn't want to come clean. He wanted to tell her the truth ever since he

46

had to cancel their date. The picnic she had made. The plan to go to the beach and sunbathe and eat sandwiches and ice cream and forget about everything. But he couldn't and she couldn't understand why.

"Not Ben," he said.

"But you are?"

The muscles in his jaw flexed and he nodded. The slight tip of his head was the burst in a dam that was barely holding.

Her hand flew to her mouth and she choked. She was thinking about how she had kissed him. How she had held his hand. How they had laughed and joked and fought over the bill. She was thinking about when he had bought her flowers – orange tulips, her favourite and he had remembered. They had been an apology gift after the first date he had had to cancel due to the sun still being in the sky. All of this was written all over her beautiful face.

"You're a vampire," she said with disgust and then laughed. "A *vampire*. This is real. All what's in the news. It's not a hoax. There're vampires."

"We're not evil. We're just like you."

"You drink blood though, don't you?"

"We're not savages."

She paused, her eyes roving the wall behind him. Then realisation flashed in them and she gasped. "My grandad. I let you near my grandad." Her eyes studied his and she gasped again. "His anaemia. It's been getting worse since you've been assigned to him." She took a step back, measuring Gabriel with a look of repulsion. He had never felt so disgusting in his entire life. "You've been *drinking* from my grandad?"

"Becca, you've got to understand that-" he reached for her again.

"Don't touch me!" She spun so her back was to him.

A coldness seeped into his bones and he watched her silently processing everything.

"I would never hurt Julian."

She scoffed. "You're supposed to be his nurse and you've been drinking his blood."

"Not anymore. But he's dying anyway. You know this. I would never drink from the young and healthy," he tried to explain, which was met by another scoff. "And it's not like I'm not giving him anything in return. Remember when he fell in the bathroom and cut open his knee?"

She turned, her eye peeking at him through her hair. "No."

"Exactly. That's because I found him and I healed him. With my blood. Your grandfather is a good man, Becca. I'm giving him a pain free exit from this world."

"How many of your patients have you killed?"

"It's not like that-"

"How many?"

Gabriel squeezed his eyes shut. "I don't know."

"You don't know? What? Because they're just food to you? They're people, Gabriel. We're people. My grandad-"

"Fine. Twelve."

She looked stricken. "…Twelve?"

He nodded. "Twelve elderly patients in the past five years. For a vampire, that's pretty low."

She scoffed. "And what? Am I supposed to be proud of you? Those people were mothers, fathers, grandparents. And you *murdered* them. What about Ezra and Lillian? What're their tallies?"

"Lillian feeds from Ben. It's consensual. Ezra goes to the clubs in the city. Like the one they raided. Also consensual."

"Does my grandad know what you are?"

Gabriel shook his head. "His mind is not what it used to be. I take care of him. And he likes me, doesn't he?"

She paused for a moment. "You've been his favourite nurse."

A silence spread out between them like it always did. He wanted to reach out and hold her but knew not to. He could see she was torn. She wanted to hate him but she couldn't. Finally, she exhaled and looked up to the moon half covered by clouds.

"You can't go out in sunlight, can you?"

"No. That's why-"

"I get it," she cut him off. "I was so mad at you. I thought I was good at reading people but you were giving me all these mixed signals."

"I never wanted to push you away."

Standing outside in nothing but a dress and cardigan, she hugged herself tightly and squinted at him through the breeze.

"Who else knows about you?"

"Just Ben," he replied.

"What are you going to do now? Everyone's got their guard up."

"We don't know. But please don't tell anyone about us."

She searched his eyes, looking for something. Something evil?

Finally, she sighed. "I won't." She passed him to head back into the church. "But my grandad will no longer be needing your services."

Once back in the function room, Gabriel headed straight for the front door, chest tight and jaw clenched.

Ezra spotted him and started following close behind. "Whoa, what's up with you?"

When Gabriel stayed quiet, Ezra grabbed his elbow.

"I'm going home," Gabriel snapped.

Ezra pulled him to a stop. Gabriel let out an angered exhale.

"Let me go. Let's not cause a scene." Gabriel scanned the hall. Several eyes were on them. Did they think this was a lovers' quarrel?

"If you tell me what's going on, there won't be a scene."

Gabriel sighed, his anger dissipating. He rubbed his forehead, suddenly exhausted. "I just got fired."

Ezra glanced over to Becca. Her eyes quickly flickered down to her glass. He looked back to Gabriel. Even though the two of them weren't bound by blood, they had been side by side long enough to read each other's expressions near perfectly. The quirk of Ezra's dark eyebrow spelled the question, *'is it anything we need to be worried about?'*

Gabriel shook his head.

Ezra's eyebrow lifted higher and his eyes flitted to Becca for a fraction of a second. *'Is she anything we need to worry about?'*

Again, Gabriel shook his head. "She's fine." But a sinking feeling hit his gut when he caught Becca and Maeve talking, voices low and heads bent together. He tried to tune into their conversation but he couldn't single out their voices. "Just keep an eye on her," he said. "I'm leaving."

Ezra nodded like a soldier and gave Gabriel a solid pat on the back. *Great job tonight, lad. Now go rest, keep your strength up.*

Gabriel rolled his eyes and left the church.

Chapter 6

Becca lifted her grandad's arm up carefully and ran the soapy sponge under it to his armpit. He sat silently on the plank-like bench in the centre of the bath she had slotted in for him. He hated being bathed. The subject used to cause so many arguments at the start, to the point where Becca would storm out of the bungalow and have to sit in her car for ten minutes to cool off before going back in to finish her duties. She used to give in when he would tell her he could clean himself. For the first month, she had let him. The names he had called her back then had hurt. They were out of anger. Anger that was a part of his disorder. And she knew it wasn't aimed at her. It was at his illness. At his own incapability. She knew that, but it didn't make the words hurt any less. He used to say that she enjoyed seeing him like this. Weak and vulnerable. That she was just like her mother and 'that arsehole she married.' Then when Becca had realised he wasn't cleaning himself properly and not changing his underwear, she had to make the decision to bathe him herself.

"You're practically going mouldy," Becca had said-- a joke that held some truth.

"Yeah, well, thought you'd be happy. You want me to rot, don't you? Your mother did," he had spat back.

"I'm not my mum," Becca had said in a small voice, a lump lodged in her throat.

These days were different. Her grandad sat patiently, his head bent forwards, allowing her to manoeuvre him like a puppet as she scrubbed him down. He kept his underwear on, and she would pass him the soap for him to clean that area himself. They had both agreed on that.

"At least let me keep a little bit of my dignity," he had grumbled.

As she washed him, she checked his body over for any suspicious marks. She didn't really know what she was expecting to find. Bite marks? Two little puncture wounds like in the movies? But Gabriel has said he had healed her grandad when he had fallen, so maybe he had healed his bites, too? Had he healed his defence wounds? Hid the evidence?

He had fed her grandad his blood. She felt sick and suddenly light headed. She sat down on the edge of the bath and tried to control her breathing.

After a moment, her grandad lifted up the soap, and when she didn't retrieve it from over his shoulder, he turned.

"Grandad," she started, pushing past the swelling in her throat. "Did Gabriel ever… did he ever hurt you?"

His big eyebrows furrowed. "Why are you asking me that?" He turned more so he could look her in the eyes. "Did he hurt you? Because if he did, I swear-"

"No, no," she rushed to quickly calm him. "He hasn't hurt me."

But he had. He'd lied to her. But then again, the truth wasn't exactly welcomed.

Her grandad nodded. "He's a good man, that one. I can see why you like him."

She gulped. *He's not a man at all.*

Becca finished bathing her grandad in silence, the two of them dancing the same dance they always did in perfect synchronicity like they shared one mind. It wasn't until he was all dry, dressed and sat in his chair when she broke the news.

"Grandad, Gabriel will no longer be your night-time care nurse." She was sat on the wooden dining chair beside him. She watched him process the information.

He blinked and frowned and looked up to her. "What? Why?"

She tried to think of an excuse that wouldn't lead to any more questions. "He found another job."

His brows furrowed, unconvinced. "And he didn't tell me?"

"Maybe he did tell you and you forgot?" She instantly hated herself. *I'm gaslighting my own grandad. Smooth, Becca.*

He nodded. "Yes. Probably." He was silent for a moment. "Does that mean he won't be coming here anymore?"

"I'm afraid so."

"That's a real shame." His eyes bugged. "Does that mean no more scones?"

Becca laughed. "I'm sure I can get you some scones."

"Perhaps you and Kathy could bake some together? You two used to love baking."

Becca's blood ran cold. He hadn't spoken her name to her in over a year. They had promised each other not to. She was the root of all their arguments, of all the early tension between them.

"We never baked together," Becca replied coolly.

"Sure you did." He smiled. She could see the child-like joy sparkle in his cloudy eyes and it was like a stab to the heart. "The two of you were always in the kitchen together."

"Mum wasn't a baker," she said. *And you weren't around to witness even if she was.* He had probably watched something on TV where a mother and daughter would bake cookies and laugh and throw flour at each other and then share them with their big, happy family. But that wasn't their family.

"When is Kathy coming to visit?" he asked, the dopey smile still filling his face.

The knife twisted deeper into her heart. "She's not, grandad."

"It would be nice to see her."

No, it wouldn't.

"Could you tell her to pop up sometime?"

Becca inhaled a shaky breath. Tears burned the backs of her eyes. She squeezed them shut and one escaped, rolling down the side of her nose.

"She's dead, Grandad. She's not coming."

He looked at her a moment and his smile fell. He sank into his chair. "Ah, that's right."

No, it wasn't. But Becca had also made a promise to herself that if her mum ever came back up in conversation, she was going to lie. Her mum being dead was a lot easier to say than the truth. She didn't want to explain their sordid family history to her grandad, only for him to forget and ask her again.

Her grandad didn't need to be reminded that he hadn't been a good dad to her mother. He didn't need to remember how he refused to go to her wedding because his illness made him hate Becca's dad for no real reason. He didn't need to remember that, even after he was diagnosed with a personality disorder and was given the right medication, Becca's mum still refused to let him back into her life.

He didn't need to know that there was an empty chasm between Becca and her mum ever since Becca had reached out to him behind her back and moved into the same village to take care of him now that he was old and alone.

No, it was better for everyone if Kathy was thought to be dead.

The mood in the basement of *Black Velvet* was sombre. The long, dark room was bordered with kegs and cages of bottles, crisps and peanuts. Right in the centre of the room stood a round table. Three chairs surrounded it where there used to be five. In them sat Ezra, Silas and Dalia. They met up every few weeks to gamble. Blood and money were exchanged as they laughed and joked. But the gatherings were never really about that.

Ezra wasn't quite an ancient. There wasn't really a specific age a vampire had to pass to become one. The title was more about endurance and experience, but Ezra liked to think ancients were six-hundred or older. And at this moment in time, Ezra was in the company of two ancients, instead of four.

Silas flung his cards across the table. They spun and danced in the air before landing all over the place. "I think it's time we stop pretending we're here to talk about the weather."

Both Ezra and Dalia lowered their cards, placing them carefully face down, as if the game was going to resume later on. All three of them looked to the empty space between Silas and Ezra. Ezra's gut twisted. Two ancients, gone, just like that. Ezra didn't know the specifics. He didn't want to know. But Tyrone and Nat had been in the club the night of the raid, and now they weren't at the table.

Ezra swirled his glass of blood before taking a sip, not daring to be the first one to talk about why they were really there.

Dalia sucked in a breath and ran her hands down her skinny black jeans as if to calm herself. "I've heard it's bad. Everywhere. Worse than here."

Silas nodded solemnly; his lips puckered. He was the oldest looking vampire Ezra knew. He must have been Turned in his late sixties, and he hadn't treated his body well in his human years. His skin was thick and leathery from too much sun exposure, and he had scars on almost every knuckle from being a hot-headed teen who relied more on brawn than brain.

"My progenies in New York have gotten in touch," he said. His voice was deep and gravelly from smoking a pipe. He had one of those voices that didn't need to be raised to be heard. "There's some kid – some small-time actor type – he's come clean. Says he's a vamp. He did the whole popping out his fangs and being burnt by silver to prove he's legit. Filmed it. The videos will make their way here soon, I'm guessing." He shook his head, jaw clenched beneath the tanned folds of his cheeks. He was never one to show emotion, so the slight flex said more than enough. Even though he always spoke with an even, loose tone like nothing really mattered, Ezra had learned to figure out when to listen. Now was most definitely a time to pay attention. "He's a big hit," Silas continued. "Fans are loving it. But you know for every fan who's fawning over him, there's a hundred humans clutching their crosses and fearing for their lives."

Dalia hugged herself, the leather of her jacket squeaking in the silence that followed. She opened her mouth several times before she spoke. "Same thing's happened in Copenhagen. Not an actor, but vamps are revealing what they are. Some ballerina, newly Turned. Did it to make her stronger and more agile but she ended up not getting work because she couldn't show up to rehearsals in the daytime. Apparently, they're loving her. Then there's a couple of nobodies filming themselves showing off their vampire abilities. Probably hoping it'll get them famous."

This was why Ezra came to them. They had progenies scattered all over the world. They were the best sources when it came to global matters. And, as much as Ezra hated to admit, they were in the middle of a global crisis.

An angry exhale rushed from Silas' nostrils and he ran his tongue over his teeth. "How are their Makers letting them do this? It goes against everything we stand for."

"I guess they're trying to control their exposure. They think it's better to be the ones revealing what they are than someone else doing it for them," said Dalia.

"But why now? This can't all just be because of the Moonlight raid," said Ezra.

Silas shook his head. "Stuff like this has always been happening. There's been vampire hunters around for as long as we've been around. We've just been able to keep a lid on things. Compel people to forget what they saw. Killing progenies that step out of line. Or simply changing the subject. Someone claims they saw a vampire? Well did you also know that deodorant can cause cancer?"

Silas stared at Ezra with his piercing blue eyes that were more fitting for a Siberian Husky, making Ezra's insides turn ice cold. He was daring him to react. Waiting for him to crack. Despite being over three-hundred years old, Silas had a way of making Ezra feel like a novice. He didn't see it as an insult. Silas was his Maker, after all. It was his job to teach and mentor Ezra.

"This is too big for the Court. They can't contain it now."

Both Silas and Ezra looked to Dalia, and by the sharpness in Silas' eyes, she'd said something wrong.

"I'm sorry, what? The *Court*?" asked Ezra. In the corner of his eye he saw Silas' jaw clench. Dalia gulped and looked to her lap.

He looked to his Maker for an explanation. Silas' nostrils flared, clearly reluctant.

"The Vampire Court," he said through a sigh. "We've been the ones keeping us a secret for the past couple of centuries."

Ezra blinked, shaking his head. "*We?*"

Silas watched him for a moment, his blue eyes studying the confusion etched across his face. He sighed again.

"I was recruited by the Court in the late 18th century. It was why I... taught you how to be a vampire the way that I did."

Ezra looked away as bloody memories attacked his mind; the heart-wrenching sensation of vampire bonds snapping. Of being the one destroying them. He stared for a long moment at the cement wall, his eyes flickering to calm the tears welling behind them. The basement plunged into a heavy silence. He could feel Silas watching him the way he always did – like some sort of twisted combination of predator and protector.

Ezra's jaw worked, shifting left to right. This *Vampire Court*... this power that he has only just found out his Maker was a part of... Their sole purpose was to keep their kind hidden for *centuries* and they had failed. His mouth moved trying to form words, before he managed to say in a voice so quiet it was barely more than a hushed breath, "Why does this feel like the end?"

Silas leaned back in his chair, his hand loosely around his glass of blood. "Because it is, Slick."

The statement was so harsh and final it knocked the wind right out of Ezra like a punch to the gut. He looked down at the table, at the back of his forgotten cards. Sudden anger roiled inside him in the silence that followed. He knew his Maker wasn't the type to hold his hand, to pat him on the back and tell him everything was going to be okay. He hadn't done that when he had Turned him, he'd made him earn his new life the hard way; so why should he expect things to be different now?

But Silas could have died in that raid. It was only a stroke of luck that he wasn't a mess of bloody goop being scrubbed off the hospital walls. Yet here he sat, working a cigarette out of the pack in his blazer pocket like they were all just a group of mates drinking and talking shit.

Panic and hysteria battled inside Ezra. He felt for their bond to try and sooth himself with his Maker's unshakable calm. But when he reached, mental arms outstretched, he was met not by a cool, still pool, but a tumultuous sea.

Silas' shining eyes cut to him across the table and their connection broke like a rope snapping. Silas stared, unblinking, as he slid his cigarette between his thin lips and lit it. Ezra gulped, too afraid to look away.

"They've gotten ahead of us," said Dalia, breaking the stifling tension. Silas looked to her and Ezra relaxed. But Dalia's back was ram-rod straight. The aloofness she had tried to trick Ezra with when he had met her last was gone. It had worn out. Now her fear was real and it was tight in her features.

"So, this is it. What do we do? Do I shut the club? Will they come for me? Are they gonna kill us?" Blood tears gathered in her dark eyes and ran down her cheeks. Her panicked questions had Ezra's blood rushing with static once again. Ezra instantly regretted being annoyed by Silas' indifference- the indifference he now knew was a ruse.

The ancient's eyes slid to her lazily. He shrugged and tapped his cigarette against the ash tray. "I guess the ball's in their court now," he said through a smoky exhale. "We've just got to sit back and see what they do with it."

Chapter 7

Gabriel stared up at the ceiling of his bedroom. He had kicked his duvet to the foot of the bed but he just laid there, his fingers drumming against his biceps. Becca had fired him. He now had nowhere to go. Lillian was either always over at Ben's or the couple were hidden away in her room. And Ezra was on a mission – with all the stuff on the News, he now had a reason to be the Big Shot. So, he was busy out and about doing God knows what to try and help them out of this shitshow. Which left Gabriel on his own, struggling to find ways to spend his nights.

   With a sigh, he sat at the edge of his bed and looked about his bedroom. He had never decorated. The walls were still painted a calming, stone grey and the only furniture he possessed was his bed, a wardrobe and a desk for his TV to stand on. Lillian had made a remark that the sparseness was so that he could up and leave them whenever he wanted. It had been a joke, but it had stung. The three of them had a complicated relationship. It had been him and Ezra for so long, and then Ezra had Turned Lillian and suddenly there were three.

He had nothing against Lillian. In fact, he thought her to be quite charming. He had been there in the first few months of her being born anew – which was when most trouble occurred – and she had fallen into the role of a progeny seamlessly. Ezra had watched over her like a proud father, teaching her how to manage her hunger, to compel when absolutely necessary, and how to heal. They had been a well-oiled machine back then, and still were. And this had made Gabriel feel like a third wheel. Like he had been a mangy stray dog Ezra had found and nursed back to health, only for him to get bored of and buy a pedigree.

He knew those feelings of abandonment he quashed nightly weren't just Ezra's doing, but it was easier to be pissed off at him than the faceless vampire who had made him.

Gabriel shrugged on a pair of jeans and a navy long-sleeved t-shirt before heading downstairs. Ezra was at the kitchen table, scanning over a newspaper. Four more were stacked by his side. His lithe frame was dwarfed by an oversized red hoodie. He had one ankle up on his knee, his gym shorts exposing his toned legs. For a guy with such dark hair, his leg hair was surprisingly sparse. It was something Gabriel usually poked fun at. But by the scrunched up look on Ezra's face, this was not the time to bring it up.

Gabriel eyed him as he took out a bottle from the fridge and poured some blood into a pan on the hob. The other vampire was so engrossed by what he was reading he didn't seem to notice his new company.

"So, we moving or what?" Gabriel asked casually, flicking on the hob.

Ezra's eyes lifted to him and his thick, dark eyebrows furrowed. "What?"

Gabriel nodded to the paper. "With what's going on… it's getting worse, right? I've been seeing more and more videos up and… well… I've lost Becca and Julian…"

Ezra was watching him curiously, a crease of anger deepening between his brows. He leaned back on his chair.

Gabriel itched under the scrutiny of his gaze but he'd already started. He shrugged, trying to look casual. "I dunno, I guess my job was the only thing keeping me here."

At this, the muscles in Ezra's cheek rolled as he clenched his jaw. "You wanna leave?" His tone was sharp and accusing – challenging.

Here they were again, conversing the only way they knew how.

"Do *you* want me to leave?" Gabriel snapped back, standing to his full height.

They stared at each other for a long, drawn out moment. Both of them daring the other to look away first. This type of standoff, if not interrupted by Lillian, would usually result in an argument, and Gabriel's dead blood was humming with anticipation. But instead, Ezra just shook his head, the tight lines of anger in his face shifting into concern.

"What's gotten into you?"

Gabriel's heart plummeted and he quickly turned to stir the blood in the pan. "Nothing," he mumbled, clenching his eyes shut and cringing at how pathetic it came out. "It's just... I have a lot of time on my hands now. I've been thinking a lot. I just-I don't know what I'm supposed to be doing with all this. I don't know how to make myself useful." He gazed out the window, at their small, decked garden. Lillian had wrapped fairy lights around the trellises and now they danced and winked at him.

Ezra sighed heavily. "You and me both."

Gabriel switched off the hob, poured the steaming blood into a mug and turned back to his company. Ezra's posture had wilted, he suddenly looked so pale and drawn out. His thick dark hair was mussed from a lack of brushing.

"How was poker?" Gabriel asked, lifting his mug to his lips and blowing.

"Not much poker was played." He tried to slam the paper closed but it floated smoothly and silently back together so he slammed his palm over it for effect. "Silas is shit scared which is *not* a good sign." He let out an angry puff of air through his nostrils. "He hides it well but I felt it. He then caught me snooping and was *not* happy."

Gabriel bit down on his tongue and took a sip of his blood. *Ooh Silas this, Silas that,* he mimicked in his head. *Oh, I'm so close to* my *Maker and I know what he's thinking.* He frowned, inwardly chastising himself for the ball of envy swelling deep inside him. He hated it. Hated that it made him think so ill of Ezra. He knew the other vampire didn't mean it. Of course, he was going to

Silas for help; it was the right thing to do. The old vampire was great to have on their side. He had made Ezra into an incredible vampire – although he would never openly admit to thinking that. But every time Ezra mentioned his Maker, it only reminded Gabriel that he'd never had one. At least, not in a way that counted.

He took a seat opposite Ezra, trying to focus on the hot blood easing his hunger and not his misdirected bitterness.

Ezra grabbed one of the papers from the pile and slid it in front of him.

"Don't know what to do with yourself? You can help me. See what's in there about us."

He'd been given the Hicklesbury Local and his lips quirked into a smile at the picture of the graffiti that covered the side of the Off License. Gary, the owner, sported a thick moustache and wore trousers that were slightly too short. This meant, to the bored youths of the village, that he was, without question, a paedophile. That was the premise of the vandalism.

"Well, it appears we're not interesting enough for the front page," he commented.

"Maybe not in this place but-" Ezra lifted his newspaper, "everywhere else, we are."

Gabriel's smile fell away. Staring back at him was a blurry security camera still of a male vampire, blacked eyed and fanged, chomping on the neck of a young woman in some sort of alleyway.

"I don't understand how this is happening. We've been around for centuries and just now they're finding this kind of footage?"

Ezra lowered the paper and rubbed his eye with a tired groan. "Apparently our kind have friends in high places. Friends that usually make stuff like this go away. But now the press is giving people awards for speaking up and giving them evidence. I guess money talks."

Gabriel flicked through the rest of his paper and found nothing vampire related until an article about how the local jewellers were bumping up the prices of their silver wares now that they were suddenly in high demand. He sipped at his mug, feeling the pressure of his fangs against his gums as he inhaled the hot aroma. For a moment, the sensation sickened him. The three of them *weren't* monsters. But he couldn't help feeling that at some point, and very soon, they really were going to be run out of this town by an angry mob with torches and pitch forks.

"I'd better head to work," said Ezra, dropping his face into his hands.

Gabriel studied him. "You sure? You don't look so good."

He ran his hands down his face and sent Gabriel a dry, heavy-lidded smile. "What? Am I lacking my usual chipper glow?" He dragged himself to his feet. "Ah well, girls love a brooding barman."

"Seriously, though. This-" Gabriel gestured to the mess of papers. "It's getting to you, isn't it?"

"It's getting to everyone, Gabriel. But we've still gotta go through the motions. And saying that-" He twirled, sending the toggles of his hoodie whipping violently around his neck, and grabbed the back of Gabriel's chair. "You better get yourself a new old man friend. Or old woman friend, to entertain your nights." He pulled a face. "That came wrong. I mean, find another *Julian*. Preferably one you like and so will not eat. And also, one without a granddaughter that will turn you into a lovesick puppy."

Gabriel sent him a sarcastic smile and drained his mug.

"We'll get to the other side of this." Ezra grabbed his shoulder and squeezed, an action that was equal parts comforting and belittling. "And hey, maybe the world will be a better place then."

"Hey boys."

The two vampires turned to see Lillian sliding gracefully into the room in all her pink fluffiness. Ezra leaned overdramatically, one foot in the air, to check the empty doorway.

"No Ben tonight?" he asked, righting himself.

Lillian sighed. "We're not joined at the hip, you know?"

"Could have fooled me."

Lillian opened the fridge and grabbed the bottle Gabriel had already half-emptied. "He's tired. Needed to get a good night's sleep."

"Makes sense. Good to know he has a breaking point."

Lillian grinned. "I can't help that I'm such good company."

Ezra headed out the room, dropping a quick peck on Lillian's temple as he did, "Can't argue with that."

Lillian poured herself a glass of blood, hers cold. She'd only been a vampire for twenty years so she hadn't learned to despise cold blood yet. So far, she was a pure vampire. She'd drank from the vein only enough for Ezra to teach her how to drink in moderation but she had never ended a human's life before. She had followed graciously in Ezra's footsteps. That was not the case for himself. Gabriel had had to learn how to be a vampire on his own. He had been attacked and drained in his home city, Thessaloniki, back in 1910. The vampire must have used his blood to heal him part way because after Gabriel had died from blood loss, hunched up and alone in an alley with his trachea torn open, he had awoken, dazed and confused and covered in his own blood but with no wound in sight. He'd almost died – again- that morning when the sun had risen and had burned him to his bones on his own doorstep as he had tried to enter his home which he no longer had access to. He needed an invitation to enter his communal property.

From then on, Gabriel had had to create a new life for himself, learn about his new abilities and control his hunger; all without a guide. This meant, for the first few years of his new life, there had been a trail of mangled bodies left in his wake. He'd cleaned up his act once he learned to control himself, and had found the guise of care nurse a good way to score an easy meal. Ezra's disapproval irked him. Compared to the vampire he used to be; Gabriel was a *saint*. But the fact that he was even still standing meant that Ezra hadn't disclosed his body count to his holier-than-thou Maker so he really couldn't think Gabriel was *that* terrible.

For Ezra, all of his killings were other vampires. Ezra had been Turned in a similar way. Attacked randomly in the night by a hungry Silas, but he was then kept and reared.

Silas was a ruthless Maker. To engrain the importance of being a 'good' vampire, the ancient had forced Ezra to kill his own vampire brothers and sisters when they stepped out of line – killing a 'breather' being the ultimate offence. Ezra had shared a story once, when they were both high from drugged blood, of him having to kill a dear friend, a vampire Silas had Turned mere months after himself. They had grown up together, so to speak, but she hadn't been able to control her urges. Once she started feeding, she couldn't stop. Not until Ezra had shoved a stake through her heart.

"Do we really need all of these?" groaned Lillian, shoving all the newspapers into a messy pile before taking Ezra's vacated chair. "I'm gonna tell Ben to stop being Ezra's lapdog, going to the shop every morning to grab papers for him."

"He's just worried," said Gabriel, leaning back. His eyes flickered to the clock on the wall. He should be starting his shift with Julian in ten minutes. A sudden stab of pain hit him when he wondered if the old man thought he'd abandoned him. He liked to think they found a good replacement care nurse. Julian deserved that.

Lillian's eyes widened. "Yeah, don't I know it. But we can't do anything, right? It's out of his control."

Gabriel sucked a breath in through his teeth. "Don't let him catch you saying that. He'll think you're losing faith."

She smirked over her mug. "He's not *God*."

He tutted, shaking his head. "Blasphemy."

She rolled her eyes and looked to the newspaper with the picture of the vampire in the alley. She gulped heavily and her jaw tightened slightly. He reached across the table and held her hand. Her eyes closed at the touch and she squeezed her fingers around his, a wordless plea that set his heart to ice.

Chapter 8

It was a quiet night. Eerily quiet. The streetlamps lit Gabriel's and Lillian's leisurely walk around their quaint little village. They had both gotten bored around midnight, lounging around in their living room feeling sorry for themselves, and so a bit of fresh air was needed. Lillian had traded her dressing gown for a cream belted trench coat. The small heels of her knee-high boots clicked loudly in the silence of the night.

They walked past the 24-hour petrol station and Gabriel furrowed his brows at the lowered shutters. "That's weird."

They both paused, double checking the huge sign above the building advertising their around the clock opening times.

"That is weird," Lillian agreed. She looked to the road. "But, to be honest, I don't think any cars have passed us since we've been out."

Hicklesbury was indeed a small village, but it was also a very common travel route. In fact, it was a very popular stop over destination for people travelling through the country. So much so that the village prided itself on their very cute and pricey boutique bed and breakfasts. And with knowing all of this, Gabriel did find it awfully strange that the roads were completely empty.

"We should go see Ezra," suggested Lillian. Her shoulders were bunched up as she surveyed their dead surroundings warily.

Gabriel nodded in agreement and they headed in the direction of the *Horseshoe*.

Becca stopped talking and just stared at her friend once she realised that her attention had drifted. Becca swirled her straw around in her rum and coke, the ice clinking against the glass. When Maeve's lips twitched up in amusement, Becca had had enough.

"I'm sorry, am I keeping you from something?" she asked.

Maeve blinked and her eyes shifted back to her company. She grinned like a giddy child and tucked her wavy, blonde hair behind her ear. "What?"

"I was trying to tell you something important and your eyes just, like, glazed over." Becca looked behind her, at Ezra and Mitch behind the bar chatting. Her stomach twisted a little. He was a vampire. The man who had poured their drinks *was a vampire*. As if sensing her watchful eyes, Ezra looked over his shoulder and their gazes locked. Her insides suddenly turned cold. She spun around in the booth, picked up her drink and took a sip, her heart pounding.

Maeve's brows furrowed. "Am I missing something? What the hell was that?"

"What?" Becca winced, the rum burning her throat.

"The way Ezra just looked at you." The twitch in her lip reappeared. "That was so intense. How do I make him look at *me* like that?"

Oh, just find out that he has a diet of human blood. Becca let out a steadying breath. She had promised Gabriel that she would keep quiet. And although their relationship was complicated – understatement of the century- after seeing all the hysteria over social media, she knew it was the right thing to do.

"I thought we came here for a drink, not to stare at the bar staff," she said instead.

"We can do both." Maeve chewed her lip then sipped at her gin and tonic, still watching over Becca's shoulder.

Becca rolled her eyes. "He's like ten years younger than you. You're basically lusting after a child." But then Becca paused in thought. How old *was* Ezra? What exactly were real vampires? Were they how they were written in books? She knew they burned in sunlight and when they touched silver, but what else? Were they actually immortal? And if that was true, how old did that make Ezra?

How old did that make *Gabriel*?

She slumped lower into the cushions of the booth, her drink nestled against her chest, hugging it as she sipped through her straw. How could she chastise Maeve for having the hots for Ezra when she had dated Gabriel? Who, on the outside might look in his mid-thirties but he could be double that? Or even more? Bile rose in her throat. Was Gabriel older than her grandad?

"Are you okay? You've gone super pale."

Becca pushed herself back up and placed her drink back on the table. "Yeah. Shouldn't have bought a double."

Becca heard the door creak and clang behind her.

Maeve's eyes lit up. "Ooh, interesting. The whole gang's here."

Becca followed her eyes and her heart did one heavy thud at the sight of Gabriel. He and Lillian crossed the floor to the bar, catching Ezra's attention.

"God, you must really be bored without Ben if you're hanging out with him," said Ezra to Lillian which was met with a sour look from Gabriel.

"What is he doing here?" Becca spun back round to Maeve.

Maeve pulled a face. "How am I supposed to know? What's the big deal?"

"I was literally just telling you that I'm still really conflicted about Gabriel. I thought we were... I dunno, getting back into it? Then things just..."

"I mean, you did fire him. That's not a way to get into a guy's pants, just saying."

"I did what I had to do. He just... he wasn't a good fit." Becca had told Maeve that her reasoning behind firing Gabriel was because her grandad didn't like him. She wasn't comfortable with lying, and since finding out about Gabriel's true nature, it felt like every second thing out of her mouth was a lie.

Becca shrank back down in her seat. "Have they noticed us?"

"Not yet." Maeve sipped at her drink, entranced by whatever was going on at the bar. "Such a strange combination," Maeve said wistfully, her head tilting.

"What?"

"The three of them. What's their deal? They fucking or what?"

Becca nearly choked on her breath. "*What?*"

Maeve squinted like the three vampires by the bar were a puzzle she was attempting to solve. *Good luck with that.*

"It's just an odd group. The three of them living together. A Gen Z, a millennial and a Gen X all under one roof. None of them related?" She started absently swirling her straw around her gin glass as she studied them. "The way they are with each other. They're so *close.*"

Giving in to the intrigue, Becca tried to subtly glance over her shoulder. Ezra now had his forearms on the bar. Lillian was opposite him, standing with her boots crossed at the ankles and her face mere inches from the barman's. Ezra's dark eyes positively *shone.* Gabriel was sat on one of the stools, head resting on his knuckles, seemingly lost in thought.

"Definitely fucking. It's some polygamy shit, I'm telling you."

Becca looked back at her friend, appalled. "Excuse me, I dated one of them."

Maeve pointed her straw at her. "Dated, past tense. And it's a good thing you got out when you did. Although, gotta admit I'm a little jealous of Lillian because that is one tasty sandwich."

"Right, I'm finishing my drink and going. I've had enough of you."

Maeve laughed. "Awh, c'mon, I'm just joking. I mean, *I'm not really joking.*" Becca shot her a tired look. "All you do is worry about your grandad. Can't you just chill out for one night and indulge me. It's not like you can escape me, we live together."

When Maeve started showing her the sad pouty look and fluttering her long eyelashes, Becca couldn't help but smile. "Fine, I'll stay. But we're not talking about those guys anymore."

Maeve shrugged and dropped back in her seat. Her eyes wandered back to the bar. "I guess Mitch is kinda cute. If he got a haircut."

Becca rolled her eyes.

Maeve laughed. "It's a small village. Slim pickings."

Ezra was sitting cross-legged on the floor of his bedroom balling his socks when there was a knock at his door.

"House meeting downstairs," said Lillian.

Ezra furrowed his brows and threw his socks into his drawer. He looked at the clock on his bedside table. It was just past eight in the evening. Lillian was never usually up this early. "Okay."

"Now."

When he opened his door, she was waiting for him, arms crossed tightly and a worried crease in her brow. Ezra reached out to her but she turned and headed down the stairs.

"Come on," she said.

Ezra followed. Gabriel was already sitting on one of the sofas, ankle on his knee and arm over the armrest. He looked calm and casual in a thin, fitted cashmere jumper and jeans. Lillian dropped into the space beside him, hands curled into the sleeves of her dressing down.

Standing in front of the TV was Ben, in his usual plaid shirt and khaki combo. He was hugging himself, his fingers digging into his biceps. When he locked eyes with Ezra, he gulped but straightened his back.

Ezra jerked his thumb to him but looked to Lillian. "Did he call this meeting?" Then he shot a glare at Ben. "You can't call house meeting. You don't live here."

"Ezra, just sit down and listen to him," said Lillian firmly, "please?"

He sank down onto the other sofa, not without shooting the human another accusatory look.

A silence followed. Gabriel shifted in his seat. "So? What's this about?"

Ben cleared his throat, clearly uncomfortable under all their watchful eyes. Even Lillian, who always had a smile on her face whenever he was around, looked grave.

"I watched the News today," Ben started. He released the hold he had on himself and started fiddling with his fingers in front of his chest instead. "The Prime Minister is acting on the vampire… conspiracy that's been going around."

Ezra's eyes automatically flickered to Gabriel and he was not surprised that the other vampire was looking back at him.

"He's ordered a country-wide curfew," continued Ben.

Ezra's confusion was mirrored by Gabriel and they both turned their attention to the human.

"What?" asked Gabriel.

Ben shuffled and scratched the back of his neck. "He's advised everyone to be indoors before sundown. It being the middle of August, people should be off the street by eight."

Ezra looked back to Gabriel but caught Lillian's eyes instead. They were huge and expectant and stuck on him. His heart sank. She was looking at him, progeny to Maker. Like he had the answers. But he had nothing.

Gabriel shook his head as if to dispel his confusion. "The Prime Minister actually was on TV talking about vampires?"

"Not outright, no," said Ben. "He just referred to the videos of people being attacked. He said the attacks were by people suffering from an ailment that made them sensitive to sun exposure. So, for everyone's safety, he has issued a curfew."

Ezra felt like the ground had been pulled from under him. His head swam. He ran his fingers through his hair, dropped his back against the back of the sofa and expelled a loud sigh into the silence that followed.

"They know about us. They're trying to talk around it to keep people calm but they know we exist. And if the government knows-" He ran his hands down his face.

"This curfew is just the beginning," finished Gabriel. "We're gonna be hunted down. We're gonna get captured and experimented on and God knows what else."

"Really?" Lillian's voice was tight with panic. She looked to Ezra. "Really? Is that going to happen?"

I don't know. I really don't know. The words lodged in his throat.

A sudden knock at the door had everyone jumping to their feet.

Chapter 9

Lillian had shot to Ben in the blink of an eye. His arms wrapped around her like he could actually protect her. Gabriel and Ezra were closest to the hallway. They both looked at each other, to the hallway, then Ezra lifted his hand in a 'wait there' motion, before stepping out of the room like he was about to sacrifice his life for the good of his country. Gabriel wanted to roll his eyes but a bigger part of him was thankful the older vampire had taken charge. After hearing about the curfew, all he could think about was the way humans treated anything 'other' in almost *every* sci-fi movie. Was this the moment right before the three of them were dosed with drugs to knock them out, only for them to wake up strapped to a hospital bed, hooked up to a bunch of machines and tubes?

He heard the door open and he stared at the wall as if he'd be able to see through it by sheer force of will.

"Oh hey," he heard Ezra say in a conversational tone, not exactly fit for being confronted by a load of suited up muscle with guns.

"Hi Ezra, is Gabriel home?" replied a familiar voice.

Gabriel looked back to Lillian and Ben. The two of them had loosened their hold on each other. When he turned back round, Becca entered the room with Ezra at her back. Gabriel blinked in surprise and took a step back.

She smiled at Gabriel then paused and looked around. "Have I come at a bad time?"

Gabriel looked back. Lillian grabbed Ben and pulled him towards the door, smiling the whole time. "We'll give you two some privacy." On the way out, she pushed Ezra along as well.

When it was just the two of them in the living room, Gabriel hooked his thumbs in his belt loops in an attempt to look casual. "So, what are you doing here?"

Becca tucked a long strand of hair behind her ear. "My plan was to stay away but with everything going on and knowing what you are-" she winced, "I have questions. Like, a lot of questions. And I would really appreciate if you gave me some answers. I just- I need to know what we're dealing with."

Gabriel nodded. "Understandable. I can give you all the answers you need." He gestured to the sofa. "Can I make you a drink?"

She sank down onto the edge of the sofa, her posture stiff but a thin smile on her lips. "Got anything besides blood?"

He returned her smile. "We have tea, thanks to Ben."

She nodded. "A cup of tea would be lovely. Milky. Two sugars."

Just how your grandfather has it.

Gabriel calmed himself as he made the brew, focusing solely on the matter at hand. Becca was here. Becca had come here to see him. To talk about vampire stuff. She had come *to him*. After the way his kind was being portrayed in the media, he had figured she'd be terrified of him. Yet she was currently sitting on his sofa and he was making her a cup of tea. Even when they had dated, she had never come to his place. With Lillian being a new-born, it wasn't fair to make her hide her nature in her own home so they never had visitors, besides Ben.

Becca's eyes flew to him when he returned. She was still sitting in the exact same position, her hands clutched together tightly on her lap, her dress smoothed over her knees. The mug trembled when she took it. Gabriel dropped a coaster onto the coffee table and she seemed grateful to be able to place down her drink.

He took the opposite sofa, sitting as far from her as he could. By the nervous energy she was filling the room with, he felt like it was the best option.

She looked around the simply decorated room. The real fireplace. The leafy wallpaper. Lillian's collection of jade turtles.

"Your house is so… normal," she commented.

Gabriel's lips quirked up. "Not what you were expecting?"

She shrugged. "You were always so adamant that we stayed at mine."

"I just needed to make sure I left before sunrise. Not that I wanted to."

Their eyes locked. The way they had back at her grandfather's house. Like there was still something between them. "I hated that. It made me feel used."

He gulped. "I'm sorry."

She held his gaze for a moment, then cleared her throat and picked up her mug. "So, I have questions."

Gabriel leaned forward, his elbows on his knees. "Of course."

She sipped, her eyes looking faraway, thinking. "How old are you?"

"A hundred and forty-five."

A small noise left her mouth, something between a gasp and an *oh*. She rested the mug on her lap, both hands circling it. "I've slept with someone twice my grandad's age."

Gabriel couldn't help but smile. "I was Turned when I was thirty-five. So, really, I've just been thirty-five for a very long time."

"I don't know if that's better."

"That's fair."

Her brows furrowed. "Can you turn into a bat?"

"No."

"A wolf?"

Someone's read Dracula. "No."

"Any sort of animal?"

"No."

She looked around the room as she delved into her mind. "Can you fly?"

"Unfortunately, no. But we can run fast."

Her eyebrow quirked up at him.

"I know that sounds lame. But, I mean, we can run exceptionally fast. Like, if we weren't trying to blend in, we'd have no need for a car."

"Do you have a reflection?"

"Yes."

She nodded. "I think I would have noticed if you didn't. And I know you can have pictures taken."

Yes, because they used to take photos of themselves together. And she would take candid shots of him because she liked to preserve memories.

"Do you need to be invited into places to enter?"

"Only places of residence. And it doesn't have to be by the owner."

"Why?"

Gabriel shrugged. "I'm not sure. I'm not sure about anything, really. I think maybe it's something to do with vampire being linked to the Devil, and they say that the Devil needs to be invited into a body- a life, to possess it. That's the only correlation I can think of."

Becca's face blanched at the mention of the Devil and Gabriel instantly regretted getting too comfortable with this topic.

"We're not evil," he rushed, making the whole thing sound ten times worse. He needed to stop saying that to her, but it seemed to have become a reflex.

She shuffled on the sofa and looked down at her tea. "Do you have fangs?"

He nodded but she wasn't looking. After a moment, her eyes found his and his voice came out raspy when he said, "yes."

"How come I haven't seen them? Haven't felt them?"

"We can retract them."

"Do your eyes do that... thing? Do they go all black like in those videos?"

He nodded. "Only when I'm really hungry and I smell blood. But I have a good diet so it doesn't really happen to me. Not anymore."

"Can I see?"

Gabriel gulped; his insides suddenly cold. He shook his head. "I can't do it on command and I would never want to be in that state around you."

"What about your fangs? Can I see them?"

"Why?" He hadn't meant for the word to come out so harsh. He suddenly felt very defensive. Like he was some sort of freakshow entertainment.

Her eyes widened a fraction, but then her shoulders sagged. "I just- I felt like I knew you. And now with all of this new information, I feel like I've lost you. I just want to know you again."

Gabriel's jaw clenched and he inwardly chastised himself for thinking anything negatively towards this amazing woman.

"You do know me," he said.

"I want to understand you."

He nodded, reluctancy making the movement stiff, and he gestured her over to his sofa. She placed her mug back on the coaster and sank down onto the cushion beside him. Her face was so close to his now. The freckles on the bridge of her nose looked like a sprinkling of brown sugar. He could hear her heartbeat, quick with fear.

"Are you sure you want to see?"

She nodded and placed her hand on his thigh. The warmth of her touch seeped into his bones.

Without another word, he parted his lips and willed his fangs to unsheathe. Their *click* rang out across the room, impossibly loud. At the sight of them, Becca's hand pulled away. Gabriel closed his mouth, the tips of his fangs pressing against his lower lip. Her eyes dropped to his chest. He looked to the wall, his fangs receding back into his gums.

He could feel her next to him; her body heat, her shallow breaths, her racing heart. But he couldn't look. He couldn't see that terror alight in her eyes.

Finally, she said, "Did you use them on my grandad? Did you bite him?"

He dared to look back. She looked sad now, and she had noticeably moved further down the sofa.

"No," he said, "I used a needle. In his arm. I told him I needed a blood sample."

"Why has he never told me about it?"

"Because I compelled him to forget."

Confusion creased her forehead. Gabriel chewed on his tongue. He really didn't want to talk to her about compulsion, it was such messy topic. But he'd told her he'd give her answers, and he was a man of his word.

"Vampires can compel humans. We can make them forget things and manipulate what you see or feel," he explained. Becca crossed her arms over her stomach, an unconscious reflex from feeling exposed. "I can only take away a few minutes, maybe a specific memory if it's not too engrained into the person's being," he added, not knowing if he was making things better or worse. "Ancients can do more. They can wipe away whole years, whole chunks of a person's life."

"Ancients?" Her voice was barely a whisper now. Clearly this was far too much information to receive at once.

"Very old vampires."

She slouched to the back of the sofa. Her eyes flickered to the closed door. "Ezra and Lillian, are they ancients?"

He shook his head. "Ezra likes to think he is, but no."

"Did you ever compel me?" When her eyes met his, tears shone in them.

Gabriel's throat tightened. He shook his head. But when a tear fell down her freckled cheek, he added. "Never. I would never do that to you. I promise you that." He reached for her and she let him take her hand. "I am answering every question you ask me. If I ever even thought that compelling

78

you was an option, you wouldn't be here right now. I would have compelled you back in the church when you saw Lillian get burned. I would have made you forget there and then. But I would *never* do that to you." He was shaking. His voice was coming out wet like he, too, was on the verge of tears.

Her eyes were locked onto his, so impossibly green and beautiful. Her lips were trembling but she didn't look away. She wanted to believe him; he could tell.

"I compelled Julian just enough so he didn't remember the pain, that's it. I promise," he added, *needing* her to believe him.

Her eyes searched his. Tears gathered on her lashes. He just watched her watching him, trying to be as open to her as he possibly could. He wasn't hiding anything, not anymore. It was so freeing and so terrifying.

"Should I be scared?" she finally asked.

"Of me? Never." He looked down at her hand in his, so pale and fragile, and he knew he would never so much as leave a bruise on her skin for as long as he lived.

"What about the others? The ones on the internet? The ones with the eyes."

"The three of us are the only vampires in Hicklesbury. So as long as you're here, you're safe. And those vampires on film, they won't be around for much longer."

"What do you mean?"

He released her hand and returned to his elbows on his knees position beside her. "Vampires have a strict code to not do anything to expose our secret. So, vamps going around attacking humans in places where they will be caught on camera-" He *tsked,* "They will be taken care of."

"You mean killed?"

Gabriel nodded.

She gulped, paling. "By who?"

He shrugged. "Other, more dedicated vampires." *Like Ezra's blood family.*

She thought about this for a moment. "But what about now? Now that, well, the secret is out."

"That's a good question." He locked eyes with her. "And it's one I'm afraid I don't have the answer to." *But I fear it won't be good.*

They both fell into a thick silence. Becca's eyes were chasing her milling thoughts around the floor as Gabriel wrestled with his own unsettling uneasiness. But he couldn't think about the uncertain road ahead right now. Becca was by his side and there were still so many unsaid things between them.

"I'm sorry," he rasped. The two words were so heavy between them. "I'm sorry for everything. For leaving you alone in the mornings. For constantly going to the bathroom when we went out for meals, but you have to know that everything I ate when we were together would just come right back up."

She laughed at that. It was small, and she tried to hide it by chewing on her lip, but the joy was back in her eyes – even if it was just for a second.

"I'm sorry I was never one of those boyfriends that surprised you at work with, I don't know, a box of cookies." She smiled and he smiled back, laughing at himself. "All of my knowledge of twenty-first century relationships has come from watching sitcoms, if you haven't already noticed."

He dropped his chin on his knuckles, gazing up at her. "I was never meant to fall for you. I've been so good. I usually keep my distance. Never get too involved with humans. But with you, I just couldn't help it. I tried. I really did."

Her cheeks flushed and she averted her eyes. "Well, I mean, we did see each other almost *every* night. It was just a proximity thing. I was-" She shrugged, "*there.*"

"No." The word was so delicate from his lips but it startled her. Her wide eyes found him. "You are incredible, Becca. You're so caring and loving and *strong*." She laughed, shaking her head. He took her hand once more, and slid across the sofa so their knees touched. "The way you took it upon yourself to take care of Julian after your Mum disowned him, you didn't even know him growing up. You owe him nothing. Yet you found him, you built a relationship with him, and he loves you *so* much."

She smiled and tucked her hair behind her ear. "I mean, he may have been a bad dad to my mum but he never did anything bad to me. I'm just doing what any granddaughter would do."

Gabriel shook his head. "You don't give yourself enough credit. You amaze me."

She took her hand from his and hugged herself, clearly not used to being so heavily complimented.

"It's not like I did it all by myself. I had you, and Claudia."

"Stop that."

She peered at him. He gazed back at her. And for a moment, everything was simple. He liked her, she liked him. They were so close now. He saw himself cupping her cheek and kissing her like he used to. She'd melt in his arms for a moment before grabbing him back and holding him close.

But the truth was out there now. It had simultaneously brought them closer and pulled them apart.

"I'd better go." She got to her feet and Gabriel was quick to follow.

"Are you sure you don't have any more questions?"

She laughed lightly. "Oh, only like a thousand more. But that'll do for now. And with the curfew starting soon, I'd better be home."

"It's not started now?"

He followed her into the hallway.

"No, it starts Sunday officially, but with everything going on, I don't want people talking."

Gabriel nodded, understanding. If everyone else was locked and bolted behind their doors, Becca walking around alone at night would have some net curtains twitching.

"How is he, by the way, your grandfather?" he asked.

"He misses you." She smiled sadly.

He missed him, too. That old man never failed to make him laugh.

"What did you tell him?"

She shrugged. "I said you got a different job." She rubbed the back off her neck and winced. "I hate lying to him."

"Who's looking after him now?"

"He's got another care nurse. Paul something. He seems nice. Grandad hasn't complained about him- *yet*."

Gabriel smirked. "I'm glad he's doing okay."

They both said their goodbyes, not holding eye contact long enough to want to make it linger, and he watched her from the door until she was out of sight.

When he closed the front door and turned, Ezra appeared from the kitchen with a smug look on his face.

"Were you listening the whole time?"

Ezra shrugged. "I was in the kitchen, not my fault I have exceptional hearing."

Gabriel moved to head back into the living room but the other vampire blocked his way. "So, you told her everything, huh?"

Gabriel's gut twisted. "I had to." *And here comes the tongue lashing.*

"I get it." Gabriel blinked in shock, to which Ezra shrugged. "I'm not saying it's gonna be easy for you two but, she's clearly into you. I mean, she willingly came into a house full of vamps. And with everything going on right now, we need as many humans on our side as we can get."

Gabriel's eyebrow quirked up, unconvinced. "Seriously?"

"Yeah. And I did a background check on her back when you were going out anyway so she's fine."

"You did *what*?"

Ezra seemed offended by Gabriel's outrage. "Just to check she wasn't some secret government spy trying to infiltrate us. And she's not, so no need to worry." He smiled. "Did you know she made her money as a teen breeding ferrets?"

Gabriel pulled a face.

"That was also my reaction."

Gabriel shook his head, trying to rid his mind of this conversation. "If you think we need more human allies, does that mean you're going to ease up on Ben?"

"Our lives may be in imminent danger but he still wears socks with sandals. We really need to think about the types of people we want on our side."

Gabriel laughed, shaking his head. Ezra spun around on the banister like it was a dancing pole, before heading up the stairs. "I shall bid you adieu, laundry calls. And then I've got to get ready for work." He paused on the fourth step. "Do I even go to work with this curfew thing going on?"

"Apparently it's not starting until Sunday. I guess it's your call."

Ezra pulled a face. "That makes no sense."

Gabriel shrugged.

Ezra continued up the stairs. "Curiouser and curiouser."

Chapter 10

Becca closed her front door behind her and sank against it with a sigh. Her mind had been swimming the entire walk back from Gabriel's. So much new information. So much to process. She got this sick feeling in the pit of her stomach whenever she thought about Gabriel, because, after everything he had told her, she still liked him. She didn't want to. She wanted to be horrified. She wanted to be disgusted. She wanted to feel betrayed by all the dishonesty in their relationship. But she understood his side. And with understanding came acceptance.

She shook her head and made her way into the kitchen. *Acceptance?* What the hell? *What, I'm just suddenly completely fine with my ex-boyfriend being a freaking vampire?* But the whole situation was so bizarre that the only way to truly deal with it was to just accept the new reality and carry on with life.

And with that in mind, she was in dire need of a drink.

She opened the fridge and did a double take. There were six bottles of wine in the fridge that had not been there before she left. *Maeve*. She laughed and selected a bottle of white, filled a glass and headed into the living room. Her housemate was sitting on the sofa, feet tucked up and a blanket thrown over her. She, too, had a glass in her hand, and a half empty bottle on the coffee table.

"I see you went shopping," said Becca, dropping into the space beside her.

"Well, if they're telling me to stay in my house, you bet your arse I'm stocking up on wine," Maeve replied with a slight slur to her words. She was in the middle of watching a makeover show. "Speaking of-" She looked to Becca, her eyes glassy and unfocused, "where've you been?"

Becca sipped her wine. "None of your business."

"When there's vampires loose attacking people, it is my business."

Becca winced, a lump thick in her throat. So, no one had *officially* stated that the curfew was because of vampires and there were people online accepting the lie that it was just some sort of illness making people act irrationally; but for people who believed what they saw with their own two eyes, vampires were real and they were here.

Maeve had reacted to the stories the way she reacted to everything. With humour. She rolled her eyes at the terrified comments over social media, she even criticized the vampires clothing choices, complaining that they had missed the opportunity to bring capes and cloaks back into fashion.

Becca and Maeve had been friends since university and had lived together on and off for the past eight years. Maeve was not the type of person to talk about her feelings. She was a very closed off person because she didn't think many people deserved to know the real her. It had come from years of trusting the wrong people and allowing herself to be underappreciated.

Becca had learned, throughout the years, to read between the lines. And right now, Maeve was worried. She needed a distraction.

"I was at Gabriel's," she said. Maeve's eyes flew back to her. She put down her glass on the coffee table and shuffled about under the blanket until she was fully facing her.

"What? Why?" she asked, positively beaming.

85

Becca froze. *Shit, I did not think this through.* "Just to make sure there were no hard feelings about the-"

"Firing?"

"Yeah."

"And is there?" She tilted her head, an eyebrow pulled up in genuine concern.

Becca smiled. "No, we're fine."

"Are you getting back together?"

Becca scoffed – a little too loudly.

Maeve grinned like a Cheshire cat. "You wanna get back together."

"What? No. No…" Her brows furrowed. "No?"

Maeve was still grinning as she leaned over and grabbed her glass. "Well, if you get back together and then he starts asking about orgies and swinging, don't say I didn't warn you."

Becca laughed. "They're *not* like that."

Maeve shrugged, sipping her wine. "Just telling you what I'm seeing."

When she leaned back, Becca caught sight of something propped against the wall beside the radiator. It took her a moment to realise what it was.

"Why is there a cricket bat in here?"

"Oh," Maeve looked to it. "It's my old one. Found it in my mum's loft. I also put my old lacrosse stick in your bedroom."

Becca pulled a face. Maeve caught it and arched an eyebrow.

"It can be used as a weapon, trust me. In high school, I dislocated a girl's kneecap with that thing," she said, miming the action and punctuating it with a click of her tongue.

Becca's heart sank to her feet. Maeve hid it well, but her friend wasn't just worried, she was scared. Becca wished she could tell her friend all the information she had gathered. That they were safe in their homes so long as they didn't invite a vampire inside. And that the only vampires in the entire village were the same people who she fantasied about having orgies with. But she couldn't tell her any of that, and so she had to let her friend sleep with one eye open and some sort of makeshift weapon under her pillow.

"There is *literally* no one here." Mitch threw his arms up and spun around gesturing to the empty pub.

"And yet we are," said Ezra, polishing an already immaculate wine glass. "Until Sunday."

Mitch's face dropped. "What? We not working anymore?"

Ezra shook his head. "I talked to Carol. She's shutting the place once curfew kicks in."

Mitch leaned back against the bar. "Man, this is really serious, innit?"

Ezra watched as realisation hit his young workmate. The mischievous spark in his eyes dulled and for a moment, he looked so hollow.

This was what had happened to everyone. Sure, the jokes and the gimmicks would continue; people would always hide under the veil of humour. But when the Prime Minister made that speech, it was like he'd shaken the whole world awake. Awake to reality. Awake to the secrets that had stayed hidden for so long.

Mitch instantly pulled out his phone and did the one thing they both knew he shouldn't but, again, humans were predictable beings. They liked to pick at scabs.

After the house meeting with Ben, Ezra had instantly found the video of the Prime Minister's speech, but when Mitch began playing it, Ezra was drawn in again. Perhaps humans and vampires weren't so different. After all, this was one titillating scab.

They both stood side by side behind the bar and watched the little screen. Ezra was a few inches taller than Mitch and so, in this position, the human's throat was in his eyeline. Mitch's shaggy red hair was tied back into a bun, exposing the pale, freckled column of his neck. As they watched the speech, Ezra's focus kept shifting to his pulse-point. His heart was racing. Ezra could hear his rushing blood singing to him.

"An ailment affecting people's mental faculties causing them to act irrationally," Mitch recited with a scoff. "Similar to *'roid rage*? Is he fucking kidding with this shit? They're vampires, dude!" He turned. "You seeing this shit?"

Ezra blinked, refocusing his hearing on the slightly tinny phone speakers. "Yeah, mad right?" He stepped away, sliding the wine glass back on its rung.

They closed the pub at 3am. Mitch' mum was waiting in the carpark to pick him up. He usually walked home. When Mitch ran to the car instead of kicking up a fuss, Ezra figured it had been his idea. The boy was being cautious. He was being smart.

Ezra wasn't ready to go home just yet. Knowing that he wouldn't be able to wander around alone at night without drawing suspicion at the end of the week, he took up the opportunity while he still could.

There was something so disheartening about seeing Mitch so agitated. For the rest of the shift, he had barely spoken. He just spent the whole time searching for vampire stories – and not to make fun of anymore. He was searching for information. Ezra wouldn't exactly call Mitch a *friend* per say, but he was probably the human he was closest to. And now he couldn't stop thinking about what would happen if he found out he was a vampire. Would Mitch be scared of him? Scared of the workmate he teased for being too serious? The workmate he'd tell stories about his embarrassing dating life to? Scared of the workmate he'd worked with side by side for the past two years?

The sudden sickness in Ezra's stomach told him that maybe he cared about his relationship with this kid more than he'd realised.

There was a bench at the end of the road, lit up by the orange glow of a streetlamp. Ezra reached it, sat down, and didn't leave that spot until the sky started to lighten.

It was 6am when Ezra finally returned home. He could feel the strain of the waking sun pulling at his consciousness. So, when he passed Gabriel's room and heard his TV on, he paused and knocked.

Gabriel called him in and Ezra opened the door. Gabriel was lying on his bed, forearm over his eyes. He was lit up by the harsh light of the TV screen but it was clear he wasn't watching it.

"What are you doing up?" Ezra asked.

Gabriel dropped his arm, or, more like his arm slipped off his face and dropped onto the bed. He sighed heavily.

"Gotta call work when they open. They left a message saying someone wants me as their care nurse." He yawned overdramatically.

Ezra smirked. Being able to fight the sun came with age for a vampire. The older you were, the longer you could resist the need to sleep. And Gabriel's state of fatigue showed that he was a mere amateur beside Ezra.

"You sure you're gonna make it?" Ezra teased.

Gabriel's eyes were closed and he was as still as the dead. "Mmhmm," he sighed. "Didn't help that I had to listen to Lillian talk about *The Bell Jar* all night. She's very excited about book club."

"She's still going to book club?"

Gabriel made a slurred noise that sounded like a mix between *I guess so* and *I don't know.*

He was asleep. Ezra found the remote and turned the TV off, then slapped him across the face. Gabriel jerked awake, his fangs unsheathing instinctively. Ezra smiled as Gabriel blinked up at him, bleary-eyed.

"No sleeping for you, princess." Ezra patted him on the shoulder. "Just another hour, you can do this."

Chapter 11

Gabriel headed up the driveway of the small bungalow, acutely aware of the eyes that watched him from behind net curtains. The curfew was an issue. Now, even when Gabriel was doing normal *human* things, like going to work, he felt like everything he did was under scrutiny.

Shaking off his unease, he rapped his knuckles on the front door. A tall, dark silhouette of a man appeared through the panel of frosted glass. The door swung open. The man before Gabriel adjusted his glasses and then folded his arms across his large chest. He was probably a little younger than Gabriel's human age, wearing a grey cardigan over a maroon t-shirt. Before words were even spoken, Gabriel could feel something off about his energy.

"Hi, I'm Gabriel. I'm guessing you're Ian Howden? We spoke on the phone," he said in his polite, work voice. He refrained from offering his hand, sensing that this man wouldn't have taken it.

Instead, Gabriel stepped backwards and ran his tongue over his teeth. He didn't like that there were two steps up to the house; that this man was looking down at him as he stood in the cold autumn night.

"Yes, hi," Ian Howden replied, his voice calm but not friendly. He was standing right in the centre of the doorway, his stance wide like he was trying to look intimidating. Gabriel could just about see that lights were on behind him, but little else.

"I'm the night-time care nurse allocated to your mother," Gabriel added, unsure of why he was still outside.

"Yes, I know who you are." Ian looked down the road. "I've seen you around the village. Only at night."

Gabriel chewed the inside of his cheek but kept his facial expression blank. "Yes, as I said, I'm a night-time care nurse. I work at night, so I have an adjusted sleep schedule."

Ian nodded. "Makes sense," were the words that left his mouth, but his tone said the opposite.

"I know I'm officially starting next week but like I said on the phone, I always visit beforehand so I don't seem like a stranger."

"That's very thoughtful." Ian seemed to relax a little, his posture loosening. Perhaps Gabriel was reading him wrong? "Becca gave you a good recommendation."

Gabriel's back bristled at the mention of her name. The way it left this man's lips had him clenching his jaw. It was as if he was tasting it, savouring it, like it meant something.

"We went to the same university, you know?" he laughed. "Funny how we both ended up here, in this tiny, forgotten village."

"Funny," Gabriel echoed, with a smile that lacked warmth.

Ian looked at him, looked him right in the eyes, and the intensity of the connection made Gabriel realise the man had been avoiding his eyes the entire conversation.

"The good recommendation makes me wonder why she requested a new care nurse."

"She gave me a good recommendation, that's all that matters," Gabriel replied through gritted teeth. He'd had quite enough of this guy's weird energy.

"Was it about the breakup?"

Gabriel shifted his weight from foot to foot, and looked down the street. So, this was this guy's deal. He had a thing for Becca. He was jealous. Was that why he had requested Gabriel to take care of his mother? To have this stand off? To have the opportunity to look down at Gabriel and make himself feel big and powerful?

This guy was a freak.

"If you don't want me to be your mother's care nurse, that's fine." He held his palms up. "I'll go."

Gabriel turned to leave.

"No. No. Wait."

The urgency in Ian's voice caught him off guard. Gabriel spun back to the door. Ian was half hanging out the doorway and when Gabriel walked back up to the steps, he stepped back into the porch. He jerked his thumb over his shoulder.

"My mum's in the living room."

Finally, we're getting somewhere. Gabriel smiled. Ian stepped further back into the house but Gabriel couldn't follow him. Not yet. He looked down at the steps, at the threshold he couldn't cross. Then, when he looked back up at Ian, he understood. The man stared back at him, his eyes daring him. A smile playing on his lips.

"It's probably not safe to stay out there. With the curfew, and all. Apparently, there are thinking lurking in the dark," he said.

The tension was suddenly palpable. The space between them full of unsaid things.

"Then I should come inside."

Now, Ian let himself smile. "Like I said, my mum is waiting."

Every word was calculated. He was making sure that nothing he said could be taken as an invitation. This wasn't about Becca. This was about him.

This was a test.

Ian stepped back again. The distance between them lengthening and stopping the opportunity for Gabriel to compel him, even though he couldn't through his lenses. Did this guy even need glasses or were they another precaution?

Gabriel stepped back and lifted the sleeve of his jacket to reveal his watch. "Look, I was only meant to pop round. But with all this small-talk – I'm running late. I've got to go."

Ian was quick to grab the handle of the door, his eyes twinkling triumphantly behind his glasses. "That's a shame. Well, it was nice to meet you, Gabriel."

There it was again. He said his name in the same way he did with Becca. Like he somehow owned it now. Owned him.

"Yeah, likewise," Gabriel threw over his shoulder as he stalked down the pathway. He heard the door shut but he could once again feel the eyes on him. He itched all over, suddenly suffocating within his jacket. His fangs pressed against his gums as anger ate at his insides.

He knows. He knows. He knows.

He couldn't get the image of his stupid, smug face out of his head.

Shitfuckshitfuckshitshitshitshit.

He'd walked straight into a fucking trap. Now the whole street knew.

How long would it take for word to get around the entire village?

If he was human, his heart would have been hammering and he'd be struggling to breathe. Instead, Gabriel just kept walking, head bent and hands shoved into his jacket pockets.

He rounded the corner onto another street and resisted the urge to just vampire-sprint home. It was always a risky decision but usually, in the dead of night, he wasn't concerned by onlookers. But now… now, things were different.

Gabriel continued on home at mortal speed, mentally ripping Ian Howden's stupid fucking head off. Did he even have an elderly mother in need? The trap had been so simple that Gabriel hated himself for being drawn in by it. But why wouldn't he have been? He never used to have to be so cautious.

Too caught up in his own head, Gabriel almost charged right into someone as he turned to head into his house. He managed to halt just before he collided with them, and realised it was Lillian. She looked up at him and her eyes shone from under the fur hood of her parka. Blood was smeared under her eyes.

"Lillian, are you okay?"

Her shoulders were bunched up, her hands plunged into her pockets, the same way Gabriel's were. For a fraction of a second, there was a glint of fear in her eyes. And then she smiled and expelled a small laugh.

"Yeah, it's nothing. I just had a fight with Ben, that's all," she said. Gabriel studied her face, the blood tears still welling in her eyes. "Honestly, I'm fine. I just want to get inside."

And then she was pushing open their front door. Gabriel followed silently behind and watched her rush up the stairs, not looking back. When he heard her bedroom door click shut, he knew their conversation would never be spoken about again.

Expelling a sigh, he shut the front door and then made his way to his own bedroom. He got halfway up the stairs before the living room door opened and out came Ezra.

"Did I hear Lillian?" he asked, confusion creasing his brows.

"Yeah. She just went upstairs."

Ezra studied him a moment. "Is everything okay?"

Gabriel's heart contracted, like a fist squeezing a sponge. "Yeah. Why wouldn't it be?"

Lillian's relationship wasn't Gabriel's problem. He had his own shit to deal with. And even though he knew Ezra had a right to know he'd been caught; he was already kicking himself enough as it was. He didn't want to deal with the older vampire telling him how he'd let them all down. That his brazen attitude had finally screwed everything up and put them all in danger. Just like he warned him it would.

The crease of confusion deepened in Ezra's brow as he looked around the room. He lifted his nose as if trying to smell something. Then he stepped into the hallway and gestured about with his hands.

"There's a weird energy. Something's off." He looked back to Gabriel.

Gabriel shrugged. "Burn some incense or some shit, I don't know," he said before hurrying up the stairs and shutting himself in his room.

His fangs were pressing against his gums once again. Anger at himself rolling in his gut. His hands turned to fists and the next moment his knuckles were colliding with the wall. Flecks of paint and plaster dust coated his skin when he pulled his hand away. He flexed his fingers and it rained onto the carpet.

He stared at the hole in the plaster, eyes wide, nostrils flared and breathing heavy. Losing his temper wasn't going to solve anything. He needed to calm down.

He sank onto the end of his bed, dropped his face into his hands and closed his eyes.

This is not good. This is not good.

Fuckfuckfuckfuck.

Chapter 12

Becca collapsed onto one of the dining chairs, slinging her work bag onto the table as she did so. It was amazing how tiring it was just sitting at a desk, answering phone calls and filling out paperwork. She peeled herself out of her coat and pushed it over the back of the chair. In the other room there was the sound of movement, and then Maeve appeared at the door holding two glasses of wine. Her short blonde hair was up in a little scruffy bun and she was wearing a unicorn pyjama set – the same thing she had been wearing that morning. She smiled at Becca and held one of the wine glasses out to her.

"Drink with me," she said.

Becca dragged herself up to her feet and grabbed her coat. Maeve followed her into the hallway where she hung the coat up on its hook.

"I've literally *just* got in from work."

"And you deserve a drink." Maeve pouted when Becca arched her eyebrow. "C'mon, you know I don't like drinking alone."

"Curfew started two days ago and you've already nearly finished the bottles you bought."

She just blinked at her and lifted the wine glass higher.

Becca rolled her eyes and went into the living room. She dropped onto the sofa and stuck her hand down the side of the cushion to fish for the TV remote. Since curfew had begun, Maeve had turned their living room into her office. Her laptop and spreadsheets were scattered across the coffee table. She worked in marketing and so she said working from home was easier than driving to and from work every day. There was an obvious correlation between Maeve refusing to leave the house and the government telling people to be cautious, even though she was adamant that the reason for the change was because she was tired of her overcrowded office that stunk of body odour and tomato pasta.

"I made chilli. There's some left over. Want me to heat it up for you?" she asked from the door.

"Sure. Thanks," Becca replied, her fingers finally finding the remote.

"And then you'll have a drink with me?" Maeve fluttered her eyelashes.

Becca smiled. "Fine. Just one."

By the time Becca had finished eating, it was 7pm and the sun was down. She grabbed her phone.

'I have some more questions.'

She read the message over several times and her heart did one heavy lurch when she finally pressed send. When there was no reply straight away, she placed her phone face-down on the armrest, tricking herself into believing she wasn't bothered if it stayed silent.

But as she sat, pretending to watch a rerun of a sitcom, her palms were clammy against her tights and she found her eyes drifting to the left. When it finally buzzed, she almost jumped out of her skin. She forced herself to wait a moment before looking.

What the hell are you doing? She rolled her eyes and grabbed her phone. She wasn't a teenager anymore, and with everything going on, replying too quickly was the least of her worries.

'Okay. I could come over if you'd like?'

She smiled down at her phone.

'Sure. I'm in all night.'

'Be there soon.'

"Who you texting?" Maeve was at the other end of the sofa, her eyebrows dancing and a knowing smirk filling her face.

Becca sent her a jokey dirty look and got up to leave the room.

"Tell Gabriel I said hi," Maeve called after her before she closed the door behind her.

Less than half an hour later, there was a knock at the door. Becca picked herself up off the top step and made her way down the stairs. Yes, she had been sat at the top of the stairs, staring at the door like an anxious teen waiting for her prom date to arrive. She knew it was dumb, but there was something about Gabriel that filled her with giddy optimism. Even after everything she knew.

Letting out a calming breath, she opened the door. And there he was, standing a few steps away down the path, hands in the pockets of his wax jacket, his natural tan washed out by the glare of the streetlamp. He smiled at her, soft and warm and delicate and not in the least bit intimidating. She had always thought that. He had a look of a man who could easily come off as imposing. He was probably just shy of six foot, broad shouldered with a scruff of beard. His dark hair was short, his curls slicked back from his face, turning them into a sea of shiny waves. The style made him look more like a mafia boss than a care nurse. But despite all that, there was something so cool and disarming about him – even now.

"Hey," he said, just like an awkward date ready for prom.

She smiled, her heart soaring. "Hey. Come in."

He stepped inside and they both lingered a moment, standing almost chest to chest. His amber eyes gazed down at her. She noted that they flickered to her lips.

Then the living room door opened. They both turned to see Maeve poking her head out. She grinned.

"Hey, Gabe, want some wine?"

Gabriel audibly gulped. Despite him coming over to her place almost every week when they had dated, he and Maeve rarely interacted. Becca figured that Maeve's bold, eccentric personality was a little too much for Gabriel to handle.

"Erhh..." he stammered, looking to Becca for help.

"We're just gonna go up to my room." Becca grabbed Gabriel's arm and steered him towards the stairs.

Maeve wiggled her eyebrows suggestively. "Yeah you are."

"Sorry about that." Becca closed her bedroom door behind them and rested her back against it. "I think she's bored."

"It's okay." He laughed softly. He was standing by her bed, eyes scanning the art on her walls. He'd been in her room countless times before, but it felt different now somehow. Now that she knew the truth about him, everything felt more intimate.

"And sorry for making you come here."

"I offered."

"I know but…" She trailed off with a shrug.

"Since curfew, the three of us have had nowhere to go. I think we've completed Netflix, if that's a thing. So, trust me, this is a welcome escape."

"You can sit." She gestured to the bed.

He dropped down obediently and unzipped his jacket, revealing a simple black jumper underneath.

"So, you said you have more questions?" he asked.

She crossed the room and sat beside him. His body turned to her instinctively, like a flower searching for the sun.

"Yeah." She cleared her throat and tucked a strand of hair behind her ear. "But first." She frowned, trying to find her words. "Why am I okay with this? Why am I not scared of you? I mean, I should be, shouldn't I?"

His eyebrows pinched as if hurt. "You should never feel like you need to be afraid of me. I meant it when I said I would never hurt you."

"But you're a v-" They both looked to the door, "*vampire*," she whispered.

He held her hand on her lap. His enveloping hers. She noticed how cold his was compared to her own.

"I'm still me," he said.

She watched their hands, feeling comforted by the way his thumb stroked her knuckles.

"I think a part of me is just thankful your odd behaviour wasn't to do with me. Is that vain?"

Gabriel laughed softly. Her eyes found his.

"It's so weird going to my grandad's now you're not there. Paul's great with him and everything, but he barely talks to me. It's like as soon as I get there, he's like *okay my shift's over,* and leaves." She tilted her head, noticing the details of his face. The dark flecks in his irises, the sharp edge to his jaw. "I miss seeing you every night."

He was watching her lips, mesmerised. They were so close she could smell his cologne. It was the same one he used when they dated. It was subtle but heady. Nothing like what the lads doused themselves in every night. No, Gabriel always had a refined, gentlemanly quality to him.

Her hand slipped out from under his and crossed the threshold between them. She watched as the muscle in his jaw flexed when she placed her hand on his thigh, his jeans rough under her touch.

"Can I see them again?" she asked, her voice now soft due to the close proximity.

"What?" he replied in a rushed expel of air.

"Your fangs."

This time, she didn't need to ask twice. He parted his lips, eyes still on hers. His top lip twitched and his fangs lengthened in one fluid motion, accompanied by a sound oddly similar to that of a pen cap. A small gasp escaped her but she didn't move away. Instead, her hand gripped his thigh and he inhaled.

She gazed at the sharp canines and marvelled at how they didn't seem out of place. No, these were his real teeth. This was the real Gabriel.

She moved closer, their thighs touching. He just watched her, silently and patiently. But the air between them was thick with tension. In that moment, they were the only two people in the world that mattered.

Gabriel was here. Back in her room. Showing her all of him. Wanting her to know all of him.

Her heart was pounding and she relished the thought that he could hear it. Hear what he was doing to her. She gazed at the tips of his fangs and wondered how they would feel against her skin. Piercing her. Marking her.

Her lips were on his then. Soft and careful. He kissed her back, the tension in his body dissipating. His hand slid to her neck, his thumb brushing her jaw. Still so careful. She pulled away. His eyes were hooded as he gazed back at her. She could tell he could see the look in her eyes. The want. The need. His fingers curled around the hair at the nape of her neck. Tugged. She gasped. And then they were kissing again. This time, passionately. Feverishly. *Hungrily.*

She pushed off his jacket and straddled him. His hands were splayed over her back, pressing her to him, then pulling her dress up over her head. He peppered kisses across her neck and chest, the tips of his fangs scraping against her like nails.

Soft mewls and moans escaped her. She kissed him harder, grabbing at his jumper, needing his skin against hers. When she pulled it free, she threw it to the ground. Her hands explored the soft grooves of his muscular chest before pushing him back against the bed and getting lost in the heat and passion.

The atmosphere in the dark basement was somehow even gloomier than last time. Dalia had dealt the cards but they hadn't even attempted to play. No, instead, the three of them sat, topping up their whisky glasses with the same bottle of blood. Dalia's blood supply was running low. Now that the word was out there, the doctors she and Silas had befriended were no longer willing to fudge paperwork and give them blood donation handouts. Apparently, since the massacre after the raid, all hospitals were on high alert, and every doctor was being watched over like a criminal.

"This curfew has fucked everything up," Dalia sneered, showing fangs. "Now I've had to shut my club. What the fuck am I supposed to do?"

"First thing you need to do is hide this stuff." Silas lifted his glass then nodded over to the freezer at the back of the room. "I've got word from the States that their vamp clubs are big business now. They've even got celebs paying good money to get bitten and thrown around a bit." He shook his head and took a swig of his drink. "So, I can bet the authorities will start snooping around more establishments here soon, now they know Moonlight was just the tip of the iceberg."

"Don't worry, I'm not dumb." Dalia leaned back in her chair. "These bottles are from home." She gestured to the one in the centre of the table. "Freezer's empty already."

"There are no curfews in other countries?" Ezra asked.

"Not yet," replied Silas. "But it's hard to tell which way the rest of the world is going to go. It'd be easier for the States to just embrace this new culture. Now that the rich are involved and it's most likely bringing in a profit."

"But they won't do that here?" asked Ezra.

"Not now they've exercised the curfew. They're already basically public announced that we're a threat. They can't go back from that now."

Ezra's body felt so heavy in the chair. Like his loss of hope was dragging him down.

"And the curfew is just the beginning," said Dalia.

Silas nodded. "It's only going to get worse for us."

An exhausted groan erupted from the back of Ezra's throat before he had a chance to quell it. His eyes bugged when both ancients' gazes shot to him.

"I'm sorry, are we boring you?" said Dalia, arching a pencilled eyebrow.

Ezra had slouched so far in his chair his shoulders were almost level with the tabletop. He shouldn't say anything. He should politely apologise. But when he caught his Maker's frosty gaze, a sudden blaze of anger shot through his heart and he straightened himself.

"I'm just sick of you two whining like there's nothing we can do about any of this. Honestly, you're like a pair of old crones who just love to bitch and moan." Dalia's nostrils flared at Ezra's fiery tone but Silas' eyes shone with sudden exhilaration. His Maker sat opposite him, one shoulder against the back of his chair, a ringed finger circling the rim of his glass. A ghost of a smile played on his tanned face.

"Last week I was informed that we have a *Court*. That there are some higher power vamps looking out for our kind and what, now that things are getting a little shaky, we're just supposed to throw in the towel? We've been around for God knows how long and we've managed to make it this far. I've got a progeny at home and I promised her I would give her a better life. This is not the end for us. I'm just not accepting that."

Ezra was shaking; fury and fear and adrenaline buzzing through his veins. The backs of his eyes burned as he looked between the two ancients.

Dalia's jaw worked, her painted red lips pursing together. She rose off her chair, fangs extended, "Look here you little *shi-*"

"Dalia."

Her mouth clamped shut and her head whipped to Silas so quick her dark ponytail cracked like a whip. The one word uttered from Silas had been barely a whisper but it had instantly put the other vampire in her place. She gulped and sank back down onto her chair, cutting a sharp glare towards Ezra before bowing her head in subjugation.

Ezra looked to his Maker. He'd never seen his eyes twinkle before, it was unnerving. Why wasn't Silas screaming at him for his insolence? His Maker was not one to shy away from using the back of his hand to remind his progenies of who was in charge. Ezra had expected the ancient to reach over the table and grab him by his collar but Silas hadn't so much as flinched.

No, instead, his smile only grew bigger.

"Ezra."

Ezra gulped, unable to look him in the eye.

"I think it's time you meet them."

"What?" The word tumbled out of his mouth.

"There's a meeting tonight." Silas lifted his glass and watched the last ounce of blood swirl around the bottom. "-with the Court. You're coming with me."

Chapter 13

Ezra had allowed his Maker to clasp his leathery hand over his own and guide him at vampire speed through the desolate city and towards the secret Vampire Court meeting.

Now they both stood, shoulder to shoulder, looking across the graveyard to the old stone church. Candlelight danced behind the stained-glass windows.

"A creepy, abandoned church. Really?" Ezra arched an eyebrow. "What, were all the gothic castles taken?"

Silas smirked. The cool night breeze made his grey hair float about his ears.

"The Court does have a soft spot for theatrics," he said.

Ezra looked down at himself; at his simple grey polo-shirt and jeans, and then to his Maker, dressed in his usual tailored blazer, trousers and dress shoes. Ezra's nose wrinkled. Was he underdressed? He was about to be in the company of the vampire equivalent of the Royal Family, or so he thought. To be perfectly honest, he still had no idea what to expect. But nevertheless, he didn't think he was in the best attire. For Christ's sake, he was wearing *Vans*.

"Don't speak unless you're spoken to. I will not have you showing me up, got it?" said Silas.

Ezra nodded.

Silas began making his way down the path between the graves and Ezra followed doggedly behind, running his hand through his styled hair and flattening his collar.

His Maker rapped his knuckles on the huge wooden door in an obviously thought-out pattern. *Secret knock? Nice.* Ezra heard a slat being pushed back then the door opened inwards. At this precise moment, Ezra envisioned some sort of occult scene. A group of vampires all standing in a circle in long black robes, hoods covering their faces. But that's not what he found.

It had been a female vampire who had opened the door. She was slightly shorter than him with straight dark hair, wearing a navy knee-length dress. A knowing smile between friends passed between her and Silas, and when her eyes hit Ezra, she cocked her head curiously but said nothing.

Ezra stayed a short pace behind Silas as they walked down the aisle between the pews, so close he almost stepped on the back of his shoes. His eyes were everywhere. At the rows and rows of candles that were alight beneath the windows and up high on mounted sconces. It wasn't until Silas stopped and Ezra stumbled to a halt beside him that he noticed the other vampires in the shadows near the altar.

Five of them were standing at the front. In the centre was a bald man, tall and lithe and dressed in an immaculate three-piece grey suit. His eyes were dark and beady, surrounded by a pool of wrinkles. Silas was no longer the oldest looking vampire Ezra had encountered. It was clear this man had been Turned in his seventies, at least.

Flanking him were four other vampires, two on either side; three males in similar smart attire, and one female. Ezra's eyes shifted to the female. She looked so striking amongst all the others. Her floor-length white nightgown style dress made her look out of place amongst the suits and ties. Her hair was jet black and fell in two sleek waves down her chest, almost to her hips. She caught him looking at her and winked. Ezra gulped and quickly looked away, only then noticing that there were other vampires sitting along the first row of pews.

"Silas, so good of you to join us," said the bald man. By the way he held himself; Ezra assumed he was more important than the rest.

"Guardian." Silas bowed his head. Ezra bowed too, still not really knowing what was happening.

When he looked back up, the bald man was appraising him. His thin lips uplifted into something similar to a smile.

"And who is this?" he asked. There was a weird, playful edge to his tone as if he were addressing a shy puppy.

"This is my progeny, Ezra." Silas gestured to him. Unsure of what to do, Ezra bowed his head again.

"Pleasure to meet you, Ezra. I've heard a lot about you."

Ezra's eyes shifted to his Maker. *You have? Because I've heard nothing about you.*

Guardian extended a thin, bony hand. When Ezra just stared at it, Silas jabbed him in the side with his elbow.

"Pleasure's all mine," Ezra rushed, taking his hand and was surprised by the strength of his grip.

Guardian then gestured to the pews. "Please, sit. And then we'll begin."

Silas and Ezra found space on the front pew. Directly in front of Ezra stood the beguiling female vampire. She locked eyes with him again and swayed her hips slightly so her dress swished about her ankles. When he adjusted himself on the bench, she smirked; her deep blue eyes teasing. Not allowing himself to be drawn in, he looked down the pew to the other side of the church. The woman who had answered the door now sat on the other bench with several others. They all had their eyes forward, like actual church goers awaiting a sermon.

"These are trying times," began Guardian. He started pacing slowly before the altar, wringing his hands. "There is an air of trepidation, of fear, of uncertainty joining us tonight, as we are all here to discuss what is unfolding all across the world.

"There is no doubt that things will never be the same again. But that doesn't have to be our downfall, if we don't allow it to be."

This is what I'm talking about. Ezra looked to his Maker. He was gazing up at Guardian like he was a prophet. They all were. Even the flirty woman in the white dress. Except, she was looking to him more like her saviour. Like he had already solved all of their problems. Was Ezra missing something?

"Our kind have survived everything that this world has thrown our way. Witches. Wars. Vampire Hunters," Guardian continued. Ezra furrowed his brows and looked around. *Wait. Witches are real?*

"But we have always learned to adapt. To thrive. And our discovery will be no different." Guardian sighed. "We are playing the long game, we always have. And, being immortal, that isn't too much to ask of us. This curfew, I admit, will cause problems. But to me, this only seems like a way to delay the inevitable."

Guardian looked around the church. Looked at every vampire individually. The pause lengthened. Some of the vampires closed their eyes as if in prayer. Others waited with wide, expectant eyes.

"The inevitable?" Ezra asked, his voice surprisingly loud within the stone building. Silas looked to him, his frosty blue eyes screaming.

Guardian smiled, again like he was a puppy learning a new trick. "Acceptance."

All the other vampires nodded in agreement, like the answer was obvious.

"You think they're gonna accept us? After what they've been broadcasting? They're making us look like monsters." Ezra could see his Maker in his peripheral vision, his eyes flashing a warning. But if this Guardian guy was going to stand up there in front of them preaching like he knew all the answers, well then Ezra was going to take this opportunity to get his.

"Right now, the human authorities are gathering as much information on our kind as they can. In other countries around Europe, vampires are complying, answering questions to ensure their continued freedom." Guardian strolled over to Ezra, his heels clicking loudly across the stones. He stopped before him, hands behind his back. "Once the humans realise just how many of us are out there, they will have no choice but to accept us. They're not stupid. They know our kind are stronger. We have the power to overthrow them and if that was our goal, we would have done it already."

Ezra gazed up at him. At the liver spots at his temple, the certainty in his dark eyes.

"They will kick up a fuss, no doubt. They want to make us the enemy before they corral us. They need a way to make it seem like they have won some sort of conflict. If they show the public that they have tamed us, the humans will believe it because they want to."

"And how exactly do they think they are going to *tame* us?" asked Ezra.

A soft laugh rumbled in Guardian's throat that sounded like grinding rocks, and he shifted his eyes to Silas. "He's an inquisitive one, isn't he?"

Silas' jaw clenched.

"We have already let them know about our ways of keeping unruly vampires off the streets. Silas has told me that you have had your own part to play in that." The smirk Guardian sent him- fanged and wicked- made Ezra's stomach roil and the bloody memories attack him once again. The phantom feeling of his slick grip on a bloody stake had his hands curling into fists on his lap. "No doubt that they will take all the credit for themselves, though. They can't have us being the heroes now, can they?"

"So, that's it? We just do nothing and everything will somehow work out just fine?" Irritation edged Ezra's voice. "Not buying it."

"*Ezra*," Silas finally snapped. "Do I need to walk you out?"

Guardian held up his pale palm. "No need, Silas. This is good. The boy's got gusto. He's passionate. It's what we need right now."

Ezra felt like the praise was supposed to validate him, but it just made him feel dirty. This man was creepy. And the way all these vamps just sat and watched, taking his word for gospel? It just seemed counterintuitive to him.

"I've received word that the human authorities are planning something," said Guardian. At this, all the vampires noticeably straightened and leaned in. *Ah, now we're getting to the good stuff.*

Guardian looked about the church before stepping back into the centre, now addressing them all.

"I was going to wait until things were clearer, but there has been talk that they are going to try and make us more *humane*."

At this, the dark-haired female vampire in white pulled a face of disgust.

Ezra opened his mouth to talk but Silas jabbed him with his elbow. Guardian caught the altercation.

"I don't exactly know how," he answered Ezra's unspoken question. "It's in the early stages but I have my best people sniffing out the information. And, with that said-" Guardian clapped his hands together, "are there any other questions?" His eyes cut to Ezra but by the stiffness of his Maker's posture, he feared he'd said too much already. When Ezra stayed silent, Guardian smiled and gestured to the group. "Meeting over."

Guardian turned and the four vampires who had been standing all gathered around him. It was clear that they were some sort of inner circle.

"I can't believe I thought it was a good idea to bring you here," Silas seethed, looking at Guardian but addressing Ezra. "You made me look like a fool."

"He seemed to like me."

Silas turned to him, his face cast in shadow, making his eyes look even more hauntingly bright. "The best thing to be to Guardian is forgettable. Now you've shown him up you'd better be on your best behaviour. He'll have his people watching the both of us." He let out an angered breath. "I'm going to try and smooth things over. Stay there and don't cause any more trouble."

Silas stood and headed over to the inner circle. Ezra folded his arms and looked down to his lap like a scolded child.

If he hadn't said anything, they would have left the meeting just as clueless as they were when they entered. It wasn't his fault this *Guardian* seemed to expect people to blindly follow his lead.

In the corner of his eye, Ezra caught a swish of white material. He looked up just as the dark-haired woman sat beside him. Ezra just looked at her, wide-eyed. Up close, she was even more stunning. Her blue eyes crinkled in delight as she chewed her bottom lip, watching him watching her.

"I haven't seen you before, have I?" she asked. Her voice was silky and seductive. Her dark blue eyes slid down his chest. "No, I'd definitely remember you."

Ezra wanted to look away, to ignore her. In the back of his mind, he knew he should. The way she watched him; it was predatory. A lioness stalking a deer. A spider coaxing a fly.

She pursed her full, red lips and frowned. "Why so quiet? You sure had a lot to say earlier."

Ezra cleared his throat. "Silas told me to stay out of trouble."

She rested her pale elbow on the back of the pew, twisting her body to his fully. Her dress was cut low, with only thin lace covering her chest.

"Now where's the fun in that?" A cold spell washed over his entire body when her fingers slid into his hair, her long nails massaging his scalp.

Ezra looked ahead. He found Silas. He had his back to him, conversing with Guardian. A soft laugh tickled his ear and that cold spell hit him again when she raked a finger down the side of his throat, from ear to clavicle.

"You have fire in you," she said and Ezra let himself look back to her. Her face had softened. She no longer looked like a temptress. Her smile was wistful as her eyes roved his face. "You remind me of a dear progeny of mine." She leaned back against the pew and faced the front of the church, but there was this faraway look in her eyes – like she was somewhere else entirely. "I should check up on him. It's been a while."

And then she picked herself up and left, leaving Ezra reeling as he watched her go. The way the thin material of her dress slid over her body like liquid had him adjusting himself once again. It wasn't until Silas grabbed his shoulder when he finally tore his eyes off the mysterious beauty.

"We're leaving," said Silas, his eyes already on the door.

Ezra obediently followed him out, meeting his clipped pace.

Silence rang between the two of them as they weaved through the graves. The moon was high in the sky, bleaching everything with its light. The wind rustled through the trees. Beyond the gates of the cemetery, Ezra could feel the expanse of emptiness. They were still at the outskirts of the city, but the absence of cars on the road was noticeable even from where they were.

Ezra watched Silas' back as they continued walking at mortal speed. He could feel the tension between them, thick like syrup. His jaw worked a few times before he managed to speak.

"Is it bad?"

"What?" Silas replied curtly, not looking back.

"What did Guardian say? About me?"

"Not much. He accepted my apology and you will not be joining us at any more meetings."

Ezra nodded. *That's fair.*

"Who's the woman in the white?" he had to ask. He'd wanted to ask since they left the church.

Silas halted and Ezra nearly walked into him. Silas turned and looked at him, for the first time in what felt like forever. He smirked.

"You mean Milah?"

Milah. The name echoed in his mind.

"What about her?" asked Silas.

Ezra shrugged and emitted a noncommittal grumble.

Silas huffed a laugh and continued walking. "Stay away from her, if you know what's good for you." His eyes slid to Ezra. "I mean it."

"Why?" asked Ezra.

"She's got a bad reputation."

"But she's part of the Court. She can't be that bad if she's part of the inner circle."

"Inner circle?" Silas tasted the words. "I guess you could call it that. And Milah's an ancient. A powerful one, at that. She may have wreaked havoc over the last few centuries but Guardian knows how important it is to preserve ancients. He would never kill her. So, instead, he made her join him."

Ezra furrowed his brows, confused. "You make it sound like a punishment. I thought the Court is here to help us? They're the good guys, right?"

When Silas didn't reply, Ezra quickened his pace so they were shoulder to shoulder. His Maker was looking off into the distance, his husky blue eyes squinting through the wind. He looked pensive; his thin lips were a tight line.

"The Court is here to protect us," he finally said. "But protection comes at a price. And Guardian is not afraid to get his hands dirty. I brought you here because I could sense your hopelessness, Ezra." His eyes found Ezra's. "Guardian is a practical man. He does what is right for our kind. We do not question his methods."

Gabriel rubbed his eyes and leaned over the edge of the bed in search of his phone. He hooked his finger around a belt loop of his discarded jeans and pulled them across the carpet, careful not to move too much and wake his company.

His phone screen lit up when he grabbed it, showing his clock. He still had a bit of time before sunrise but he was cutting it fine. Beside him, Becca stirred. He placed his phone on the bedside table and rolled back over. Her long brown hair was splayed over her pillow. She was facing away from him. He brushed her hair from her neck, exposing her freckle-covered shoulder. Her breathing was heavy and even as he pressed his lips to her back. She smelled like vanilla and perspiration. Her pulse danced against his lips.

A soft grumble left her and she burrowed her face deeper into the pillow, groaned louder and rolled over. She rubbed her eyes and blinked several times before she focused them on him.

"What time is it?" she mumbled.

"Nearly seven. I've got to go." He brushed her hair behind her ear.

She groaned and buried her face into his chest, inhaling his scent. "*No*."

He laughed softly and kissed the top of her head. "I'm sorry."

She pulled away and dropped her head back onto her pillow. She tried to pout but when Gabriel tilted his head, she smiled.

He kissed her again, on the lips, before sitting up and shoving on his jeans and boxers. Her eyes followed him as he walked around the bed in search of his jumper.

"You never asked me any questions," he said. His jumper was by the dresser. He grabbed it and shoved it over his head.

"Yeah…" Becca looked at him sheepishly, the duvet bunched up in front of her naked chest. "I may have just said that because I wanted you to come over."

Gabriel smiled. "You don't have to trick me into seeing you."

She shrugged, playing with her fingers. Gabriel sat at the foot of the bed, putting on his socks

"Actually, I do have a question. Well, actually *Maeve* has a question."

112

He looked over his shoulder, eyebrow arched.

"Not about you being… *y'know*. I haven't told her," she rushed. "No, it's more of a question about your living situation."

Gabriel turned to face her. He couldn't help but smile when she blushed and looked down.

"What is it?" he asked.

She rubbed her hands up and down her arms. "She wanted to know if you, Ezra and Lillian were…" She pulled a face, and looked to the wall as if she'd find the rest of her thought painted on there. "She thought that maybe the three of you had ever… or were…together?" The last word came out as an almost squeak.

Gabriel just looked at her for a moment, a laugh threatening to escape his lips. She caught his eyes then threw her duvet up over her face.

"Sorry I asked," she mumbled.

"Are you asking the man you just slept with if he sleeps with his housemates?"

"Kinda."

Gabriel crawled over the bed, careful of her legs. He straddled her middle and pulled the duvet from her face. She looked up at him, cheeks flushed.

"I know there's been a rumour going around about me and Ezra but no, it's strictly platonic. The same with Lillian. Although Ezra and Lillian were together in the past. And now she's his progeny. It's how they met."

Becca's eyes lit with intrigue; her embarrassment forgotten. "His progeny?"

"Ezra Turned her."

She blinked, surprised. "Oh." Her brows furrowed. "I never even asked you how someone becomes a vampire."

"A human has to die with vampire blood in their system. That vampire is then the progeny of the vampire whose blood was used."

"So, Lillian had Ezra's blood in her when she died?"

Gabriel nodded. "That makes him her Maker."

"Who's yours?"

Gabriel gulped. His eyes must have shown something because Becca stiffened under him and her pulse quickened.

He let out a hard sigh, his shoulders slouching. "I don't know."

Becca stayed silent, her eyes drifting to his chest. He leaned over, his hand slipping to the back of her neck as he kissed her forehead.

"I'd better get going."

She nodded against his lips. "Okay." Her hand wrapped around his forearm. "Last night was fun."

Her lips found his. The kiss deepened and he let himself be taken by her.

It was moments like this when he wished he could be human so he could stay the morning and they could make love again. Then he wouldn't have to hold back. He could give all of himself to her. He wouldn't have to resist his natural instincts to bite and drink and mark her. He wouldn't have to fear his own strength; have to calculate every touch so to not leave a bruise.

But he was a vampire, and Becca was human. *Vampire and human relationships don't work.* Ezra's voice pierced his mind. He kissed Becca harder, his fangs pressing against his gums. She welcomed the added pressure and moaned into his mouth.

No, me and Becca are different.

He was going to prove Ezra wrong.

Chapter 14

"You would not *believe* what I got up to last night," said Ezra, his back to Gabriel as he cleaned the glasses and mugs in the sink.

Gabriel smirked from the table. *I could say the same.* But he wouldn't. He wasn't the type to kiss and tell.

"Go on then. Colour me intrigued," he said instead.

Ezra let out an overdramatic sigh using his whole body. Gabriel could see the reflection of his face in the blackness of the window.

"I'm afraid I can't. Silas told me to keep things on a need-to-know basis."

Gabriel rolled his eyes. *Then why bring it up then? So you can brag more about your attentive Maker?*

Lillian strolled into the kitchen- a welcome distraction.

"How's you and Ben?" Gabriel asked to change the conversation, knowing Ezra wanted him to continue to pry.

Lillian blinked at him, seemingly surprised to be acknowledged. She furrowed her brow and then when Gabriel mirrored her confusion, something seemed to click in her mind and she batted away the question with an obviously forced laugh.

"Oh, that? Yeah, everything's fine."

Ezra looked over his shoulder. "Something happened with you and Ben?"

"No. No, we're fine." She opened the fridge and grabbed a bottle.

Ezra tutted, "Shame," then grabbed a tea towel to start drying what he had washed.

Lillian playfully swatted him around the back of the head before joining Gabriel at the table with a mug of blood.

"So, you got that job then?" she asked, "the old lady?"

Gabriel's gut twisted. He could picture Ian Howden's eyes. The knowing glint in them. "Erh, no. Turns out she didn't like me very much. Nothing personal. It happens when they go senile."

"Huh." Lillian took a sip. "Just thought that's where you were last night. House was empty."

"I do have a life other than work."

"Alright, no need to get tetchy."

Gabriel opened his mouth to apologise for his abrasiveness when a loud smash coming from the living room had them all turning towards the door. Lillian and Gabriel then both looked to Ezra who had already slung the tea towel over his shoulder and was heading towards the noise. The two of them got to their feet and followed him.

Their big bay window at the front of the house had been smashed. In the centre of the room was a brick with a note tied to it with string. Shards of glass covered the wood floor. Ezra crouched to pick up the brick as Gabriel moved to the window to look outside.

His insides ran cold at what he saw. On the street were two dozen people staring right back at him.

"We know what you are, you freaks!" shouted a man Gabriel recognised. His jaw clenched. It was Ian Howden. He'd rallied a group.

Gabriel turned around. Ezra had unravelled the note. *WE KNOW YOUR SECRET* was scrawled in big, black letters.

Fuckshitfuckshitfuckfuckfuck.

"Oh, God." Lillian wailed from the doorway. Her hands were covering her mouth, red rimming her eyes. "Oh, God, I'm so sorry. I'm so sorry. This is all my fault. I'm so sorry. Oh, God."

Gabriel furrowed his brows, confused. Ezra moved over to his progeny but she backed away.

"Lillian, what are you talking about?" Ezra asked, his voice surprisingly calm considering the shouts of abuse streaming in through the broken window.

She sniffled hard. "The other night. Book Club. Angela was wearing rings. She grabbed my arm. They were silver. They burned me." She wiped at her face, smearing blood up to her hairline. "They all chased me out the house. Calling me a monster. Telling me how disgusted they were that I thought they'd want to be my friends."

Then Gabriel understood. Her hurrying home in tears. It had had nothing to do with Ben. She'd fucked up just like Gabriel had.

"You're monsters! How dare you come to our village!" screamed a woman from outside.

"Bloodsucking motherfuckers!" joined in another.

And then there was another noise. This time it was hitting the walls like heavy rain. Gabriel and Ezra moved back to the window. Something red splattered across Ezra's face. He shut his eyes; jaw clenched, unimpressed. It was paint. The group outside had tins of it and were splashing the front of their house, flicking paint brushes and ladles full of it.

"Go back to where you came from!" shouted a man Gabriel was pretty sure worked at the corner shop. He'd buy biscuits for Julian from him.

"Yeah, go to Hell!" shouted someone else. A woman. Laura's mother on the village committee.

A man threw another brick, smashing another window pane. It would have hit Gabriel right in the chest if it wasn't for his vampire reflexes.

Ezra's nostrils flared, his dark eyes wide and shining against the splatter of red paint. His hands balled into fists. His whole body tensed with anger. Gabriel just watched, unsure of what to do,

117

as Ezra pushed past Lillian and headed out of the front door. Lillian ran to the window and Gabriel instinctively stepped closer to her side as they both watched.

Ezra flung the front door open and strode down their short path. The mob instantly quietened, and even though Ezra was still at least ten feet away, they all took one collective step backwards.

"Sorry, I couldn't hear you back there. What did you say?" asked Ezra in a conversational tone. He folded his arms across his chest, flexing his boy muscles in his thin, black t-shirt. The tea towel was still over his shoulder.

The mob all looked to one another. Clearly their pack mentality had worn off.

Then Ian Howden stepped forwards and Gabriel felt his fangs press against his gums.

Ian Howden pointed at the window, at Gabriel.

"I know he's one of them," he seethed. "A vampire. And they know she is, too."

Lillian sucked in a sob by his side. It was then Gabriel noticed the four women in their forties all bunched together at the back. The Book Club.

Ezra looked to them and Gabriel could see his face now. It was dark but the streetlamps lit up the scene perfectly. He arched a dark eyebrow, still so cool and collected. There was almost a smirk on his face.

"You lot attacked Lillian?" he asked with a dry laugh and took a step forward. The women all clutched each other. "I heard you drove her out of your home. That right?"

"Sh-she lied to us," said one of the women. Gabriel was pretty sure her name was Linda. "She put us in danger!"

"Okay, so." Ezra put his hand to his chin, thinking. "You thought that Lillian being at your little book club put you in danger. So, what? You come here, now knowing she's a vampire, and vandalise her house? Where is the logic there?"

They all just looked to each other.

"So, you see, now you've put yourselves in danger because no one messes with Lillian *or Gabriel*-," He shot a look to Ian Howden, "and gets away with it." The cold smile fell from his face, and what was left made a shiver crawl up the back of Gabriel's neck. For a moment, Ezra looked *evil*. For once, Gabriel could picture him killing, covered head to foot in the bloody mess of his fellow vampire brethren. It chilled him to his core. "I suggest you lot go run back home now-" He parted his lips. The light of the streetlamps shone against his extended fangs, *"before I tear... your fucking... throats out!"*

Ezra roared so loud it echoed down the street. The mob screamed and scrambled away, knocking into each other like bowling pins as they ran towards their cars.

"We are good people!" he called after them. "We wanted nothing but to live here peacefully and you come to *our* door and threaten *us*?"

When Ezra turned back, Gabriel caught a glimpse of dejection in his eyes. It was like a part of him had shattered. The evil was gone and he was lost. Then he blinked hard, scrubbed the back of his neck, grabbed the towel from his shoulder and headed back into the house.

Lillian ran to Ezra and by the time Gabriel got to the hallway, she had thrown her arms around him and buried her face into the curve of his neck.

"I'm so sorry. I'm so sorry you had to do that," she blubbered.

He held her tight, eyes clenched shut. "It's okay." He planted a heavy kiss on the top of her head. When he said, "We're going to be okay," his eyes found Gabriel's. There was a seriousness to his gaze. A directness. It was a knowing look. Like Ezra knew the roll of the dice. But what Gabriel couldn't tell, was if he should be relieved or terrified.

Ezra placed the bucket of soapy water by Gabriel's feet and joined him in his attempt to scrub the paint off the wall of their house. The mob had done a thorough job. The paint reached up to the second floor, covering the windowsill of Ezra's bedroom window.

After the nasty confrontation, Lillian had gone upstairs to get cleaned up and the two of them hadn't seen her since. It was obvious she was having a hard time, and blaming herself was not helping her situation. Ezra wasn't mad. The humans were actively searching for vampires. He would have bet any amount of money that Angela had used those silver rings on all of her guests, finding any opportunity she could to touch them and test. It was only a matter of time before the three of them were found out.

Gabriel bared his teeth as he scrubbed and scrubbed and scrubbed at their brickwork.

"This is ridiculous," he hissed, stopping and taking a step back to review his progress. He hadn't achieved much. "They've made our place look like a fucking Jackson Pollock painting." He looked to the broken window, which they had covered with cardboard and several layers of binbags. "Who gave them the *right*?"

"They're scared. It's human nature to blindly attack what they don't understand," said Ezra, crouching on the pathway and dunking his scrubbing brush into the water.

Gabriel scoffed. "Yeah, well, they're gonna be even more scared now after you threatened to kill them all. What were you thinking?"

What had he been thinking? He'd been thinking about what Guardian had said. How they all just needed to trust him and play along and hope things work out in the long run. Why? Because they're immortal so waiting should be no big deal?

No, this was their home. This was their reputations. This was their *lives*.

He started scrubbing the wall beneath the bay window, watching the suds turn pink.

"They hurt Lillian and… I don't know. Something in me just snapped," he said, punctuating his words with harsher scrubs.

When Gabriel didn't respond, he peered at him. The other vampire had his brush against the wall, but his mind was somewhere else. Ezra knew the lost look in his eyes well. He was thinking about how he had been Released. How his Maker had broken their sire bond as soon as it had been created. How he didn't have a Maker to protect him and love him the way Ezra loved Lillian.

But he had Ezra. And Ezra tried to be the Maker he never had. He just needed Gabriel to let him.

"And then I saw Mitch's mum out there," Ezra added, bringing Gabriel's thoughts out of that dark place. His attention came back to Ezra.

"Your barman?" he asked.

Ezra nodded. "I got a text from him before asking me why I never told him. He hates that I didn't trust him. Said he thought we were mates."

"He might come around. Becca did."

120

"Yeah." Ezra sighed, scrubbing with less vigour. "It's just shit."

The brickwork was cool against Ezra's back as he sat at the front of the house, eyes to the moon. Gabriel was by his side, legs outstretched across the flagstones. The bucket of pink, soapy water sat between them. They had scrubbed away most of the paint, but it had left splotchy stains behind. It seemed very fitting. Now that their secret was out, they couldn't just wipe it away and forget like it never happened.

Or could they?

They could compel them to forget?

No, there's too many of them. Ezra shook his head. That was a stupid idea. He couldn't erase an entire village's memory.

Footsteps brought Ezra's attention to the street and he perked up at the sight of Ben heading towards them, shoulders bunched up against the cold wind. *Wow, things really must be shit if I'm happy to see this guy.*

Ben spotted the two of them on the ground and a deep worry line creased his forehead.

"Hey," he said in that sighing way people used when something bad had happened.

Ezra jerked his thumb to the front door. "She's upstairs."

He looked behind them, to the boarded-up window and the stained brickwork.

"Are you guys okay?" he asked, slotting his hands into the pockets of his thick, wool-lined denim jacket.

"What do you think?" Ezra snapped.

"*Ezra,*" chastised Gabriel, sounding tired and deflated. "He's being nice." Gabriel showed Ben a tight smile. "What he means is, we've been better."

"What does this mean for you guys? Are you leaving?"

Ezra could see the worry in his eyes and a part of him relented. Ben was just afraid for Lillian, the same as he was.

"No," Ezra rasped. "We're not going anywhere. This is our home. If people don't like us being here, well, fuck them."

He could feel Gabriel's eyes on him, watching him unravel. Ezra looked to him; to his partner who'd been by his side for centuries. To the one person he knew he could count on no matter what.

Gabriel's eyes spoke to him. *We've got each other. That's what matters.*

Ezra sent him a weak smile. *This is it. Whatever happens, happens.*

PART II – The New Diet

Chapter 15

It had been weeks since the attack on their home and the three vampires were stuck in a rut. Gabriel and Ezra had both lost their jobs. Feeling too vulnerable in her own home, Lillian now spent most of her time at Ben's now.

All over the world there were more and more stories about vampires being exposed. A group in Florida had even taken it upon themselves to gun down a couple of vampires living in their apartment block. They weren't charged with murder because, apparently, it wasn't murder if the victim's heart wasn't beating to begin with. This sparked outrage across the country. In the USA, vampires were protesting for Equal Rights while, in the UK, vampires were protesting for the curfew to end and for businesses to stay open late so they could go back to living their normal lives. And all over Europe, there was an obvious divide between lovers and haters. Asia was dealing with things a little better, there seemed to be order there that the rest of the world was apparently incapable of.

After the news of Gabriel, Ezra and Lillian being vampires had travelled around their entire village, Maeve had refused to let Becca see Gabriel in fear for both their lives. She had managed to contain Becca for just over a week before they had fought and Becca had stormed out of the house in anger, heading straight to Gabriel. She'd worn her hood up and entered through the backdoor, like that was going to fool the neighbours. At first, Gabriel had also tried to keep her away for her own protection. Not protection from him, but from everyone else. But when Becca had showed up on his back doorstep, eyes full of so many questions, he had given in almost instantly.

Now they were sitting on the sofa together, her head resting on his chest, watching a police drama. She had remarked how stupid she felt after realising she had never noticed his lack of heartbeat. Becca had fully accepted him. Hell, she was even afraid *for* him. If only the rest of the village was as understanding as she was.

They spent most evenings cuddled up together now. Ezra was up in his room, trying to stay out of the way. And if he wasn't hiding up there, he was in the city gathering information and bringing back worryingly few bottles of blood.

Gabriel couldn't help but feel like his whole world had suddenly shrunk down to the size of a pea. He hadn't left the house since the attack so the only way he found out information from the outside world was through Ezra or the News – and it was hard to know what to believe.

A knock on the front door had Gabriel jerking up to attention and almost making Becca topple to the floor. She managed to right herself and looked to Gabriel in confusion. By the time he got to the hallway, Ezra was at the top of the stairs. He raced down them and beat Gabriel to the door. Both vampires looked to each other. Gabriel pushed Becca back into the living room as Ezra opened the door.

Two uniformed police officers stood several paces back, their feet barely off the pavement. Their car was parked across the road. Gabriel spotted another a few doors down, this one with another two officers in the front.

The man sized them both up.

"Ezra Garcia? Gabriel Matsouka?" he asked.

The two of them remained silent. Gabriel's mind began to head down a dark road. *This is it. This is when we get taken. It's over. We're done.*

"Is Lillian Reynolds home?" asked the female police officer.

"No," Ezra said, pulling the door closed so it was pressed against his side. "What do you want?"

"Where is Miss. Reynolds?" she asked.

"How about, why are you here?"

Gabriel looked to Ezra. Something had changed in him the night of the attack. There was a wildness about him. Like he was a caged bear just waiting for someone to dare to poke him. Waiting for a reason to snap. *Asking* for a reason to snap.

"Mr. Garcia, we have reason to believe that the three of you in this residence have been lying about your identities," said the male officer.

Ezra ran his tongue over his teeth. "That right?"

Gabriel could feel the tension from Ezra's body, like he was standing beside a spring coiled too tight.

"Is it true what your neighbours say about you? Have you been impersonating humans?" continued the male officer.

Ezra smirked. "Impersonating humans? What are you getting at?"

The two officers shifted their stances, clearly uncomfortable. The female officer gripped her bullet proof vest and squared her shoulders as her partner's jaw worked and eyes shifted.

"You're vampires," said the female officer and her partner noticeably cringed.

Ezra jabbed Gabriel in the side and they both burst out laughing like they had rehearsed this whole scene.

The male officer scowled and crossed his arms over his chest. The woman reached for something on her belt and then there was a blinding flash of light. Gabriel's cheek and neck burned like he'd just been doused with acid. He hissed, stumbling back into the hallway. He felt Ezra doing the same but he couldn't see through the pain and the bright light. He grabbed at his cheek, smelling and tasting his own burning flesh.

The light blinked out and Gabriel found Ezra by the stairs, holding onto the bannister for support. His throat and chin were red and blistered. Blood painted the neck of his t-shirt. The female officer was still on their path, now a few steps closer, a torch raised in her grip.

"UV light." She smirked. "I heard that it burns vampires."

By her side, her partner looked horrified. He was at the pavement, his head snapping between the house and his backup.

Gabriel's jaw clenched and he fought back a wince when he felt his skin tear. The back of his hand was also an angry red. "What do you want from us? We're not hurting anyone."

She reached into her back trouser pocket and the two of them both braced for another attack. But this time, she pulled out a brown folder folded in half. "Well, we're here to make sure of that."

Ezra stalked up to her, his chest rising and falling in anger. The officer held the torch up higher in warning and Ezra paused at the threshold of the door, his top lip twitching like he was ready to show her his fangs. She held out the folder in her other hand and he snatched it off her.

"What's this?" he asked.

"A new law states that all vampires must follow the new government mandated diet," she reeled off like she had practiced it in the mirror a hundred times.

"What?" Gabriel came up behind Ezra as he opened the folder to reveal a bound document inside.

"To protect the human population, from now on, vampires are ordered to follow the new guidelines."

"Animal blood?" said Ezra, skim-reading.

"Yes." She gestured to the folder, still keeping the UV torch held ready. "Inside is information about which butchers are supplying. There are also coupons inside. The three of you have a monthly allowance. You will exchange the coupons for the animal blood. Each month you will receive your new allowance in the post."

"Allowance?" Gabriel echoed. "Like rations?"

She smiled at him politely but it didn't wash away the distain in her eyes. "Stick to the diet and there will be no problems."

"And if we don't?" Ezra's eyes flicked up from the document.

"The three of you have been registered as vampires. You are now in our system, along with thousands of others. If we find that you are not adhering to the new law, you will be punished in a way that we see fit."

By the haunting look in Ezra's eyes, Gabriel could tell he could read between the lines. Gabriel gulped. *Mess up, and we're dead.*

"Where can we find Miss Reynolds?" she asked.

"I don't know," said Ezra, staring her down. He waved the folder between them. "But I'll make sure she gets her *coupons.*"

The officer smiled, so tight it crinkled her whole face. "Great. Thank you for being so understanding, Mr. Garcia. Mr. Matsouka." She nodded to Gabriel.

"Doesn't seem like we have a choice in the matter," Gabriel replied.

"It's called a law for a reason." The smug look she sent his way had Gabriel's fangs pressing against his gums.

"Have a pleasant night, gentleman," she tossed over her shoulder. She met her partner at the pavement. The two vampires watched as they crossed the road to their car.

Becca jumped from the sofa when Gabriel returned to the living room, followed closely by Ezra. She ran to him and went to touch his cheek. Her fingers hovered over the swelling redness there. He could already feel that the burn was partially healed.

"What happened?" she gasped. "I was about to come out but then I heard you cry out and I panicked. I'm so sorry."

Gabriel waved her away and gestured her to sit back down. "No, no, it's fine. It's best you stayed away."

She tucked her dress under her knees as she sat, keeping her hands under her legs as she gazed up at him. Ezra sank onto the opposite sofa and opened the folder on his lap. His cheek and neck were also starting to heal. It now just looked like a patch of sunburn.

"I heard everything," Becca said. "About making you drink animal blood. Is that right? Would that work?"

Ezra expelled a heavy sigh and shook his head, scanning the pages. "I have no idea. I mean, I guess vampires have drunk animal blood before in desperate times but it's usually a last resort sort of thing. But living on it?" He shook his head again.

"And we can't stock up on blood from Dalia?" asked Gabriel.

"I've been grabbing what I can but her supply is almost out."

Gabriel frowned. "Guess we are all gonna have to use Ben."

Ezra shook his head more vigorously and pulled his phone from his jeans pocket. "Not a chance. Lillian's stopping feeding from him, too. I'm getting her over here."

Gabriel watched him typing. Ezra could just command her to come using their sire bond but he'd said long ago that he didn't like her feeling like she was his pet.

"If she gets caught with Ben and the police start asking questions, we're fucked," Ezra said.

"What about me?"

They both looked to Becca.

She shuffled uncomfortably, still sitting on her hands. Her eyebrow quirked up helplessly. "If they see me with you guys, will they think you're feeding from me?"

Ezra closed the folder and wagged a finger between them. "Just to clarify, you're not, right?"

"No, no. Not at all. I'd never do that," rushed Gabriel.

Ezra sent him a withered look. "No, you'll just feed off her senile grandad instead."

Gabriel's jaw clenched and he sent Ezra a warning glare. *Shut the fuck up.*

He turned to Becca. She was now hugging herself and looking at the wallpaper, clearly uncomfortable.

"Anyway, it probably is best you stop coming here. At least until the police are confident that we're not a danger to anyone," said Ezra after a stiff silence.

"Says the guy who threatened to kill everyone," said Gabriel under his breath, rolling his eyes to Becca.

Ezra sent him a dry look. "I was antagonised."

Gabriel sank down onto the sofa beside Becca. She slid her hand into his on his lap like it was muscle memory.

"I know. But from now on, I feel like no matter what we do they're gonna paint us as the bad guys. Even if we're just protecting our property. They want a reason get rid of us," said Gabriel. Becca's sudden squeeze of his hand made his dead heart lurch.

Ezra was back to reading the folder. He nodded. "I think you're right."

The front door banged open and Lillian stomped into the living room, pushing off her hood. Her eyes darted to Gabriel and Becca then she found Ezra half hidden behind the open door.

"So, what's the big emergency you needed me home for?" she asked, her voice casual. Then her brows pinched when she noticed the very official looking file open on her Maker's lap. Ezra slid further down the sofa and patted the pace beside him.

His jaw was tight and helplessness shone in his eyes as he looked up at her, "I think you'll wanna sit down for this."

Chapter 16

Becca stood behind her grandad, combing his surprisingly thick, white hair as he sat silently in his chair flicking through his five TV channels. His box got all the channels but he 'didn't trust' any channel beyond five. He'd managed just fine with those channels back in the day, he was fine with them now.

He stopped at the morning news updates and Becca's stomach flipped when she read the scrolling headline. '*Breaking News: Vampires, they're out there!*' The media was inundated with more and more cases of vampires. When a few celebrity heartthrobs were outed as being fanged, it had seemed to curb the haters. And it had also led to an onslaught of new memes. These ones comparing 'outed' vampire actors to other actors and band members that 'suspiciously' hadn't aged in the last decade.

Ezra had told her and Gabriel to stay away from each other. She understood his reasons, of course, but she couldn't help sucking her teeth to contain her annoyance. They had *only just* gotten back together. And now that Gabriel was no longer weighed down by his secret, things had been going great. It wasn't until Maeve had camped outside her bedroom one night – well equipped with a sleeping bag and midnight snacks, to make sure she didn't sneak out to see him – when she realised how oddly unfazed she was by the fact that her boyfriend drank blood and had been dead for over a hundred years.

But despite Maeve's disapproval, Gabriel was a big part of her life, and the sooner everyone accepted that, the better.

With that in mind, she cleared her throat and tested the waters. "So, what do you think of all of this, Grandad?"

Her grandad huffed a laugh and grumbled, "One thing about living in Santa Carla I never could stomach: all the damn vampires."

Becca smiled, holding a section of his hair from his scalp so she could painlessly untangle a knot. She guessed the reality that they now found themselves in wasn't so far from the films he watched and memorised. It was actually quite a relief he was getting more and more absorbed into the land of make believe. Maybe he was safer there.

She finished combing, smoothed his hair behind his ears, and planted a soft kiss on the top of his head.

"The vampires don't scare you?" she asked.

He scoffed. "Those biker boys? Bunch of fancy lads, they are."

"You don't think they're evil?" She sat down on the dining chair pulled up beside his. On the screen there was a blurry CCTV image of a dark figure on a street, there one moment and gone the next. The video was then slowed down to show that the figure hadn't vanished, but had instead darted out of shot at lightning fast speed. Becca then understood what Gabriel meant when he said he could *run very fast.*

"Evil?" her grandad scoffed again, which led to an onslaught of dry coughs and wheezes. Becca handed him his glass of water and he gratefully glugged down a mouthful. "Hard to say what's not evil these days," he continued. "But can't say these guys are much worse than us."

It was a harrowing thought, but one Becca didn't necessarily disagree with.

She heard the front door open and got to her feet. "Claudia's here."

Her grandad grumbled.

"Play nice," she said, hearing the care nurse heading down the hallway. "I'll be back to check on you after work."

———————————

With the curfew still very much ongoing, Ezra had approximately forty minutes between sundown and closing time to receive the monthly supply of animal blood from the butchers. The whole system was already heavily flawed. What would happen in summer when the sun set later? Had they even thought that far ahead?

But despite this new law making him feel like a pitbull forced to be muzzled and monitored simply for being a pitbull, he took the car and headed to the other side of the village with his stupid little coupons stuffed into his jeans pocket.

He parked around the corner and strolled down the empty high street. The butcher's shutters were already halfway down, signalling to customers in a polite way that they were still open but to not enter while they were cleaning.

Ezra opened the door and ducked inside. Behind the counter, a stout man was wiping down the glass surfaces. He spotted Ezra and his lips formed a thin line.

"Can't believe I've been dragged into this," he mumbled, shaking his head as he turned and threw his cloth into a sink behind him.

"Sounds like you know why I'm here," said Ezra, trying to sound as casual and non-confrontational as he could - which he was finding more and more difficult with each passing night.

This was not the village he called home anymore. These people were no longer neighbours, friends, even strangers. No, they were all his judge, jury and possible executioners.

Ezra stopped before the counter. All the leftover meats had been covered, waiting to be put away. The butcher – who he had served plenty of times at the pub and was pretty sure was named Lyle – placed his hands firmly on the lower part of the counter, leaned forward with squared shoulders and looked Ezra directly in the eyes. It was an attempt at a threatening stance, but then he seemed to remember that vampires could compel through close eye contact – something that had been discovered and broadcasted the week before. He then jerked back, his lip curled with contempt like Ezra had actually attempted to play with his mind.

Ezra clenched his jaw. They were always going to think the worst of them. Just like a pitbull.

"I have your blood," said Lyle, taking another step back. "Got your coupons?"

Ezra pulled the silly things out of his pocket. They looked like ticket stubs. The three of them had received a row each. Four stubs to a row. Apparently, each stub should last them a week. How they figured that out, he didn't know. Possibly from the vamps who were cooperating for freedom in return? Did that make them exempt from this stupid charade?

He slid all three rows onto the top of the glass display counter. "I'll take them all."

"You can't do that."

Ezra ran his tongue over his bottom teeth to suppress a groan of frustration. "What?"

Lyle nodded to the coupons. "You can only use yours. They have your name on them." He fanned out the coupons and tapped on the row addressed to Mr. Ezra Garcia.

Ezra swiped a hand down his face. "But Gabriel and Lillian live with me. See, the same address. I'm picking them up for them, too, so they don't have to deal with this shit."

Lyle shrugged and grabbed his row of coupons, leaving the others behind. "I'm just following the rules. I'll go get you *your* supply."

The butcher headed into his back room, shoulders back and a swagger in his step. Ezra spun on his heel to face the door and let out an inaudible scream of irritation, before clearing his throat and fixing his face into an expressionless mask just in time for Lyle to return.

Swinging in his tight grip were four white plastic bags, two in each fist. He dropped them onto the counter top and they all lolled to the side. The bags were larger than Ezra had expected. He figured possibly at least six pints of blood in each.

"I've gotta ask-" said Lyle, folding his thick tree trunk arms across his chest, "How'd you manage it? To kid us all."

Ezra started collecting the bags. "We're not so different from you. Those depictions you see on TV, read about in books, that's just fiction. This is just as much our world as it is yours, it's time you realised that."

The stubborn line in Lyle's forehead softened. Ezra lifted the bags as if toasting a beer, and nodded his thanks before leaving, making sure to dodge the shutters.

By the time he returned home, both Lillian and Gabriel were stretched out on the sofas in the living room. Now neither of them really had anywhere to go, they had resorted to living in their comfy, housebound attire. Gabriel had swapped jeans and fitted jumpers for plaid pyjama trousers and a long-sleeved white t-shirt with moth holes around the collar. Lillian was dressed head to toe in pink flannel and was currently using her fluffy dressing gown as a blanket.

She twisted her head awkwardly to look up at Ezra as he entered the room. His easy smile was met with a scowl. Breaking the news to her that she could no longer see Ben had not gone down well, despite the precaution being for his own safety.

"Oh, it's you," she mumbled, slapping the cushion she was resting on before burrowing her head deeper into it and bringing her attention back to the TV.

"Who else would it be?" said Ezra, ignoring her icy tone.

"What's that?" Gabriel sat up and nodded to the freezer bag at Ezra's feet.

"Just been to the butchers. It's our new meal plan."

Gabriel's eyebrow quirked up and even Lillian shifted up into a sitting position and eyed up the bag.

"There's only one bottle left in the fridge," she said, "of the real stuff."

Ezra grabbed the bag and made his way to the kitchen. "Well, let's hope this stuff is as good."

He heard shuffling feet across the wood flooring and didn't need to look back to know the two of them were following.

Inside each white plastic bag was another, thicker plastic bag that contained the blood. Without needing to ask, Gabriel took the empty glass bottles from under the sink and placed them on the table. Getting the blood from the bags into the bottles was an awkward ordeal, but between the three of them, they succeeded with the transfer without spilling much.

"This is for all of us?" asked Gabriel.

"Apparently, you guys have to go yourselves to get your share. But we can all use this 'til we run out and then grab yours. Easier to just do it that way," Ezra explained. "And I think it'll be a good idea to move to this now and keep the bottle of real stuff in the fridge for back up in case of an emergency."

"What kind of emergency?" Lillian had picked up one of the new bottles and was inspecting in warily.

What kind of emergency? Ezra didn't want to find out.

She lifted it to her nose and sniffed. Her fangs sprung free with their tinny click and a surprised *oop* escaped her.

Gabriel laughed softly. "Well, that's a good sign."

Ezra smiled at his progeny, who was gazing up at him with that cheeky glimmer in her eyes he had always loved. He crossed to the cabinet and grabbed three mugs. "Guess we'd better sample this stuff, eh?"

Both Gabriel and Lillian took their seats at the dining table and watched while Ezra grabbed a saucepan and heated up some of the animal blood. A silence fell between them. It almost felt like some sort of ceremony, or ritual.

Ezra stirred the blood, watching it stain the wooden spoon. The smell grew thicker and headier as it warmed and soon his fangs were also trying to force themselves free. The pressure against his gums was welcomed. Gabriel was right, it was a good sign. It meant his hunger was reacting. It meant his body yearned for this blood just like it did with human blood. Maybe the humans were onto something?

He poured the blood into the three mugs and brought them over to the table. He slid into the chair beside Lillian and they all sat there in silence, looking down at their drinks. Gabriel's top lip twitched and his fangs popped free. The sound triggered Ezra's to finally unsheathe.

Lillian, the youngest of the three and so less able to resist her hunger, was first to pick up her mug and lift it to her lips. Ezra and Gabriel both watched her drink. Ezra gulped when she gulped, as if he was somehow drinking it with her. Fear fluttered in the pit of his stomach. He wasn't sure why. It was just animal blood. He'd heard of vampires drinking it before. But never had they been forced to drink it. To live off it.

What if she couldn't stand it? What would that mean for her?

She settled the mug back on the table. Her eyes flickered between the two of them. A delicate smile played on her lips.

"Well, what are you waiting for?" she asked.

"What's it like?" The mix of nerves and excitement in Gabriel's voice made Ezra's fearful flutters worsen.

"Try it."

Both Gabriel and Ezra picked up their mugs, locked eyes and drank. *Whatever happens, happens.*

The hot, thick liquid slid down Ezra's throat. His eyes closed as he basked in the sensation. It wasn't as sweet. Not as *rich*. But it hit the spot.

He placed his mug down and leaned back in his chair. Gabriel still held his mug at his chin, his eyes on Ezra.

Ezra shrugged casually. "It actually isn't bad."

Both Lillian and Gabriel grinned at him; their teeth stained a wicked red.

Maybe this won't be so bad after all.

Chapter 17

Becca let out a hearty yawn as she got out of her car and headed up her driveway. The living room curtains twitched and by the time she had grabbed her keys from her coat pocket, Maeve was standing in the doorway.

"Where the hell have you been?" Maeve demanded.

Becca furrowed her brows and followed Maeve's eyes as they scanned the road erratically.

"I was at work, like I am every day." Becca pushed past her and headed into the kitchen. Maeve followed a very close step behind her.

"You're usually back by seven. It's nearly eight."

"I had to stay behind. Some people in the office are refusing to go to work because of what's going on so we're short staffed."

"And rightly so! You shouldn't be going to work, either!"

Becca inhaled and exhaled a slow, calming breath as she dropped her lunch container into the sink. Not only was she now overworked in the office, she had to come home to her frantic, paranoid, overdramatic friend judging everything she did.

"Maeve, we've talked about this. If you want to work from home, that's your decision. But I'm still going to work. I'm still going to see my grandad. I'm still trying to cling to some form of normality."

Maeve scoffed. "Normality? Seriously? You're dating a *vampire*."

Becca spun to her, anger now sizzling deep in her chest. "Yes, who you are refusing to let me see."

She blinked, dumbfounded, and pressed her fingertips to her forehead as if trying to contain a headache. A headache caused by Becca's stupidity. "Because he's a *vampire*." She dropped her arms and her narrow shoulders wilted. Genuine concern filled her eyes and the anger in Becca diminished.

"Becca, please. You really don't see it? There's a reason you're so chill about Gabriel. He's done that compelling thing to you. How else would you be fine with all this vampire stuff?" Maeve's voice was calm with a hint of pity. Becca suddenly felt like she was at an intervention.

Becca smiled softly and closed the distance between them. "I appreciate your concern, I really do. But you've got it all wrong. Gabriel promised he'd never compel me. He has no reason to. I fell for him when he was taking care of my grandad and my feelings haven't changed since finding out the truth."

Maeve rolled her eyes to the fridge, her lips a thin line of silent disapproval. She paused for a moment, thinking. Really thinking. Becca could see her mental cogs turning. Worry tightened her features and Becca gulped. She hated how afraid Maeve was. She didn't like being annoyed at her. But Becca hated it when other people acted like they knew what was best for her when she'd done a pretty good job at looking after herself.

"How do you know you can trust him?" Maeve finally asked, her voice a broken whisper.

Becca shrugged. "I just do."

"I still don't want you seeing him."

"I know." Their eyes met. "But I hope you'll find it in you to trust him, too."

Maeve scoffed, but it wasn't vicious. "He's a man. I'll never trust him."

Becca smiled. "Fair enough."

Maeve crossed the kitchen and opened the fridge. "I've got one bottle of wine left. And you're drinking with me. I'm not taking no for an answer. You're not leaving me in the lurch like last time."

Becca grabbed two wine glasses from the drying rack. "Well, I guess if I don't have a choice…"

Gabriel had retreated into his bedroom and had his TV on for background noise as he flicked through new memes between replying to texts from Becca. Just because they couldn't see each other, didn't mean they couldn't stay in contact.

The memes, as stupid and nonsensical as some of them were, eased his trepidation somewhat. If people could laugh and make jokes, their discovery couldn't be that doomed, could it? And after drinking the animal blood to find that it actually was pretty decent, things weren't looking as dismal as he had first thought.

But leaving the house? He hadn't gotten *that* comfortable with the new normal just yet.

A tentative knock on his door had him looking up from his phone.

"Come in," he said.

The door opened and Lillian appeared sheepishly. "Am I interrupting?"

Gabriel sat up, shoving his pillow between his back and the headrest. "Like there's anything to do."

She came in, shut the door behind her, and perched on the edge of his bed. "Can I talk to you about something?"

"Of course."

She sighed heavily, playing with the cuffs of her dressing gown. "I wanna see Ben."

The ache in her voice made Gabriel's eyebrows pinch with sorrow.

"I know you do," he said. "I miss Becca, too."

139

"Will you talk to Ezra? I know I'm his progeny but you're his best friend."

Despite knowing Ezra for centuries, Gabriel was still surprised by how taken aback he was whenever they were described as being best friends. The term was so… human. There should be a whole other label allocated to what Ezra and Gabriel were to each other.

"But he's right, Lil."

"But they've already seen me with him! They know we're dating! What's the point in being apart now? This is when I need him the most." She hugged herself tightly.

"Have you spoken to Ben lately?"

"Yeah, a little. On the phone."

"And what're things like on his end?"

She shrugged. "He's had a few death threats."

Gabriel's jaw clenched. *Has Becca had death threats? If she had, would she even tell me or pretend like it's nothing so I don't worry?*

Lillian squeezed her eyes shut and winced. "I know it's selfish of me to wanna see him but this is a lot, and he makes me feel safe."

"Safe?" Gabriel laughed softly. "The safest place you can be is under this roof with Ezra. You heard him that night when they attacked. If anyone caused you harm, he would not hesitate to rip them apart. Especially now."

She peered at him. "You've noticed it, too? How he's changed?"

The sudden severity in her tone took him off guard. He'd predicted they would have skated around the subject, not for her to hit it head on.

Gabriel nodded and grabbed his other pillow to hug to his chest.

"He's told me about what Silas would make him do," said Gabriel. "I know he'd spared me most of the gory details. But I was never able to picture it. Ezra's so… collected. He's so methodical and protective and just… *not a killer*. But that night, faced with our taunting neighbours. Just being so overwhelmed with their hate. He had this look… and everything he'd told me; I could see it then."

Lillian nodded down at her lap. "I saw it, too. And I've felt it. In our bond. Like a rust." A heavy pause followed. "It's part of the reason I wanna leave. Get out of this house. This shift in him, I don't know how to take it. And every time I look at that boarded up window, I hear their threats and see the hate in their eyes.

"I love being a vampire, but not right now. Right now, I just want to pretend. I want to be with my human boyfriend and cook him meals and play the housewife."

Gabriel watched her for a moment. He felt for her, he really did. She had looked so lost these past few nights. And being the third wheel when Ezra and Lillian were on good terms was one thing, but being the third wheel when there was tension between them? That was something else entirely.

"I'm sorry, Lil, I really am. But I'm on his side on this."

Lillian was still a new-born, meaning she was a lot more unstable than himself and Ezra. Who's to say she wouldn't snap if provoked? And Ben was now getting death threats. The two of them seeing each other was far too risky.

Gabriel's phone vibrated on the duvet and they both looked to it. He smiled at the screen.

"Becca?" Lillian asked.

Gabriel instantly regretted the smile.

"I'm glad you're back together. She really likes you, Gabe. And I can see she makes you happy."

Gabriel met her eyes. "This is all just temporary. Things will calm down soon."

She smiled wistfully and stood up. "I hope so."

Around midnight, Gabriel felt a little peckish and so he headed to the kitchen for another mug. He met Ezra in the hallway, throwing on a zip-up hoodie and heading for the front door.

"Where you going?" Gabriel asked.

Ezra was patting all his jeans pockets, looking harried. "To see Silas."

"Why?"

He paused and finally looked at Gabriel. "What do you mean, why?"

"I mean, why are you going to see Silas? Because it can't be for more blood."

"No. I'm going to get updated on what's going on." He looked confused. "Like always."

"I'm coming with you."

He looked even more confused. "And why's that?"

"Because I've been cooped up in this house for too long and I'm bored, that's why." *And also, I want to know what the hell is going on with you.*

"Oh, so when you're bored you can follow me around but when I do it, I'm *in the way?*"

"You followed me to *work*. I could have been fired."

"And you got fired anyway without my help." Ezra arched a dark eyebrow. "And me meeting Silas is also basically work."

"I'll be well behaved. You won't even know I'm there." Gabriel started heading to the kitchen backwards. "I'm gonna put some blood in my thermos and I'm coming with you. Don't go anywhere."

Ezra sighed heavily and sank onto the stairs, pulling out his phone.

Afraid Ezra might dart off, Gabriel just poured a bottle of blood from the fridge straight into his thermos and then met Ezra back in the hallway.

Ezra stood and eyed Gabriel warily as he shoved on his wax jacket and boots. Luckily, he had changed from his scruffy house wear to his slightly less scruffy home attire – a simple black t-shirt and some scuffed up jeans.

"You don't even like Silas," said Ezra.

"It's not that I don't like him." Gabriel paused to wriggle his foot into his boot with a little extra force. "I just don't really get him."

"You don't get him?" Ezra followed him as he opened the door and headed down their path. Gabriel paused on the pavement, waiting for Ezra to lock up. "What does that mean?"

"He may look all crisp and proper, but he's kind of a brute. You think he has your best interest at heart then makes you do unspeakable things."

"Well." Ezra jogged to catch up and they both headed to the car that was parked a few spots down. "He hasn't made me do those unspeakable things for a long time. And with that in mind, no talking about how you used to chew your patients."

Ezra unlocked the car and they both got in, Ezra in the driver's seat.

"Oh yeah, because that would be the first thing I'd bring up," said Gabriel sarcastically.

Ezra started the engine and double-triple checked the road in silence before inching out of the tight parking spot, as if there were actually going to be any cars driving past. Gabriel chugged down a few gulps of his thermos before slotting it into the cup holder. Once they were on the empty main road out of the village, he piped up again.

"Silas' ways may not be kosher, but sometimes you've got to be tough and teach the hard way," said Ezra.

Gabriel shook his head. "It's just – for someone who hates killing, he sure kills a lot. And makes you kill."

"Killing killers," Ezra stated simply, not looking from the road. "Vampires are always one step away from being the monsters that humans think we are. It's why I was so pissed at your antics. Silas knows this, and he just wants his progenies to play by the rules. It's fine if you don't get it. I mean, I don't expect you to. You don't have a-" Ezra's words seemed to turn to dust on his tongue. He cleared his throat and narrowed his eyes at the darkness ahead.

"Because I don't have a Maker? Is that what you were going to say?" Gabriel asked, eyeing his profile.

Ezra's pale fingers wrung the steering wheel but he said nothing.

"Because you don't need to remind me, Ezra. I'm well aware." There was venom in his words that only seeped into his tone when discussing this particular topic.

"I'm sorry," Ezra said in a small voice, his eyes still forward.

Gabriel wasn't finished. "Just because I was Released doesn't mean I can't see when someone is taking advantage of their authority."

"Do I need to turn this car around?" Ezra finally looked at him. The steeliness in his big, dark eyes took Gabriel by surprise. "Because you're not coming to the meeting with this attitude."

"I'm just saying he-"

"Well, don't," Ezra cut in, gripping the wheel hard. "I am who I am because of him. And if you insult Silas, you insult me. So, either shut up, or get out." His jaw worked as his eyes flitted between the road and Gabriel. "Do I need to pull over?"

143

Gabriel shook his head and sank lower into his seat.

The car then plummeted into a stiff, uncomfortable silence.

Gabriel's wariness and -okay- *slight* dislike for Silas came from a good place. Usually he could push it back and it replace it with mild irritation and jealousy that Ezra was kept when he was tossed aside, despite them both being Turned in the same way. Randomly in the night when they were minding their own business.

But the dislike had resurfaced since Ezra's weird shift in personality. Even the argument they had just had didn't feel like their usual type. There was usually an element of comradery in their jibes. But that look Ezra had just sent him, it was cold and hard and *fierce*. Gabriel knew that Ezra would never hurt him physically. He'd never end him the way he'd ended his murderous brothers and sisters. If he had it in him, he would have done it already.

But the way he'd looked at him just then… Gabriel was damn sure he'd have pulled the car over and dumped him on the side of the road like an empty beer can.

Chapter 18

Gabriel hadn't set foot inside a vampire bar for at least the better part of a decade. He had dabbled in the sordid vampire culture when he had travelled to Milan. But it had taken him a few years to realise he didn't actually enjoy the scene- he just felt like he was supposed to.

From the outside, *Black Velvet* looked dark and mysterious, with black panelling along the front and blacked out windows. The neon sign above the door was switched off. Ezra unlocked the door and Gabriel followed him through the empty, silent room. The red strip lighting under the bar and booths were the only sources of light as they crossed to the back room and down an industrial-looking stairwell. The basement was slightly brighter, lit by two fluorescent strip lights. In the centre of the room was a large, round black table with three chairs. The one closest to them was occupied. Gabriel's jaw clenched at the sight of the head of grey waves.

At the sound of their entrance, Silas turned in that easy way of his, like he didn't have a care in the world. His bright blue eyes were like two glowing gas lights.

"Ezra," he said in greeting. His deep voice rumbled, amplified by the surrounding concrete. His eyes slid from his progeny. "Gabriel."

"Silas," replied Gabriel, matching his cool, indifferent tone.

"It's been a while. How are you keeping?"

The two of them stopped before him.

"I'm coping," said Gabriel.

"Indeed." Silas turned back to the table, an indication that the two of them should join him. "It is all we can do."

"Where's Dalia?" asked Ezra, looking between the two empty seats.

Silas sighed and gestured to the chair before Ezra. He sank down onto it.

"I'm afraid Dalia is no longer with us."

Ezra's brows furrowed. "She left? I know she wanted to travel to Iceland but I thought she'd at least say goodbye first."

Silas shook his head. "That's not what I meant."

Realisation dawned on Ezra and he seemed to sink into himself.

Silas gestured to Gabriel, who was still lingering. "You might as well take her seat."

"But, how? What happened?" Ezra was shaking his head, his voice suddenly sharp and accusatory.

Gabriel took the vacant seat, feeling like he was stepping into someone's grave. He didn't know Dalia personally, but it was just as hard to see the grief in Ezra's eyes.

"I'm not too sure," said Silas leaning back in his chair. He frowned slightly as he played with the fancy looking lighter in his hand, flicking the cap up and clicking it back shut. "She's not answering her phone. Her flat is empty. Looks like no one's been here for a few nights. There have been some incidents in the city. Of vampires being… attacked." He sucked on his teeth, his nose crinkling with contained anger. "*Killed.*"

Ezra didn't even look like he heard him. His eyes were roving the table top, skittering like he was trying to solve a maths equation in his head. He shook his head slowly.

"She was killed?" His voice was barely a whisper.

"It appears so. Like you said, she wouldn't just leave. She wouldn't abandon this place."

The muscles in Ezra's cheek flexed and he worked his jaw from side to side.

"So, people found out she was a vampire?" asked Gabriel after a heavy silence. Silas was watching his progeny. A sheen of pity glimmered in his ghostly eyes.

"This new diet has painted a target on our backs," Silas drawled. His gaze slid to Gabriel. "Once you're in the system, it's only a matter of time until some human takes matters into their own hands and starts striking off names." He looked between the two of them. "They haven't got you on there yet, have they?"

At this, Ezra's eyes bugged. Both he and Gabriel gulped. They didn't say anything, but there was no need to. Silas sighed heavily, clicking his lighter shut. His tanned, leathery thumb stayed firmly pressed onto the lid.

"How? How were you caught?"

Ezra shuffled in his chair; his hands stuffed into the pockets of his hoodie. His head was bent in subjugation, like a son being scolded for having a house party when his parents were out of town.

"A silver ring," he lied, his pocketed hands flipping outwards as he shrugged. Of course, he wasn't going to tell his Maker what had *actually* happened. That he had *voluntarily* bared his fangs to the village and revealed his true nature. It didn't matter that he'd done it to protect Lillian and Gabriel. He had broken Silas' rule. And when you broke Silas' rule, you met a grizzly end.

Would Silas actually kill Ezra? Gabriel suddenly felt lightheaded. *No, he wouldn't kill him. He'd get one of Ezra's brothers and sisters to do it for him.*

Silas licked the top row of his squared, white teeth. His nostrils flared. The thumb pressed down on his lighter turned white with strain.

"How could you be so *stupid*? I taught you better than that," Silas hissed. His eyes then slid to Gabriel. "What's your excuse?"

Gabriel opened his mouth to speak, but nothing came out. He cleared his throat. "I was refused entry into a house."

Silas' steely glare softened a fraction. "See, that I can understand. But a ring?" He cut back to Ezra. "That wouldn't even trick a new-born."

"I don't know what to tell you." Ezra shrugged again, but this time, he straightened up and met his Maker's eyes. "It happened and now the truth is out and we're on the system and we have our shitty little coupons so we can drink our shitty animal blood and that's just the way life is now."

An icy silence fell over them. Frozen; Silas stared at Ezra. His crystal blue eyes were wide and burning with quelled rage. The fury tight in his features was so terrifying, Gabriel could barely look. But there was Ezra, staring right back at him. Defiance lowered his dark brows. His shoulders were squared. Hands no longer in his pockets, his arms were folded on the table.

Oh no. Not to him, Ezra. Anyone but him. Don't do this. Not now.

The silence dragged. The basement was so deathly quiet, if they'd been human, Gabriel was sure they'd be hearing each other's hearts beating.

The pressure of Silas' thumb on the lighter lifted. An action so miniscule that in any other situation it would have gone unnoticed. Then the tightness in his jaw settled and he leaned back ever so slightly in his chair.

"How is the animal blood treating you?" Silas asked in a tone that was as close to conversational as his deep, gravelly voice could manage.

Ezra continued to stare. His eyes narrowed a fraction, making his long eyelashes tremble.

"It's okay," Gabriel chimed in. He couldn't stand the tension anymore. "It's not as bad as we thought it'd be."

Silas' thin lips pulled up into something resembling a smile, and his eyes finally pulled free from his progeny and stuck to Gabriel. "That's good to hear."

From then on, the meeting resumed. Gabriel and Silas did most of the talking. They discussed what was happening with this *'New Diet'*. It seemed all European countries were following suit and there was a chance, if it was successful, it would be taken up by the rest of the world.

Ezra commented every now and again, in that grumbly, snappy tone he had recently adopted. Back slouched and arms folded high on his chest. To which Silas would acknowledge his contribution with a look and little else.

When Silas ended the meeting, Ezra said a quick goodbye and hurriedly stalked back up the stairwell.

"Gabriel."

Gabriel paused on his way to follow Ezra out. Silas was standing by the table, his hands slotted into the pockets of his neatly pressed trousers. He crossed the floor to Gabriel. His strides were leisurely but purposeful.

"I trust you will keep an eye on the lad," he said, stopping before him. His eyes studied Gabriel's face and there was a sadness in them that turned Gabriel's stomach.

Gabriel nodded. At such close proximity, the ancient vampire was incredibly imposing. The ancient was an inch or so shorter than Gabriel, but he had an almost palpable aura of many lives lived.

Silas nodded back, placed his hand on Gabriel's shoulder and met his eyes. With that look, he said everything without having to move his lips. And then the touch was gone, and he left. A lump lodged in Gabriel's throat and pressure built behind his eyes. He turned to say… what? He didn't know. But there was no one there. He was alone in the basement.

"You took your time."

Gabriel shut the passenger side door and clipped in his seatbelt. Ezra was in the driver's seat, checking his phone on his lap.

"Let's just get back home," Gabriel replied.

Ezra slipped his phone into his pocket, started the car and drove off without a word.

Gabriel just sat there in silence while his mind whirred. That touch. That look Silas gave him, it had carved him in two.

So that's what it felt like to have a Maker?

Gabriel had entered that basement ready to sit there silently seething, staring daggers into the ancient. But once he had sat around the table that was forgotten. And he had left that basement with, dare he say it, respect for the man?

Silas' words rang in his ears. They imprinted on his mind like a command.

Gabriel looked to Ezra, who was slouched back in his seat, driving with one hand down the empty city road.

"Are you okay?" Gabriel asked tentatively, then shook his head and looked to the road. *Strong start.*

"Never been better."

"Are you sure?"

"I just want to get home."

Gabriel sighed and thought for a moment. He needed to approach this topic delicately.

"You've been acting different lately," he said.

Ezra's eyes widened at the road in that *yeah, obviously* way. "There's been a lot going on lately."

"Silas is worried about you."

Ezra arched an eyebrow and scoffed. "Yeah? And since when have you and Silas been the best of friends?"

Gabriel studied his profile; the tightness of his jaw, the flickering of his eyes.

"I'm worried about you," he said.

"Well, there's no need to. I'm fine," Ezra gritted out.

"No, you're not."

"Yes, I am."

"No, you're-"

"Since when did you know me better than I know myself?" Ezra cut across him and pinned him with a glare.

"Since I know something's wrong with you but you're refusing to talk about it. You can talk to me, Ezra. You know I'm always here for you."

150

Ezra pressed down harder on the gas and Gabriel grabbed his seatbelt when he saw the dial go past sixty.

"*Ezra*," Gabriel cautioned.

Ezra now had two hands on the wheel, his knuckles bone white. His eyes were ahead, looking somehow focused and distant at the same time.

The dial pushed past sixty-five. "*Ezra*."

There were no other cars on the main road and luckily, the road was straight. But the look in his eyes had Gabriel feeling like Ezra was almost hoping he'd lose control of the car.

The dial pushed past seventy. Gabriel's back pressed against the seat. "Ezra, will you quit playing around!"

And like a switch being flicked, Ezra suddenly eased off the gas and his grip on the wheel loosened. A small, surprised breath escaped him and he blinked for the first time in a long while.

"Pull over," Gabriel ordered, and he did without a word.

When they were safely parked on the curb and the engine was switched off, Gabriel unbuckled his seatbelt and turned to his companion. Ezra had the back of his head against the headrest, staring down at the bonnet, arms dropped like forgotten things by his sides. His jaw worked in that way of his, before he sniffed hard and looked down at his lap.

"It was all for nothing," he said in a small voice. Gabriel just listened in silence, watching him collecting his thoughts. "All this time I've been trying my damned hardest to be this *poster boy* vampire. This version of us that might just be okay. Hell, I've killed *so many* of our kind. So many, I've lost count." He pulled a face of disgust and looked to Gabriel. Red rimmed his eyes. "How sick is that? It's like they never even mattered. And I did all that for what? For the safety of humans? For the same people who ganged up on us and vandalised our home? Who taunted us and screamed abuse at us? Who *killed* Dalia?" He blinked and tears fell. He batted them away, smudging them. "How is that okay? How are we still the bad guys?"

Ezra was shaking as he stared at Gabriel, eyes wide and pleading for him to make some sort of sense of this situation.

Gabriel's shoulders sagged. "It's because they don't know us. And they don't want to try."

"We got burned. By a cop. In our own fucking hallway."

"I know."

"That's not okay."

"I know."

"But we're supposed to be okay with it?"

"Yeah."

Ezra shook his head and looked to the road. His eyes shone in the glare of the streetlamp.

"Well, I'm not."

Chapter 19

The park was desolate. The absence of people only amplified the sound of the wind rustling the leaves and the tinny clang of abandoned cans rolling across the concrete pathways.

Gabriel relaxed back against the wooden bench and gazed up at the full moon. Now that it was the beginning of October, the nights were getting longer. It was only 7pm and the sky was a beautiful inky black.

In the corner of his eye, he saw Becca rub her gloved hands together before wedging them between her thighs. White clouds left her mouth as she let out shuddering breaths.

"You're cold," stated Gabriel, and unwound his scarf. She smiled as he wrapped it around her neck.

"Are you sure?"

"I don't need it. It was more of a fashion choice. But it looks better on you, anyway."

She snuggled against his side and he wrapped his arm around her, pulling her even closer.

"Are you sure we're okay?" she asked, her voice muffled by the scarf.

"It's been a month. We've had no other attacks on our house. Sure, Ezra and I have had some funny looks on the streets but people just seem to keep their distance now." He squeezed her quilted arm reassuringly. "And now we're on a nice, stable diet of animal blood, they've got nothing to fear."

That wasn't quite true. But he had kept all the grizzly stuff from Becca. She didn't know about Ezra's vampire friend going missing – most likely dead. She also didn't know about the growing number of cases of human on vampire hate crimes in the more densely populated areas of the UK. Gabriel had not joined Ezra again on his meetings with Silas, but Ezra would come back with grimmer reports every week. It was not helping his mood swings but at least now he felt able to come to Gabriel when stuff was playing on his mind; even if it was just to vent.

"I'm so glad Maeve is staying with her mum for a few nights so I can actually breathe. I do feel bad for her, though. All this stuff is really getting to her. Does Ezra know you're seeing me again?"

Gabriel's eyes shifted to his lap. Guilt lay heavy in the pit of his stomach. No, he hadn't told Ezra about this little meet-up. But he had been cooped up in the house for *over a month.* Surely, he was entitled to a reward? And what he doesn't know can't hurt him.

The last time he left the house was to get his monthly supply of blood from the butchers. The exchange wasn't the most pleasant of interactions. The butcher had refused to make eye contact and spoke only in angry mutterings and grumbles. It seemed to be a human condition, that when they were alone, they were mostly harmless. But get those same people in a group? They seemed to coalesce and become bodies sharing one fearless, mindless, immovable mass.

Gabriel kissed Becca on the forehead but said nothing. She closed her eyes and rested her head against his shoulder. Her hair blew across his face and he smiled at the way it tickled his nose. Underneath the smell of her vanilla shampoo was something else. It took Gabriel a second to place the familiar metallic scent but then there was no doubt about it. It was blood. Becca's blood. Now locked onto the scent, his hearing attuned to the sound of her slow, steady pulse.

This was different. Sure, Gabriel often unwittingly sensed the melodic thumps of the beating hearts about him, but to smell it? He was pretty sure Becca had no open wounds, so why was the smell of her blood invading his senses?

He shuffled on the hard bench; brows drawn in confusion. She seemed to take his movements as a way to get her attention. She lifted her head and pressed her lips to his. It was a soft, innocent kiss but it had Gabriel fighting off the urge to unsheathe his fangs. He cupped her jaw and deepened the kiss. She mewled in delighted surprise and grabbed his jacket at his chest to pull him closer.

There, alone on the park bench in the moonlight, they were like two teenagers in love that had sneaked out of their houses to be with each other because they just simply couldn't bear to be apart any longer.

Becca's heartbeat quickened. Gabriel could feel her pulse against his fingers as his hand cupped the back of her neck. The kiss became even more frivolous. She gasped and writhed against him. His skull screamed at the intense pressure of his fangs against his gums.

The whistling of the wind was gone. The scuttling of night time wildlife had disappeared. The clinking and clanking of litter ceased to exist. All Gabriel could hear was blood pumping through veins. It enveloped him like a warm, intoxicating embrace. He wanted to touch it; to taste it; to bathe in it.

Gabriel jerked back, breaking the kiss. He suddenly felt light -headed, like his brain was starved of oxygen.

"What's up?" Becca asked but her voice sounded far away.

Gabriel blinked hard and focused on her. "Nothing." He cleared his throat. "I just thought I saw something."

Becca pulled away from him, her hand clasping her coat and scarf closed around her throat. "Really, what?"

The noises around him came rushing back, like he'd peeled away the film they had been stuck behind. Becca's pulse still sounded like a war drum but he was thankful she was no longer wrapped around him.

"It's fine," he finally said, more to himself than her. But just at that moment, something did catch his eye. Down by the pond not too far from them, there was a dark figure behind a cluster of trees. It lurked from trunk to trunk in a way that didn't quite seem right. It disappeared behind a tree and Gabriel waited to see it reappear on the other side. But it didn't, and he was sure he felt an odd shift in the breeze. The type of subtle change he was all too familiar with.

More articles were cropping up about vampire bars and clubs being searched and closed down. Ezra was sitting at the dining table, phone on his lap as he skim-read his way through different online newspapers. There was no mention of *Black Velvet*, but he knew it was only a matter of time.

The back door opened and Lillian entered the kitchen, head bent down so her hair covered her face. Ezra arched an eyebrow at the curious thing she held loosely by her side.

"What's that?" he asked.

She expelled a sad sort of laugh and looked up at him. Her face looked so drawn-out and defeated. She lifted the thing and presented it on her open palm. It was a bone, like from a t bone steak. There were even still pits of meat left on it.

"Where did that come from?"

She gestured to the garden. "It just bounced off my head."

Ezra dropped his phone onto the table. "What?"

"There's loads of them in the flower bed. Bits of bone. Rubbish. Styrofoam."

Ezra looked past her through the doorway as if he could see his neighbours over their high fence. "They threw that at you?"

She nodded. "Asked if I needed it for a devil summoning." She made that sad laugh again. "We're vampires, not witches. I think they're confused."

"Did you say anything back?"

She tossed the bone into the bin with a loud thud then leaned against the kitchen counter. "I shouldn't have to."

156

"I'm sorry they're being like this. Out of everyone, I thought our neighbours would at least be civil," Ezra sighed. "Just for the amount of banana bread you've baked them alone."

Lillian crossed her arms over her chest, knuckles wrapped inside her flannel sleeves. Then Ezra saw her eyebrows lift and her eyes brighten. A silent plea that would shortly be followed by a not-so-silent one. He braced himself.

"Are you sorry enough to change your mind?" she asked, her voice soft like a lost child.

"You were just attacked putting the recycling away in your own back garden. If that's not proof enough that we need to lay low, I don't know what is."

Her nostrils flared but he could see her fighting to stay calm.

"But don't you think us hiding away is only going to make us look guilty? Like we *have* a reason to hide."

"We do have a reason. Them. Gabriel was right. Nothing we do will be make them fear us and hate us any less."

"Then we should just live our lives." Lillian pushed herself off the counter and stood tall in the centre of the room. "I'm not ashamed of who I am and I'm sick of letting those narrow-minded dicks think that I am." Her eyes shone at him. "Just let me see him."

"I'm sorry."

Her jaw jutted out and she looked away, the way Ezra did when he was irritated. Spend enough time around the same person and you start to pick up their mannerisms.

"Stop saying that when you're not. If you were, you'd do something."

Ezra leaned back in his chair, sizing her up. "You think I'm not doing anything? What, you think this is nothing to me? I am trying to protect you. The both of you."

"Oh yeah?" Her eyes found his. They were wide and alight with anger now. "And where is Gabriel, by the way?"

When Ezra pressed his lips into a thin line, she smirked wickedly.

"Exactly." She let out an angry huff and stormed out of the room. "You can't keep us to yourself forever."

Ezra closed his eyes took a deep, calming breath. *Oh, but I wish I could.*

Dalia's death, along with the carnage of the *Moonlight* raid had Ezra's nerves stretched so thin he feared they'd snap and he'd unravel like an old cardigan. If having Lillian hate him was the price to keep her safe, he was willing to pay it. At least, that's what he told himself.

When he heard Gabriel come home, he didn't have the energy to ask where he had been. He couldn't face being lied to right now. Instead, he just listened to him head upstairs and shut himself in his room.

Ever since Ezra had told Gabriel what was on his mind and his anger continued to boil just below the surface, he tended to stay out of Ezra's way. They used to be like two young bucks, butting heads and locking antlers at a moment's notice. Now, whenever a conversation began to get heated, Gabriel caved instantly. And there was this look in his eyes that read *I see you; I know you and I'm here for you.* The pity wasn't exactly welcomed, but it was better than Lillian thinking that he was being difficult for the fun of it.

Chapter 20

The vibration of Gabriel's phone jerked him out of his reverie so violently that he instinctively launched said phone across his bedroom like a grenade. He frowned at the dint it left in the plaster and got off his bed to retrieve it.

His head had been somewhere else. Not just somewhere else. Somewhere very specific. On that park bench. With Becca. With lovely, sweet Becca, who he adored so very much. And for a moment, adored so much he was almost salivating.

Her name lit up on his phone screen and he inwardly cringed.

He hadn't dreamt. He hadn't had a dream since he had been Turned. But if his unconscious mind did have the capability to conjure images and stories and fantasies, he was certain he would have endured a salacious concoction of perverted, twisted tales involving gorging on Becca's life essence.

What had gotten into him? He was an old vampire. He could control himself. It was so out of character for him to nearly give in to his hunger.

Maybe it was because he hadn't been around her in such a long time? They did used to see each other every night. He had built up a resistance to her allure. And then meeting her after a long stretch apart, he was just like an excited puppy. It was harder for him to control himself.

He was just happy to see her that was all.

Yes, that's it.

It was like when they made love. At such close proximity, when emotions were running high and pheromones were all mixed up in the action, he would get the urge to bite. But he didn't. He was respectful. He could contain himself.

He was a gentleman.

I am a gentleman, he recited, before opening the text. Or, should he say *sext.*

I am a gentleman, he reiterated as he sank back down onto his bed with a smile.

A thud brought Ezra's attention to the hallway. Shuffling footsteps followed. Curious, he got off the sofa and found Lillian supporting herself on the banister while zipping up her boot. She was wearing her trench coat. A large camel coloured suede duffel bag sat in the centre of the hallway.

"What's going on?" Ezra asked. It was the first time he had seen her in actual clothes since the attack on the house.

"I'm leaving," she replied without looking up. She slid her other foot in her boot and zipped it up. "I'm done. I tried. But I'm sick of this."

A flurry of fear danced in Ezra's gut. "*Lillian.*"

"No." She snapped, finally looking at him. Her eyes flashed a warning. "I'm moving in with Ben. Don't try to talk me out of it. I'm not a child and you are not my father. You can't *forbid* me from seeing a boy."

"I may not be your father, but I am your Maker."

"And you want me to be happy, right?"

"I want you to be alive," he gritted out.

She gestured upstairs. "Hiding out in my room isn't living. The three of us cooped up in here isn't living."

A lump lodged in his throat at the pained strain in her voice.

"We're a *family*," he almost pleaded.

"Ben is my family."

"That's not the same and you know it."

She shook her head. "Just because you don't have anyone except us doesn't mean you can keep us all to yourself."

The backs of Ezra's eyes burned and the fear inside him ignited into anger. "I had people, and they died, Lillian. There are bigger things going on right now than you not being able to see your boyfriend. Do you not get that?"

She stepped up to him. "I get it. And if this is the end of the world, I'd rather spend my last night with Ben than you."

Ezra almost choked on the lump in his throat. She sent him one last furious look before grabbing her bag and heading towards the front door.

"Don't make me command you."

The words rang out between them and seemed to linger there, suspended in the deafening silence that followed.

Slowly, Lillian turned on her heel. Ezra watched, frozen. Her eyes roved his face, trepidation drawing her brows together.

"You wouldn't." Her words were barely a whisper. It was a statement but there was a questioning lilt in her tone.

No, he wouldn't. Never in the twenty years they had been Maker and progeny had Ezra ever dirtied their bond by commanding her to do anything. They loved each other, anything that she did for him, she did willingly. It was how it was supposed to be.

But this was the first time Lillian had ever challenged his authority.

They just stared at each other for a moment. The silence was so thick between them it was stifling. Ezra felt for their bond, his touch tentative. She was there, still attached to him. He reached further, feeling along the tie as delicately as if it were a trip-wire. That's how thin their bond was now. So fragile. One sharp pluck and all could be lost.

Lillian's eyes searched his, registering his reaching. Her jaw set and Ezra flinched as she threw her walls up and blocked him out. The tie reverberated erratically but didn't snap. He wouldn't let it snap. Not ever.

"Lillian, *please.*" The pressure of tears scratched the backs of his eyes, but his voice stayed firm.

"If you command me to stay-" her voice was strong and sure as she stared him down, "I will never forgive you."

He clutched at their bond like it was a root and he was dangling from a cliff. The chasm below waited hungrily, ready to be fed. As he looked into his progeny's eyes, he saw that root splintering.

That was the cold, hard truth. She couldn't lie to him.

Ezra bowed his head in defeat. The sound of the door shutting had him flinching like it was a gunshot.

Ezra didn't know how much time had passed as he sat at the dining table, ruminating over his own failure. It wasn't until Gabriel came into the kitchen when he finally looked up from the crumb on the table, left behind by Lillian's cherry Bakewell tarts. She had obviously been baking them for Ben, he should have known. Gabriel had a dumb smile on his face that didn't need explaining.

Gabriel took out a bottle of blood from the fridge. "Want a drink?"

"Sure."

He crossed over to the hob. "Shall I make one for Lil?"

"No. She's gone."

Gabriel turned to him, pan in hand. "What?"

"I said she's gone."

"Gone? Gone where?"

Anger set Ezra's jaw. "She's just gone, okay?"

Seeming to understand Ezra's desire to drop the subject, Gabriel turned back around and started heating the blood in silence.

The smell of the warming animal blood filled the room and had Ezra falling into yet another spiral.

Did Lillian take any of the animal blood with her? Did she take her coupons? Was she going to drink from Ben? Was she going to get caught drinking from Ben?

He knew Ben lived alone but surely his neighbours knew he was dating Lillian and so would be watching him like a hawk. Will they vandalise his house, too? Or worse, will they attack her there? They would know it was just the two of them in the house and Ben wasn't a fighter.

Ezra hoped he had scared the village enough that they would stay the hell away from his progeny. Although their neighbour had thrown a bone at her head in their own back garden, so it was anyone's guess.

Ezra's stomach roiled. All this uncertainty was making him feel sick.

Gabriel passed Ezra his mug and sat opposite him at the table. Ezra watched his companion as he searched his mind for some sort of conversation. No doubt wanting to find an easy topic but coming up short. Nothing that mattered was easy anymore. But Ezra was quite thankful for the comfortable silence that followed. He was far too rattled for small talk.

When they'd finished their drinks, Gabriel washed the mugs, dried them and put them back in the cupboard. That wasn't like him. He usually just dumped them in the sink and let Ezra clean up after him. It was funny what a guilty conscience did to people.

"Right, I'm just going out for a walk. Need to get some air," said Gabriel, folding the tea towel into a neat square by the sink.

Ezra chewed his tongue and kept his face neutral but Gabriel refused to look in his direction as he left the room.

Ezra didn't know what he preferred; being lied to or told the truth. Either way, he was losing them both. At this time, he wished he could be more like Silas. To be so focused on keeping his progenies in line and safe, no matter if it meant them hating him. Maybe the fact that Ezra and Lillian

163

had been involved before he had Turned her was what had muddied the waters of their bond. A part of him still saw her as the lonely woman who would sit at the end of his bar every Friday night without fail, ordering a different type of gin every time and claiming she was being 'naughty' when asking for a third.

Things had been easy back then. Even their affair had been simple. Her husband hadn't paid enough attention to her to even notice she had been leaving the house more often, and in much finer attire.

But now, Lillian was his only progeny. His only true responsibility in this world. Gabriel's safety also constantly played on his mind, but deep-down Ezra knew he could fend for himself if necessary. Lillian, on the other hand, was still just a new-born. She needed him. But how was he supposed to make her understand that without pushing her further away and into Ben's arms?

Ben. Boring, beige, human Ben.

He had lost is progeny to *him*?

The world must truly be ending.

Chapter 21

Lillian replied to Gabriel's text just as he rounded the corner to Becca's street. *I'm staying with Ben. There's nothing you or Ezra can say that will bring me back.* The words stung but Gabriel knew better than to get mixed up in this fight. He just hoped Lillian knew what she was doing.

No pleasantries were exchanged in the hallway. As soon as Gabriel took one look at Becca in her black satin lingerie, he'd scooped her up in his arms and carried her up the stairs. Becca let herself be taken, wrapping her legs around his waist and kissing him deeply. Their texting back and forth had worked them both up into quite a heated frenzy. In the back of Gabriel's mind, he reminded himself to not get too carried away. But he had already seen her once; this won't be a repeat of the park incident. He was used to being around her now. He couldn't even smell her blood as his lips explored her neck and shoulder.

Gabriel reached her bedroom and kept hold of her as their bodies met the bed. They helped each other out of their clothes, thankful there were no buttons to slow them down. With Maeve still staying at her mothers, they had the place to themselves and took advantage of being able to be as loud as they wanted.

Right now, in this moment, Gabriel could forget about all the nastiness outside. He was with Becca. Becca, a human, who liked him just the way he was. There was no hate here. Just love and understanding.

They rolled over so Becca was over him, her smile still somehow white in the grey darkness of the room. She stroked his naked chest, admiring every bump and ridge of muscle like she was reading braille.

She flipped her long, dark hair over to one side and Gabriel's fingers dug into her thighs at the smell that hit him as powerful as a wave. Blood. Again. No vanilla this time. Just pure, undeniable, irresistible *blood.* He looked down at his hands, thinking he may have possibly scratched her and she was bleeding, but she wasn't.

Becca closed the distance between them. Now chest to chest, the aroma almost suffocated him. She started kissing his neck and his fangs sprung free. His hands slid into her hair and he tried to shift his attention to the way her silky waves wrapped and slipped through his fingers.

She bit his earlobe. He bit her back.

Blood exploded into his mouth, hot and thick and so so rich. He crushed her against him and drank, getting lost in the delirium. He'd never tasted anything like it. So fresh and real and exactly what he needed.

Becca jerked against him and the sound of her sob shocked him out of his trance. He unlatched his fangs and let go of her. She clambered off him and crawled to the bottom of the bed. Gabriel rubbed his eyes and felt the thick, pulsating veins beneath them. His head felt heavy. His body felt fried. He groaned, wiped at his mouth then looked down at his bloodstained fingers.

Blood. Becca. Becca. Blood. Oh no. Ohnononononono.

She was at the foot of the bed, staring at him with her camisole clutched to her chest. Her heart was pounding. It hammered inside his skull.

He'd bitten her. He'd bitten his Becca.

His eyes darted around the room and mapped out where all his clothes were before jumping from the bed and dressing in vampire speed. In seconds, he was fully dressed and at the door.

"I'm sorry," he rushed. She was still staring. Eyes wide and frantic. Blood was knotted in her hair. It stuck in wet swirls over the open wound on her neck. "I'm so sorry."

He headed down the stairs. Footsteps followed.

"Gabriel, wait."

He turned to see her on the landing, the camisole covering her front.

"I said I would never hurt you." He could still taste her. "I'm so sorry. I don't know what happened."

Clear tears shone in her eyes. "It's okay."

Gabriel shook his head and dropped another step. "No, it's not. I would never do that. I know I would never do that. And I did. I don't know why that happened. I need to go."

He continued down the steps.

"Gabriel, *please*."

The anguish in her plea halted him at the front door, but he couldn't face looking at her.

"It didn't hurt that bad. I'm fine. Please, don't run away. We can sort this out."

His dead heart ached.

"I'm sorry," he repeated, and left.

Gabriel charged down the streets at human speed. He was in no rush to get home and face Ezra but his mind was too frazzled to walk any slower.

What is happening to me?

Becca had seen him in the state he had never wanted her to witness. Black eyes, pulsating veins, blood covered fangs.

Her blood. On *his* fangs.

He stopped at a drain and leaned over to throw up but his body refused to expel the delicious mistake. And that's what made him feel so sick inside. Her blood had made him feel alive. And that part of him that had told him to not get carried away was now telling him to go back to her house and finish the job. Drain her dry. Do it. Do it.

Do it.

"No!" he cried out into the night, clawing at his chest and stomach, ready to tear himself in two.

This wasn't him. Gabriel was a good vampire. He was a good *person.*

"You!"

Gabriel spun around to see a woman barrelling towards him from across the road, waving her fists in the air. "You sick bastard!"

She grabbed him by the front of his jumper and shook him. Her face inches from his; her cheeks boiling red.

"You sick bastard," she wailed, eyes bloodshot. "What have you done with my daughter?!"

For a terrified moment, Gabriel thought that she was Becca's mother who had somehow tracked him down but then he recognised her. She was on the village housing committee. Her face was always on the leaflets that were shoved through their letterbox telling them to keep their front gardens clean.

"What are you-"

"My daughter!" she bellowed; her wails now becoming something almost demonic. "My Laura! I know it was you! You or one of your other sick friends!"

Gabriel grabbed her wrists and tried to prise her hands off him without hurting her.

"I'm sorry I don't know what you're-"

"You will be sorry!" Spittle flew at his face. "I know you've taken her. My Laura. She's been gone for two days!"

"I don't know anything about your daughter." This closeness was becoming a problem. The racing of her heart. Her blood was pumping so fast. So fast. So nice and fast.

With a little extra force than he was planning to use, he managed to dislodge her from his jumper and jumped backwards to distance himself. She stepped forwards to grab him again but he threw his arms up to block her.

"I'm sorry your daughter's missing but I can promise you, I have nothing to do with it."

Her eyes narrowed. "I saw you talking to her at the church party. Snooping around. You like them young and pretty, do ya? You sick freak! Give her back!"

She went to choke him but he vampire-sprinted away, down the street and all the way back home.

Gabriel sank onto his front wall in front of his house and let out a deep exhale. What the hell had that been about? He shook his head and tried to pull himself together before he headed inside.

Ezra was watching TV in the living room. Gabriel sank onto the opposite sofa noisily, making Ezra arch an eyebrow.

"Enjoy your walk?" he asked.

Gabriel furrowed his brows. "A girl's gone missing."

Ezra finally looked at him. "What?"

"I was just accosted down the road by Janet Timperly, the annoying housing committee woman. Apparently, her daughter's missing. She thought I had something to do with it."

Ezra thought about it for a moment. "That's weird. But it's probably nothing. She's a teenager, right? Probably with her boyfriend or something."

Gabriel scratched the back of his neck. This whole night had left him feeling all kinds of wrong. "Yeah, probably."

But he didn't believe it was nothing, and by the way Ezra glared at the TV, he didn't think it was nothing, either.

"I spoke to Lillian," said Gabriel, needing to shift the attention off him. Ezra noticeably tensed. "How're you doing?"

His eyes narrowed even more but they didn't leave the screen. "I just don't know how I'm supposed to get through to you guys."

"What have I done?"

Ezra grabbed the remote and forcefully turned off the TV. Then he turned to Gabriel, his pale face glowing a soft orange in the lamplight.

"I'm insulted that you think you can actually lie to me."

Gabriel lowered his gaze. Of course, Ezra knew about Becca. But he hadn't said anything about it. He hadn't chastised him for going behind his back. Nothing.

"I'm sorry," said Gabriel.

Ezra scoffed. "No, you're not. You think I'm being paranoid. You think I'm being too strict on you guys. But if I was being too strict, Lillian would be here right now and not off with her human lover-boy, blocking me out."

Ezra ran his fingers through his mussed-up hair, resting his hand at the nape of his neck. "I'm tired," he admitted, looking down at the floor. "I'm tired of being the only one here grasping that we're living through history. This time, right now, is going to change everything for us. How our discovery is dealt with will lead to either acceptance or our eradication. Our mere existence is on a knife's edge."

"I know that."

"No, I don't think you do. Because all you care about right now is hooking up with your girlfriend."

The feeling of Becca shuddering against his body as he drank from her had him running his palms down his thighs and rolling his neck. His gums ached as his fangs threatened to burst free.

He shook his head. "Well, you don't need to worry about that anymore. I'm staying here, by your side. Barricade the doors for all I care."

A silence followed as Ezra studied him. Gabriel shuffled even more uncomfortably, knowing that Ezra could read him perfectly.

"What happened?"

Gabriel shrugged, trying to act nonchalant as the image of Becca's bleeding neck goaded him to go back and finish what he started. "Just what you said, vampire and human relationships don't work."

PART III – THE MASSACRE

Chapter 22

Becca was lost in thought as she pushed open her front door and was scared half to death when Maeve jumped out from the living room and crushed her with a hug.

"Oh my God, Maeve, I didn't know you were back today," croaked Becca, her lungs being squished by her friend's stronghold.

"Did you miss me?" Maeve held her at arm's length, beaming.

"Of course."

The truth was Becca had been thankful she had left for a week. Maeve was her best friend but she could also be a bit of a burden. It was nice to have some breathing room. But after the last night with Gabriel, she was actually quite delighted to have her company again.

Maeve grabbed her hand and pulled her into the living room. "What have I missed? Tell me everything."

"Can I at least take my coat off first?" Becca laughed. Maeve let her go, allowing Becca to shed her winter coat and chuck her work bag onto the kitchen table, before joining her on the sofa.

"I don't know what to tell you, nothing's really happened." Becca shrugged, avoiding eye contact. "Grandad's doing well. He's starting to like Paul. Still hates Claudia," she laughed. "And works fine, I guess."

"And?"

"And… what?"

"What about *you*? I'm glad your grandad's alright and everything but he's not your whole life. You know that, right?"

"Of course," Becca scoffed but found Maeve looking sceptical. She shook her hair out, some of it had still been caught in her collar, "Well, nothing else has really happened."

Maeve's eyes widened and she almost lunged across the sofa to pull Becca's hair back, exposing the square plaster on the crook of her neck. Becca tried to slap her away but it was too late.

"What happened?" she gasped. Their eyes met and the disappointment shimmering in her friend's eyes made Becca feel like absolute garbage. "You saw him, didn't you? You promised you wouldn't!"

"It's not as bad as it looks." Becca smoothed her long hair back over the plaster.

Gabriel hadn't spoken to her since he had run away. He had messaged her after he left saying '*I'm so sorry. We should stop seeing each other. It's what's best for both of us.*' She had tried to call him but he ignored it. She was quite thankful he hadn't answered because, at the time, all he would have heard would have been her blubbering down the phone.

"He bit you." The words were coated with disgust. "Did you… let him?"

"No," Becca blurted. "It was an accident. He apologised. It's fine."

Maeve shook her head like a disappointed parent, and looked down at the carpet.

"My mum told me some stuff. In her town there's been some serious shit going down with all this vamp stuff. People attacking vamps. Vamps attacking people. Turns out a local DJ she went on a few dates with after my dad is one." Maeve's voice grew wet with brewing tears. "I'm scared, Becca.

I'm really scared. I wouldn't have left you if I wasn't. But my mum's all alone, I had to make sure she was okay. And, in truth, trying to keep you away from Gabriel was stressing me out. I couldn't sleep."

Becca closed her eyes, her gnawing guilt twisting up all her insides.

"You can't see him. You just can't. I don't care how nice he is to you. I don't care how nice he was to your grandad. He's no longer his care nurse so he no longer needs to be in your life. In *our* lives." Maeve looked back up at her, her eyes shining silver with unshed tears. "He's not welcome in this house, okay?"

Becca's jaw had seized shut as if her own revulsion of herself had seeped into her bones and turned her own body against her. All she could do was nod, releasing tears of her own.

"I mean it." Maeve held her gaze, looking so strong and intense it was frightening. This wasn't the Maeve Becca knew. She wasn't pretending everything was fine anymore. She wasn't making up excuses for her skittish behaviour. She was no longer drinking the pain away.

She was facing her fear head on, and if Becca wasn't in the firing line, she would have found it admirable.

"Becca, tell me he is out of our lives for good."

Becca nodded and when Maeve's eyes narrowed slightly, she cleared her throat and managed to say "I promise" in a croaky whisper.

"Aha! Thought you were going home did'ya? Well, bam!" Ezra flicked Gabriel's little red counter from the Ludo board off the coffee table.

Gabriel sent him a dry look before stretching across the floor to retrieve it.

"I hate you," he mumbled.

Ezra smiled. "So close, yet so far. Back to the start you go."

Ezra already had two of his counters safe at his base while Gabriel was still yet to get any of his counters around the whole board.

They were both sat on the floor in the living room. Other board games were scattered all around them. They had found the collection in the basement when they had first moved in, and they had stayed there untouched until a week ago.

Gabriel had stuck to his word and hadn't set foot outside of the house for the past week. After Ezra told him about Lillian's trouble with the neighbours, he hadn't even gone into the garden.

While hiding in the house together, Ezra and Gabriel had simultaneously grown together and apart. Ezra was no longer acting like a teenage on steroids and Gabriel's lovesickness had just turned into actual sickness whenever he thought about Becca. He could no longer think about her without thinking about her blood. And whenever he thought about her blood, he went lightheaded and the world tilted dangerously.

But the board games had brought out both of their competitive sides. They were both gloating winners, and sore losers, which led to a lot of arguments followed by petty sulks. But it was all superficial. These were the types of arguments they were used to. The types of arguments that their friendship had been built on. They were finally starting to fit back into their old moulds.

Sometimes ignorance was bliss.

Ezra had even stopped going to see Silas. He had confided in Gabriel and told him that he no longer felt the need to keep up with the deterioration of society. He couldn't do anything about it, and he had finally realised that. Sometimes all you could do was sit back and watch the world burn.

Ezra took a swig of his mug of blood, quickly followed by another before placing it back down next to the board. "I've still got two counters left. You've still got a chance."

"Don't patronize me." Gabriel threw the dice.

Ezra smirked. His hand was still gently clasping his mug. It had been his second of the night and it had only just passed midnight. He'd been drinking a lot more than usual. They both had. At this rate, they were going to run out before they got their new round of coupons.

Yelling from outside brought both of their attentions to the big bay window. It was still boarded up and the lack of glass combined with their vampire hearing made any little commotion outside hard to ignore.

They both shared a look before getting to their feet. Ezra pulled back the curtain at the side of the window that was still intact. There was someone on the front step of the house across the road. It looked like a tall man with dark hair, wearing jeans and a zip-up dark hoodie. He was banging on the front door incessantly. Upstairs, a couple were looking out the bedroom window, shouting at him to leave them alone. The man didn't reply, only kept pounding his fists on the door like he couldn't even hear them. He then crossed over to the downstairs window and started banging on that. The woman upstairs was clutching her husband, shaking him to go and do something.

Gabriel knew of the people at that house. The wife was a primary school teacher and the husband worked in finance. Neither of which were the type to cause any drama. They were definitely not the type of people to have people angry beating down their door.

The stranger smashed through the window and the teacher screamed in terror.

Ezra quickly moved to the door and Gabriel followed. He stayed in the doorway as Ezra stepped out onto their path. Because they both hadn't left the house in a week, they were both still dressed in their *no one is seeing me tonight* outfits. Gabriel's was a simple black t-shirt and plaid pyjama trousers, Ezra's was a baby Yoda graphic tee and gym shorts.

"Hey!" Ezra called over.

The man didn't react, but the couple upstairs saw Ezra and started banging on their window.

Oh, now they want us around, Gabriel held back a sneer.

"Hey!" Ezra called louder, walking to the end of their path. "Hey! Leave them alone!"

The man's head snapped round and Gabriel jerked back in surprise. The man's eyes were completely black like two inky orbs.

"He's a…" Gabriel's words faded when the vampire began stalking across the road, heading straight for them.

The vampire snarled; fangs fully extended. Ezra almost tripped over his own sliders as he scrambled into the house, pushing Gabriel back as he did. The two of them were in the hallway, Ezra keeping Gabriel at his back as the vampire reached their pathway.

"Hey, mate! Calm down!" Ezra threw his hands up, but the vampire continued his pursuit. The veins under his eyes were thick and purple and pulsating. It was how vampires looked when they were hungry. Extremely hungry.

The vampire entered their house. Ezra shoved Gabriel into the living room, keeping himself between him and the stranger. The stranger snarled again, saliva dripping from his fangs. He grabbed Ezra by his t-shirt and Gabriel heard Ezra's fangs unsheathe. The vampire went for Ezra's neck, ready to bite, but Ezra was quick and managed to twist out of his grip and land a punch square in his nose.

Gabriel tripped over the boxes of board games as Ezra continued to shove him further and further back, his eyes never leaving the stranger who now looked disorientated but even angrier.

Ezra grabbed one of Lillian's jade turtles and slammed it into the stranger's head. The intruder careened backwards, hit the wall, then bounced back and threw himself into Ezra. Ezra flew backwards, dragging Gabriel down with him and they both crashed into the coffee table. Its legs broke under their weight and tipped them both sideways. Ezra quickly pushed himself back to his feet while Gabriel was still coming to his senses. He felt Ezra snatch one of the broken legs from under his hip and managed to focus his eyes just in time to see Ezra smack the stranger across the face with the wooden leg, sending blood splattering up their wallpaper. Then he used the leg like a baseball bat and hit him upside the jaw. Gabriel heard the wet crunch of his fangs sinking into tongue. While the vampire still stumbled, Ezra drove the jagged end of the leg right through his chest and he erupted into a disgusting flare of bloody, vampire pulp. It splattered across the walls, the sofas, the cabinets, *Gabriel.*

Gabriel rolled to the side and heaved. Nothing came up, but he heard the soggy *plop* of chunks of vampire goop rolling off him as he moved. He wiped a slick hand down his wet face so he could see clearly. Ezra was in the centre of the room, covered in red from head to toe. The table leg was still grasped tightly in his hands. He was shaking; his eyes wide and distant.

Gabriel pushed himself up onto his elbows and in the sticky, gloopy silence of the room Gabriel could finally picture Ezra out there in the world doing Silas' bidding. This whole other side of him that Gabriel had never seen was now brought to the light.

Ezra was a killing machine. And he had just saved both of their lives.

"Ezra." Gabriel's voice sounded odd to his own ears. It was like he was reminded that he was even there in the room. Part of him had felt like an observer as Ezra had single-handedly taken care of their sudden ambush.

At the sound of his voice, Ezra jerked and dropped the table leg. It landed in a pile of goo with a wet squelch. Ezra spun and found Gabriel slowly rising to his feet. Ezra's whole face was red; making his usually deep brown eyes look like glistening honey.

"Are you okay?" He grabbed Gabriel and helped him stable himself.

"Yeah." Gabriel looked to their broken table. To the Ludo pieces mixed in with all the blood and guts. "What the hell was that about?"

"I have no idea. I thought there were no vampires here except us," said Ezra, which sparked a memory. The strange figure in the park when he had been out with Becca. Gabriel thought he had felt the wind change like how it did when vampires moved but he hadn't been certain.

"Why would he attack *us*?" Ezra continued. "He tried to *bite* me."

Gabriel turned in a slow circle, his eyes scanning over the slaughter scene which had once been their quaint living room. He lost his footing, slipping on the stringy gore. Ezra caught his arm and stabled him effortlessly with his vampire-quick reflexes.

They both stared at each other. Gabriel could see his own confused and panicked expression reflected in Ezra's huge pupils.

Gabriel's jaw tightened and his words rushed through his gritted teeth, "What the fuck is going on?"

Chapter 23

It had been a long, long time since Ezra had last killed a vampire, and he hadn't missed it one bit. Not only did the killing of his own brethren make him feel like he was chipping away at his own morality, but the mess of it all was just damn right annoying.

Ezra seethed, snarling at his own reflection in the bathroom mirror as he fought with his hair. He'd showered *twice*, and that stranger's bloody entrail-goop still refused to wash out. If this meant he had to shave his head, there would be hell to pay. His hair was a part of him. He already couldn't grow a beard, and his chest hair was non-existent. The hair on his head was all he had!

The brush snagged a knot and he angrily yanked at it until the brush pulled free. Within its cushiony bed was a slimy, red hairball like a blood clot. Ezra grimaced. At least Gabriel was taking the lead with cleaning the living room.

After about another half an hour of brushing and rinsing and brushing some more, Ezra towelled his hair so it would dry in its signature intentionally mussed up way, and redressed into a long-sleeved white t-shirt and black gym shorts. Blood had stained his towel. It joined the rest of his ruined clothes in the laundry bin.

He turned to make his way slowly down the stairs to meet Gabriel and offer help, but he barely made it past the door before a screaming in his head had him losing his balance. He felt his shoulder hit the doorframe but all of his senses were muddled. His mind was somewhere else. He couldn't see. Well, he couldn't see what his eyes were looking at. Instead, his vision tunnelled and then the deep blackness dissipated to reveal Lillian. She was on the floor; knees tucked her chest. Blood covered her pyjamas. Her hands that were clasped over her mouth were slick with it. Bloody tears were rubbed across her face. She was rocking and shaking and chanting.

I'm sorry. I'm sorry. I'm sorry. Imsorryimsorryimsorry.

The scene blinked away as quickly as it had come like a TV being unplugged. The sudden shift had Ezra feeling like he'd been yanked out from under water. He shook his head. Black dots still danced at the edges of his vision. It took a second for him to register his surrounding again.

He'd seen Lillian.

Lillian wasn't here.

Lillian was at Ben's.

Lillian was covered in blood.

Oh fuck.

Ezra bounded down the stairs, taking two at a time and slipped his socked feet back into his tossed aside sliders. In the corner of his eye, he saw Gabriel get up from scrubbing the floor.

"I have to go," Ezra rushed, waving a hand in his direction. He swung open the front door and managed to catch Gabriel call out '*Oh, just leave me to clean up after your murder, then*' before vampire-sprinting to Ben's house.

Panic clutched at his throat like two icy fists and static energy sizzled through his dead veins as he sped through the village.

Ezra knocked frantically on the door out of ingrained politeness before he kicked it open without awaiting a response, making shards of wood spit from the broken lock. The smell of fresh blood hit him so hard he felt dizzy. His fangs unsheathed instinctively.

He paused at the threshold. He silently prayed for the pushback. He had never been granted entry into this residence. If he was able to enter without resistance, it only meant one thing.

Ezra lifted his foot…

…and stepped inside.

Those icy fists squeezed tighter.

The tug of Lillian's presence along with the heady stench of blood sent Ezra straight to Ben's bedroom. He slammed the door open so hard it bounced back from the wall.

Lillian screamed from her hiding place behind the chest of drawers by the back wall. Her blue eyes shone at him like a terrified cat. Blood was matted in her hair; on her hands; on her bare feet.

Oh, Lillian, what have you done?

Spread across the double bed was Ben. Well, what was left of him.

He was facedown, arms folded beneath him and legs twisted over each other as if he'd been rolled over. A huge chunk of flesh had been ripped from the side of his throat and the torn open artery had soaked the duvet black with blood. He was dressed in a t-shirt and boxers, so the bite marks that covered his arms and legs were clearly visible. There was another chunk of him missing from his inner thigh, and the huge bite on his calf exposed pink bone.

There was so much blood it was dripping from the sheets onto the carpet. It was sprayed across the back wall and up the wardrobe. Smudged bloody handprints painted an erratic path from the bed to where Lillian now hunkered down.

Hunger stirred deep within Ezra so violently he had to lean against the doorframe as his vision swam. He could feel under his eyes ready to ripple. The veins under there wanting to bulge, and his eyes wanting to turn black. But he focused his attention on his screaming progeny and stalked towards her.

"What happened?"

She was still crying long, ragged sobs. Ezra yanked her hands from her mouth and she collapsed against his legs.

"Lillian, what the hell happened?" Anger made his words come out sharp and harsh.

"I don't know," she wailed back, clutching his leg and smearing blood over her bare thighs.

Ezra dropped to his knees, grabbed her shoulder and forced her to look at him.

"Lillian."

"I woke up and he-he was like that." Her eyes darted to the body. She shook her head and whined. "I don't remember doing it. I don't remember anything."

"But you did? It was you?" A vampire had just attacked him and Gabriel in their home. Maybe one had come and attacked Ben? Was it too much to hope?

But Lillian nodded fervently. "I can t-taste him."

That's when Ezra noticed the blood on the inside of her lips and the red stain on her teeth. He hung his head.

"And you don't remember attacking him?"

She shook her head. "Last thing I remember... we were watching a film and I was starting to feel hungry. He was going to call you to ask for the coupons and... and that's it. Everything went blank."

Ezra held her hands on her lap. They both looked down at them. His freshly cleaned and her so bloody.

"I'm gonna call Gabriel and he's gonna come and get you. Okay?"

Her grip suddenly tightened. "No. No. I can't go. I can't leave him here. Not like this. No."

"Shh." Ezra held her gaze with such intensity she stopped sobbing. "Okay. I'm going to take you downstairs and you're going to wait in the living room until Gabriel and I have this all cleaned up. Sound better?"

She gulped hard, wincing like she'd swallowed glass. She tried to shift her gaze to the body but Ezra moved his head to block her view. The wrinkles in her forehead deepened and she chewed her lip, pained, but then nodded.

Ezra helped her to her feet and kept behind her as he guided her out of the room. She kept trying to look back but Ezra's strong grip on her arms prevented her. It took them a while to get down the stairs. Lillian's body seemed to be stiff but fragile at the same time. With every step down, Ezra feared she'd shatter in his hands.

He carefully guided her down onto the sofa and when he let go, she looked to the bloody trail through the house and whimpered.

"I just don't understand what happened. I've never killed." Fresh blood tears ran down her already marred face. "I've never killed. I would never kill." Her lips quivered. "Oh, Ben."

Ezra wished he had something to say. Something to lessen the blow. But he was just as confused and bewildered as his progeny. First, the strange vampire attacked him, and now Lillian killing Ben? Nothing was making sense anymore.

After making sure Lillian would stay where she was and wait, Ezra went back into the hallway and called Gabriel.

"You gonna come back and help me finish this or what?" Gabriel said immediately upon answering the call.

"Actually, I'm going to need you over here. Now."

Gabriel paused. "Why? What's going on?"

"I'm at Ben's." Ezra looked down at his blood-stained clothes. They had been fresh just ten minutes ago. Bloody footprints had seeped into the carpeted stairs. "And bring the cleaning supplies."

"Isn't this what they do in films?" Gabriel asked as he and Ezra rolled Ben's body up in a tapestry-style rug they had found in the spare room.

Ezra fixed the rug securely with two belts, before they straightened, stepped back, and assessed their work. Ezra shrugged. "It works."

The bloody bedding was bundled in bin bags by the top of the stairs. The carpet was still a horrific mess. Gabriel had tried to clean the walls but had only managed to turn the arching blood splatters into swirling red stains.

Ezra may have killed a lot during his vampire life, but those kills had been premeditative. They had been cleverly articulated. He had always taken the necessary precautions to keep the clean up to a minimum.

He had also never killed a human. And by the state of the bedroom, they bled *a lot.*

"I still don't understand how this even happened. She loved the guy," said Gabriel, surveying the new murder scene. Two murder scenes. Two locations. One night.

"She didn't know what she was doing. Like I said, she doesn't even remember."

"Maybe it's psychological. You know, when people live through a traumatic event, the mind erases it to protect the person."

Ezra shook his head. "You saw those bite marks on him. She tore him apart. That's not Lillian." His eyes dropped to the rolled-up rug. Blood was already staining it black.

I would never kill. Her voice rang in his ears. And the way she'd looked at him when she said it. She believed it. And he believed her.

There was something definitely wrong here.

Ezra's hands turned to fists by his side. Hot anger suddenly stabbed him through his gut.

"I should have just commanded her to stay. If I'd forced her to stay with us this wouldn't have happened," he seethed.

"Then why didn't you?"

The question hadn't been accusatory but it still made him flinch.

"I didn't want to lose her." Ezra hung his head in shame. "I was protecting myself. And now she's downstairs tearing herself apart."

A heady, confusing mixture of anger, self-doubt and fear burned through him, searing through his insides like a forest fire. Ezra cried out and slammed his fist through the door in one fluid, destructive motion, the breaking of the wood giving him a flare of ugly relief.

"I'm so sick of this shit!" he screamed. Every muscle in his body felt too tightly coiled. His jaw clenched so hard his teeth were grinding together. He felt ready to split in half. To tear his own self open and rid himself of his build-up of emotions.

He was losing it. He'd let Lillian go and now Ben was dead. A strange vampire had burst into their home and attacked him and when he'd killed him, it had felt *good.* And he was so hungry now that warning images flashed in his mind of him on the floor, lapping up the blood from the carpet like a feral dog. He hadn't felt so exposed and raw and furious and terrified since the night he'd been Turned. The sudden stark reminder hit him like a blow to his brain.

"Ezra," Gabriel tried to reach out to him but he batted his hand away so violently that Gabriel stumbled into the bedpost.

Blood tears scratched the back of Ezra's eyes as he watched Gabriel watching him. His gaze was apprehensive. Then, in unison, the two of them looked down at the body between them.

"Ben's fucking dead," Ezra said, releasing an ugly sob.

"Wow. I didn't think you cared so much. I thought you hated the guy." A ghost of a smile twitched on Gabriel's lips, but Ezra shook his head, not in the mood for his friend's attempt at humour.

"He was a person. Every life matters. He mattered. He mattered to Lillian so he mattered to me."

Gabriel's face went solemn. "He mattered."

The fizzling static through his veins and the tightness in his chest cast Ezra's mind back to that night. A coldness washed through him. Not on his skin, but bone deep. The memory hadn't resurfaced since he'd buried it. Buried it so deep he hadn't told a soul. And right then, in that moment, as Ezra looked at his friend who had just helped him roll up a body, he knew he couldn't hide it any longer.

"I didn't die the same way you did."

Gabriel's brows furrowed. "What?"

"I told you I was attacked randomly in the night like you, when I was Turned. I lied."

"What are you talking about?"

Ezra ran his hand through his hair – now sticky with blood, again – and then crossed his arms tightly over his narrow chest, suddenly self-conscious.

"I tried to kill myself." He shrugged, pressing his fingers into the grooves of his ribs as if physically keeping himself together. One moment he wanted to be pulled apart, now he was determined to stay in one piece. His head was all over the place.

"A friend of mine – he died. Some illness, I dunno. Probably something easily treatable now. But he was ill and we both thought he'd get better, but he didn't. I couldn't handle it. I went to his grave. It was just some mound of dirt with this shitty little cross." His tears finally escaped. He wanted to bat them away but he was afraid of loosening his own hold on himself.

He could picture Christian on that bed, his body overheating as he shivered and mumbled incoherent fever dreams. Ezra's hands clasped around Christian's. His lips to Christian's sweat-coated knuckles. Squeezing, praying for him to squeeze back.

"I-I cut myself. I was bleeding out. I couldn't face the world without him. I wasn't ready. I was weak." He bowed his head, too ashamed to face Gabriel even though he knew he wouldn't judge. "Silas found me. He Turned me. He gave me a second chance. A reason to keep going. He taught me how to be strong."

A long, heavy silence filled the room. Ezra chewed his lip and dared to look up. Gabriel looked confused. He studied Ezra's eyes for a moment.

"Why are you telling me this now?"

"I fear I'm falling back." Ezra gulped hard. "I'm supposed to be the one making sure you and Lillian are safe. I made that my job, and I've failed. Ben's dead because of me. Someone – a human – died because of me." A hard, brittle sob escaped him so suddenly he pressed his fist against his lips to suppress it. "Silas will kill me. Or he'll make me kill Lillian."

"No." Gabriel stepped over the body and shook him. "I would never let that happen. He hasn't gotten to me after I killed my patients. He's not getting to Lillian. And he's definitely not getting to you. Not after everything you've done for him. It isn't happening." The determination in Gabriel's voice almost made Ezra smile. A warmth spread through his chest. Not anger this time. But something welcoming. Rejuvenating. "You might think it's your job to protect me, but this is a two-way street."

"Just because you don't like the thought of me being the boss," Ezra smirked.

"That's because you're not." Gabriel smiled and clipped him round the ear. "Now, quit your blubbering, we've got a body to shift."

Chapter 24

A solemn silence hung in the car as they drove to the woods on the outskirts of the village. Every time they hit a bump and their cargo shifted, Ezra winced and flicked his eyes to the rear-view mirror to check on Lillian.

Gabriel hadn't been able to move her from the sofa. But, to be honest, he hadn't tried very hard. She had this haunted look about her now. Ben's blood was still all over her pyjamas and it had dried black under her fingernails.

She had just been sitting there staring at the wall. There was this emptiness in the room like her presence didn't fill up the space she inhabited.

Gabriel had shaken her shoulder lightly and told her Ezra was going to get the car. She hadn't even registered him. Not even a blink. He could only take a few minutes of her eerie stillness before he left the room and waited out in the hallway for Ezra's return. And when he did, Ezra managed to usher her out the door – talking to her in a soft, encouraging tone like a father to a toddler.

A shiver ran up the back of Gabriel's neck as they drove through the night. He was very aware of Lillian in the backseat, even though she was as quiet as a ghost. Ezra was the opposite. He was just as quiet, but his silence had mass. It was thick and tense and roiling. His inner battle was etched within the tight lines of his face. The flex of his jaw muscle. The twitch in his eye. The quiver in his lip.

Gabriel frowned down at his lap, his mind wandering to what Ezra had said back in Ben's bedroom. Why had he waited this long to tell Gabriel how he had really been Turned? If he thought Gabriel would have thought less of him, he couldn't have been more wrong. He actually felt like he understood him so much more now. And the respect for Ezra he pretended not to have had grown. So much so he feared he'd struggle to hide it from now on.

Ezra had cared for someone so much that he hadn't been able to imagine a future without him. In all the years they had spent together, Ezra hadn't seemed to connect to anyone else to that magnitude.

And now for him to think that he was failing because he respected his and Lillian's relationship too much to command her against her will? Gabriel's dead heart ached for him. Ezra had told him that it was his job to protect the both of them. But it wasn't. He could have left Lillian just like Gabriel's Maker had left him. He was bound to her, but that bond could be severed.

And as for Gabriel? He was just a fellow vampire he'd gotten high with one night and decided he was worth keeping around. He didn't owe Gabriel anything, and yet he gave him everything.

Ezra cared. He cared *so much*.

Gabriel looked up to see that they were now surrounded by trees.

Ezra slowed the car to a crawl and parked up on a dirt path just off a narrow lane. He scanned the woods. "We're here."

Lillian stayed in the car as Gabriel and Ezra grabbed the shovels out of the boot and started digging into the compact earth in the light of the headlights. For once, Gabriel was glad to have the big clunky vehicle and the boot space it provided.

With the amount of killing Gabriel had done over the years, he was surprised that this was the first time he was digging a grave.

Ben's grave.

Poor, naïve, little Ben.

He was genuinely upset by his death. The guy had been a bit odd; he called Lillian cheesy pet names and play card games against himself. But he had been harmless and so full of bubbly optimism. Gabriel suddenly felt guilty about how he had chided him for his positive outlook as he dug deeper and deeper into the earth.

This is so fucked up.

With their vampire speed, they dug the hole relatively quickly and soon it was time to drag the body out of the boot and along the dirt. Ezra's face was pinched, his lips drawn into a grim line as the two of them released their hold of the rug and the dead weight flopped against the packed dirt beside the grave. Gabriel looked to the bare feet poking out of the end. They looked so white in the glare of the headlights.

The car door squeaked open and Lillian stepped out. New tears marred her face as she hugged herself tightly and jogged to Ezra's side. Ezra pulled her close and planted a heavy kiss on her forehead.

"Do you want to say anything?" he asked against her hair.

She pressed her bloody knuckles to her lips and shook her head. "I'm so sorry."

Without another word, Gabriel bent down and rolled the body. It hit the bottom of the grave with a definitive thud. Lillian let out a distraught mewl and pushed herself from Ezra. He reached out to grab her but she put her arms up and walked off into the trees. The two of them watched her pink flowery pyjama set fade into the night.

"Aren't you going after her?" Gabriel asked, yanking his shovel from where he'd stabbed it into the earth.

"She just needs a minute. Let's get this filled before she comes back."

They both got to work shovelling the loose soil over the body. Gabriel made sure to cover Ben's feet first so he didn't have to keep looking at them.

"Guys?" Lillian's voice travelled to them through the darkness. She appeared, looking like the lone survivor of a horror film. "I found something."

Gabriel and Ezra shared a look before dropping their shovels and following her deeper into the woods.

The three of them surrounded the body. Ezra toed its side with his foot; his once white socks now black with dirt. A testament to why people shouldn't wear sliders outside the house. It was funny how Ezra would call Ben out for doing the same thing. But apparently sliders and sandals were two *very different things*.

"So, it seems this is a popular body-dumping spot." Ezra frowned.

The body was female, late teens to early twenties, dressed in jeans and a cropped jumper. The death had been by vampire judging from the gnarly chunks missing from her middle, thighs, and neck.

Gabriel bent down and brushed the dirt and leaves to reveal her face. Two lifeless eyes stared fearfully up at him. He jerked back at the familiarity of them.

"It's Laura," he said.

"Who?" asked Ezra.

Gabriel straightened. "The girl who went missing. Her mother grabbed me in the streets. She thought I'd done something to her."

Ezra nodded in recollection. His brow furrowed deeper as he studied the body at their feet. "Are you sure you *didn't* do something to her?"

A small gasp escaped Lillian.

"What?" Gabriel was appalled. He gestured to the bloodied, violated body of the poor girl. "You think *I* did this?"

"Well, Lillian doesn't remember killing Ben."

"And it seems like you've forgotten that only hours ago, we were attacked by a vampire in our home."

"Wait, what?" Lillian shook her head, perplexed.

Ezra waved his hand towards her dismissively, not taking his accusatory glare off Gabriel. "It's fine. I killed him."

"I didn't do this!" Anger and fear coated Gabriel's throat like tar. "That other vamp probably did. Why would I? It makes no sense."

"Why would Lillian kill Ben?"

"They were living together. A vampire and a human at close proximity. Throw in feelings and passion and hunger into the mix and, like you said, it's a disaster waiting to happen." He knew he was talking too fast – like a guilty person. "Same thing happened with Becca and me."

Ezra blinked. "What?"

Gabriel gulped. *Whoops.*

"Gabriel." Ezra's tone was as firm as a grasp around the back of his neck. "What did you do to Becca?"

"Well, she's not dead, if that's what you're thinking." Gabriel's whole body tensed. He knew he was exuding defensive energy. And he was defensive. But not because he'd killed a young girl for no reason.

"*Gabriel.*"

Gabriel's eyes clenched shut. His hands turned to fists by his side. "I bit her, okay? It was an accident. We were in bed and things got out of hand. But as soon as I realised what I'd done, I left. I knew I couldn't trust myself around her. I haven't seen her since. I promise."

A heavy silence followed. All he could hear was the rustling of leaves blowing across the dirt. Gabriel opened his eyes. Both Ezra and Lillian were looking at the body, shoulders slumped and brows knitted together.

"That was the first time you'd bitten her?" asked Ezra. His tone was neutral, like a cop just gathering facts.

Gabriel nodded. "I'd never bite her. Well…" He hugged himself. "I promised I never would. I guess my promises don't mean much, huh?"

"I believe you."

Gabriel and Lillian looked to Ezra. He squatted, studying the mangled wounds on the body. They knew it was a vampire attack because they knew what they looked like, but to the untrained eye, the bites looked like the workings of a wolf.

"We're not this reckless. Our kind doesn't kill like this." He straightened and met both their eyes. "Something's not right here."

Freshly clean from the fourth shower of the night, Ezra towelled his hair and redressed into yet another t-shirt and shorts combo. He sank down onto his bed, draping his forearm over his eyes to block the streetlight that seeped through his curtains.

What a night.

Two dead bodies. Or three, if he counted the dead vamp – whose remains had completely ruined both of their sofas. All in one night. Ezra couldn't shake the feeling that something was happening. Something was changing. He'd had a similar feeling right before the *Moonlight* raid and their kind had been exposed.

The raid felt like a lifetime ago. The world had changed so much since then. Vampires were on the News every night. On the front cover of almost every newspaper. Ezra discovered that a *Vampire Court* was a very real thing that not only existed but his Maker was a member of.

Ezra thought back to the meeting with the Court and figured that when Guardian had said the humans were coming up with a solution to make their kind more humane, they were talking about their new diet. He wondered what Guardian made of this change. From what Silas had told him, it was Guardian's job to protect their kind and now that meant just nodding along to whatever the human authorities proposed. As angry as he was at the time, he was starting to see the logic behind it. Humanity needed to know that vampires weren't a threat. Which was easier said than done. And from what Ezra had witnessed tonight, the truth was plainly obvious. Vampires were a threat. Now more than ever.

A knock on his bedroom door pulled him out of his thoughts. "Yeah?"

Lillian popped her head around the door. "Hey."

Ezra rubbed his eyes and propped himself up onto his elbows. "Are you okay?"

"Can I… can I stay in here with you tonight?" She closed the door behind her. Lillian had also showered and cleaned herself up. Her hair was still wet and hung in ashy blonde waves down to her shoulders. She had swapped her flowery pyjamas for a pink and grey checked long-sleeved nightshirt. "I just… I don't want to sleep alone."

Ezra was lying on top of his duvet but he still pulled down the left side of it with a smile. "Of course, hop in."

She smiled back sheepishly and tip-toed across the room then dived into the bed and threw the duvet over herself. She shuffled around until she was in a comfortable position then peered at him from the pillow. "I know it doesn't really matter once I'm asleep, but I just don't want to lie there in that bed…" Her brows knitted, pained. "I feel so empty. I'm trying to remember what happened but at the same time, I don't want to."

"Remembering won't bring him back. It'd only make things worse."

She nodded. "But it's what I deserve. I deserve to know what I did. I shouldn't be saved from that. I killed him. I should know how it felt. I need to live with that."

"Lillian, you've been a vampire for twenty years and you hadn't ended a life until tonight."

"You still haven't. Not a human."

Ezra dropped his head onto the pillow and gazed up at the ceiling. "No, but ending a vampire's life doesn't feel any better. Even when you're told they deserve it. A life is a life."

A silence filled the room. Ezra turned to Lillian. Her eyes, shining in the darkness, shifted from side to side the way they did when she was thinking something over.

"Do you really think that vampire you killed, killed that girl?" she asked.

"It seems more than likely."

"But where did he come from? I thought we were the only ones here."

"I don't know. I thought we were, too. Maybe he was just passing through."

"And he attacked you?"

"He was at the black-eyed stage of hunger."

Lillian frowned. "I must have looked like that to Ben. He must have been so terrified."

"Let's not think about that now and try and get some sleep." Ezra crawled under the duvet and a soft giggle escaped Lillian when he wrapped his arm around her and pulled her close. She cuddled up to him and pressed her face against his chest just like she used to.

As he held her close, Ezra closed his eyes and felt for their bond. The last time he had done this it was as thin as spider's silk. Now it was strong. The strands were interlaced and woven together by trauma. He sensed her on the other end of the rope, quivering so much it sent tremors down their tie. Ezra opened himself to her and poured out an artificial sense of ease. He wished he could gift her the real thing but the truth was, he was just as fragile. But she was his progeny and she was hurting. So, he passed down the makeshift calm he created for himself down to her without a second thought.

The tremors eased. She stilled. Content for the moment, until the façade fell free.

He kissed her damp hair and she sighed softly. He thought back to how they used to sleep like this, back when she still had her humanity. Her heartbeat would quicken at their closeness. Her skin blushing under his deftly touch. Her breath tingling his neck as she trailed kisses along his throat. Her body warm against his.

Now she was still and cold, like a block of marble sculptured into the form of a forlorn woman by deftly, precise hands.

He didn't blame Lillian and Gabriel for giving into the allure of human companionship. Afterall, Ezra wasn't immune to the charm.

Playing house was all fun and games until the bitterness of reality set in.

Chapter 25

Ezra woke to Lillian still cuddled close against him. He lay there for a moment, her arm a lead weight across his chest. She looked so peaceful in the deadened state of vampire slumber. He almost wished she didn't have to wake up and face her emotions. But she was still a new-born, which meant she still had a few blissful hours of sleep before her body and mind became active again.

A twinge in his stomach and a pressure in his gums had him finally crawling out of bed a few moments later and he plodded down the stairs. To his surprise, Gabriel was sat at the table reading a dog-eared novel, so worn that the front cover was practically dust. Ezra sent him a curious look before opening the fridge and noticing that there was only one bottle of blood left. He took it out and poured around a third of it into a saucepan.

"I think it's been a decade since I last saw you reading," Ezra commented.

Behind him, Gabriel grunted. "Trust me, it's not ideal. But our living room is ruined so it's not like I can relax on the sofa and enjoy the telly."

Ezra turned on the hob. "You do have a TV in your room."

"I'm not hiding away in my room. Sucks enough being stuck in the house."

"Hey, we went on a drive last night."

"Yes, to bury a body."

Ezra frowned, stirring the heating blood. "Well, looks like we need to take a trip to the butchers anyway."

"But we've only got Lillian's coupons left. She'll have to go."

"I'll go with her." Ezra turned. The novel was now closed on the table. "Wanna join?"

"Another family outing?"

Ezra smiled. "Despite the circumstances, it's nice having us all finally on the same page. Solidarity, you know?"

"What? Now that our only forms of escaping this trio are either dead or scared of us?"

Ezra turned back to the hob. "Like I said, not ideal circumstances." *Circumstances we could have avoided if you had both just listened to me.* Ezra's jaw clenched. His fangs unsheathed and sliced through his tongue. His own blood exploded in his mouth, the taste mixing in with the smell of the heating animal blood. The world tilted and he lost his footing. A familiar fuzzy feeling pressed against the backs of his eyes. The sensation that spiked right before his eyes turned black. He steadied himself, shook his head and sheathed his fangs. The feeling lingered then faded away. He cast a look over his shoulder to see Gabriel too busy picking at the ruined spine of his novel to pay him any attention.

Ezra cleared his throat and poured his blood into a mug. "Have you drunk tonight?"

"Yeah, a little. But as soon as Lillian wakes, we should head out. Feel like I'm gonna need more to get through the night."

Ezra sank down into the chair opposite Gabriel and looked down at his mug of blood. There was still enough in the saucepan for another mugful but it definitely wasn't enough.
After finishing his mug and refilling it, Ezra stood at the threshold of their living room and cast his eyes across the mess that was still left behind. Black blood filled the grooves of their wooden flooring and he knew it was still sticky to the touch. Pink swirls stained the wallpaper. The destroyed coffee

table had been thrown into the basement, but the legs were scattered about the house – makeshift weapons for them to easily grab in case their break-in wasn't a one-time thing. Ezra smirked, remembering the meme that Mitch had showed him depicting that very scenario.

Gabriel appeared at his side, gazing at the blotchy, sticky sofas longingly. He had another mug of blood in his hand. They both sipped at their drinks.

"We'll be able to properly clean them, right?" asked Gabriel.

"They'll need a deep clean. And you know no company will set foot in our house. It'd probably be best to just throw them out." Ezra looked to their boarded-up window. "Let's just shut the door and pretend this room doesn't exist for the time being."

Ezra woke Lillian reluctantly. He had wanted to leave her alone, but the butchers would have been shut by the time she had woken up naturally. She didn't particularly seem pleased when Ezra told her they had to take a trip to get more blood, noticeably wincing at the mention of leaving the house.

Her movements were sluggish as she left his room to get dressed. Ezra made his way back downstairs and heated the remainder of the blood so he was able to pass it to her as soon as she entered the kitchen. She smiled appreciatively but there was a lack of warmth in it.

She wandered back out of the room in search of her coat and boots.

"How's she doing?" Gabriel asked lowly.

"Not great," Ezra sighed. "She stayed in my room last night. She's seemed to stop crying but she feels so… lost. I reach out to her and it's like she's been ripped full of holes."

Gabriel frowned. "I can't imagine what she's going through. If I hadn't stopped myself with Becca. If I'd…" He shook his head and folded his arms across his chest. "Just doesn't bare thinking about."

The streets were empty up until they reached the high street and even then, Ezra only noticed a few gangs of youths lingering outside a convenience store, and a woman walking her dog.

The shutter of the butchers was halfway down like last time he had visited but the three of them paused when they crossed the road and got a better look. There were dents in the metal, like someone had gone at it with a hammer.

Ezra entered first, followed closely by Gabriel and Lillian.

The shop was a mess. Ezra pressed Lillian close to his back protectively as he scanned the scene. Steaks, sausages, burgers and all other sorts of meat were strewn about the counter and the tiled floor like someone had dived over the display.

"What happened?" asked Gabriel.

Ezra felt Lillian's fingers dig into his sides through his hoodie. A fearful whimpering sound brought his attention to the back room. He followed the sound, keeping Gabriel and Lillian at his back. More whimpering sounded when he pulled back the heavy plastic sheet curtain and entered the back room. Stainless steel worktops ran along the walls. It looked like the shop had only been half cleaned. There were still lumps of offal in the sinks, and blood smeared the worktop. Blood droplets marred the floor tiles.

Ezra dabbed his finger into a tiny puddle of blood and lifted it to his nose. His fangs sprang free at the scent.

Human blood.

He sent a look to the other two and Gabriel read it perfectly. He took hold of Lillian's coat sleeve and pulled her towards him. Fear flashed in her eyes as she lost contact with Ezra. But Gabriel held her close and took a step back towards the doorway just as Ezra had mentally instructed.

Ezra closed his eyes and tuned his hearing. He listened out for the whimpering and caught a muffled voice.

"Oh, God, please. Please, save me. Please."

It was coming from the walk-in fridge.

He crossed the room and paused, his hand on the handle, before throwing open the door.

A terrified shriek caught him off guard. Behind him, he heard Lillian echo the terror.

Lyle the butcher was crouched in the corner of the fridge, a bloody cleaver clutched in both hands. He stabbed the air, his face scrunched up in anger and fear. The fizzling feeling hit the back of Ezra's eyes again. He clenched his jaw to hide his fangs.

"Come to finish me off, eh?" he bawled.

There was a messy wound on Lyle's bicep. The blood was glistening. Fresh and oozing.

Ezra lifted his palms. "We just came for the animal blood."

Lyle sneered. "They only told me about you three. Didn't tell me there were more of you. Barging in here trying to tear me to pieces. I ain't going down without a fight, I can promise you that!"

He shakily got to his feet, not taking his hands off his cleaver. He jabbed it towards Ezra some more. "C'mon then."

Ezra saw himself lunge. Saw himself tear open the man's trachea. Saw his own face red with blood.

He shook away the invading image. His hands turned into fists by his sides as his gums throbbed and jaw ached. That wasn't him. He could control himself.

"I'm not here to hurt you. Another vampire did this to you?" he asked, trying to stay calm but his hunger climbed up his throat and added a strain in his voice.

Lyle charged, a battle cry ripping from deep within as he swung the cleaver. Ezra jumped back, narrowly dodging a clean slice across his middle. He sensed commotion behind him then Lillian was at his side. Her eyes trained on Lyle's wound and the whites in them clouded over with inky black. Her fangs unsheathed. Lyle cried out again and took a swipe at her. Lillian swerved and knocked him to the ground. She went to straddle him but Ezra grabbed the hood of her coat and tore her away, throwing her into Gabriel.

"Get her outside!" Ezra cried and Gabriel obeyed, the two of them becoming a blur as they sped out of the shop.

Lyle was rolling on the floor, crying into the tiles. The cleaver had been knocked from his hands.

Ezra shook his head. The butcher wasn't his problem. He had an out of control progeny to take care of.

He turned and paused. A cold shiver ran up his spine as Silas' voice whispered through his mind.

Take care of her. You know what you have to do.

Ezra sheathed his fangs. *No. Not Lillian.*

Outside in the street, Gabriel had Lillian pinned against him with her back against his chest. She writhed in his hold, clawing at his arms to try and tear free. Her eyes were still black, hollow pits; the veins beneath them thick and pulsating.

She spotted Ezra and lashed out, fangs gnashing together like a rabid animal. Ezra froze. He'd never seen her like this before. Her mannerisms. The way she seemed to have taken a backseat in her own body and let something else, something feral and savage, take the wheel. She was acting exactly like the stranger vampire who had attacked him.

Ezra held his palms up to show her he didn't wish her any harm. She still thrashed against Gabriel. Gabriel's teeth were bared as he struggled to contain her, his fangs glinting in the light of the streetlamp.

"Lillian, it's me. It's Ezra. Your Maker." He stepped closer and she snarled, saliva dripping from her fangs.

He reached for their bond and winced at what he found. Their tie. It felt… tainted. Slick with something wrong. He tried to grab hold and slipped. He could sense her on the other end. The holes he'd found before had filled with something foul, like an infection in a wound.

Something black flashed in the corner of Ezra's eye and then Gabriel and Lillian were on the ground. Somebody was on top of Gabriel, a knee pressed hard against his ribs. Lillian crawled free and sprung to her feet.

The attacker growled and sneered and snarled as it grabbed at Gabriel's jacket. It was another vampire. This one was female with cropped black hair. Gabriel grabbed her head, hands on either side and pushed back as her fangs inched closer and closer to his throat.

A garbled cry ripped from his mouth as he pressed his thumbs into her eyes. Lillian grabbed her from behind and tore her off, throwing her against the wall of the butchers.

Everything was happening so fast. With their vampire speed, the fight was just a mess of dark, blurry shapes.

Ezra tried to focus. Tried to organise his priorities.

Lillian. Get Lillian to safety.

Ezra wrapped his arms around her from behind. He could feel all her muscles, heavy and solid like concrete. She managed to tear herself free and lunged at the stranger. And then Gabriel joined in the fray. The three vampires punched and kicked and clawed at one another. Ezra could tell Gabriel was trying to grab Lillian to pull her away but Lillian was responding with fury. The stranger, between the two, bit and clawed at whatever came her way.

It was time. He had to. There was no other way.

Ezra gulped hard. An icy sensation spread across his heart as he opened his mouth and commanded, "*Lillian, stop.*"

Lillian suddenly froze, like a toy with a dead battery. Her arms dropped to her sides and she turned to her Maker obediently, black eyes wide and expectant.

A scream ripped from the stranger. She spun from Gabriel and plunged her fist straight through Lillian's chest. Deep inside, Ezra felt their bond snap like an elastic band -a plug ripped from its socket- as Lillian exploded.

Blood and gore splattered so violently that Ezra was knocked onto the road. He lost his footing and fell. The back of his head cracked against the asphalt and everything went black for a moment.

His mind whirred. Cringing, he grabbed at the ground but ended up pawing something warm and squishy. Bile rose in his throat.

He opened his eyes to blurry redness. He groaned, swiping thick, lumpy blood from his eyes. There was a hollowness in him, so stark it made him gasp and wretch.

He pushed himself up onto his elbows, the back of his head still throbbing, and tried to focus on his surroundings.

The pavement looked like the butchers sink.

A sob lodged in the back of his throat at the sight of Lillian's coat in the centre of the gore. He turned to find Gabriel but he was gone, along with the stranger.

Ezra got to his feet and spun in a slow circle.

The street was empty.

He was alone.

And Lillian was dead.

Chapter 26

Becca hurried out the building before her manager asked her *ever-so-politely* if she could stay behind another hour. She had had to park her car down a side street that morning because their tiny company car park had been full. The light on the outside of their building had been broken for over a week and was most likely not going to get fixed anytime soon. Becca wasn't one to complain, despite being acutely aware of how her heartrate sped up as she headed through the darkness at a clipped pace. She took her car keys out of her bag and slotted them between her fingers, clutching them so hard they stabbed into her palm.

A wet, sloshing sound piqued her fear. It was coming from close by. A little voice inside her told her to the other way. But it was coming from near the exit of the car park. She could go the other way, but that meant walking all the way around the building in the pitch black.

She slowed down her pace, walking between the few parked cars that were left to be less exposed. The sound grew louder and she moved closer. Then she saw where it was coming from and froze.

Through the windows of a car, she saw the person slouched against the tyre of the next car over, eyes closed and head lolled against his shoulder. Black glistened down the man's smart, white shirt. Becca pressed her knuckles to her mouth as her body trembled with fear.

Another person was crouched beside the man. No, not a person. A vampire. Sucking on his neck. *Slurping* at the blood that trickled down his front.

Becca forced herself to keep moving, thankful for the car between them. She edged sideways, keeping her eyes on the vampire – knowing that the image would stay etched on the backs of her eyelids for the rest of her life, but too afraid to look away.

She managed to reach the exit of the carpark without catching the vampire's attention. As soon as she was on the other side of the wall, she ran, her low heels clacking against the pavement.

Her car unlocked with a button and she had never been so appreciative of the function until now. Her hands were shaking so much she knew getting her key into the slot would have been like threading a needle in an earthquake.

The roads were close to empty, as usual, so she floored the gas, not caring about the speed limit. She was about halfway home when her phone started buzzing in the passenger seat. Maeve was calling her. Her tongue pressed hard against her cheeks and she swallowed the urge to answer it. She wanted so desperately to talk to someone, but she was already swerving on the road and going fifty in a forty zone. The unanswered call was followed by a text.

'Get home. NOW.'

Becca's heart was lodged in her throat. *I'm trying.*

She parked up on the opposite side of her house and tried to run straight through the front door, but it was locked. After a cacophony of frantic knocking and trying the handle, the door swung open and Maeve dragged her inside.

A small suitcase, the one Maeve used when she would stay at her mum's, was standing by the shoe rack. Beside it was her cricket bat. For the first time in months, Maeve was wearing outside clothes. Her faux fur black coat had been thrown over a baggy t-shirt and gym leggings. Trainers were on her feet in place of her usual slipper booties.

"You won't believe what I just saw," said Becca, breathless.

"The Pattinsons are dead." Maeve grabbed her and shook her.

"What?"

"The Pattinsons. At number 23. They're dead. Found in their garden. Ripped apart." Maeve was shaking her so violently that Becca felt her neck crack. "It was vampires! There's so many of them now! They're all here!"

Becca opened her mouth to speak but found herself without words. Maeve pushed her towards the stairs. "Pack a bag, we're going. I've already packed most of the essentials."

"But, where?" Vampires were everywhere. There was nowhere *to go.*

"I don't know. I don't care. But I'm not staying here waiting to get eaten!"

Becca paused on the third step. "But Gabriel said vampires have to be invited into a place to enter."

"And you invited him here!" Maeve was red in the face; eyes bugling and neck veins throbbing.

"He didn't kill the Pattinsons." Maybe the vampire she had just seen in the carpark did. Not Gabriel. She had to believe that.

"How do you know? He bit you, didn't he? He's not the man you thought he was, Becca." Her chest was rising and falling heavily with her angry breathes. "I'm taking the lead here. Now get upstairs, grab a bag and let's go."

Becca obeyed. She had never seen Maeve so frantic before, it seemed the wise choice not to get in her way.

She threw a change of clothes, her phone charger and a pack of her grandad's medication into a backpack before heading back down the stairs. All her important things were already in her workbag.

Becca got into the driver's seat and Maeve slid into the passenger side after throwing her suitcase and bat into the backseat. Becca took one last look at their little house, wondering when she would be returning, before heading off down the road.

Beside her, Maeve was chewing her nails and breathing in short, heavy spurts. "We could go to my mum's. For now."

Becca nodded. "I just need to get my grandad first."

Maeve's eyes shot to her, alarmed.

"What?" Becca caught the look. "He's coming with us. I can't just leave him here to die."

"He's dying anyway!" Maeve exclaimed then quickly clamped her mouth shut when Becca looked at her appalled. She corrected herself, "He'll slow us down, Becks. We have to go. Now."

Becca's grip tightened on the steering wheel as she turned the corner in the direction of her grandad's bungalow. "He's coming with us."

"*Becca.*"

"I'm not gonna abandon him!"

Maeve fell silent. Becca glanced at her. She saw the understanding in her best friend's huge eyes. A lump swelled in her throat and the backs of her eyes burned with brewing tears.

Silence hung in the car for the rest of the journey, even Maeve's erratic breathing had calmed somewhat.

It wasn't until Becca parked the car outside her grandad's house when Maeve spoke again. "Do you need my help?"

Becca shook her head. "Paul will be there. He can help me get him in the car."

Maeve nodded, and as soon as Becca shut the door behind her, she reached over the seat, locked it and lodged her bat upright between her knees.

Becca rushed up the driveway and unlocked the front door. As soon as she stepped into the house she was hit with the smell. The smell everyone knew even if they couldn't place exactly *how*. It was oddly metallic. Like old pennies.

Blood.

A lot of it.

Becca charged through the corridor and nearly tripped over Paul, lying on the kitchen floor by the open back door. His head had been almost torn completely off. Bile crawled up Becca's throat at the sight of the stringy, meaty mess of exposed tendons. Blood had pooled around the body, running under the kitchen units. It had a dull, tacky look to it, like the top film of it had dried over. That meant it had been spilled a while ago.

"Grandad," Becca gasped, and shot into the living room. Her legs gave out beneath her and she dropped to the floor, the carpet burning her knees through her tights.

Her grandad was sat in his chair, arms limp on the armrests. Head back, slack-jawed. His chest had been ripped open – rib bones sticking out like red, clutching claws. His whole body was soaked in blood and when Becca's eyes trailed to the floor, she threw up onto the carpet. Some sort of organ was by the fireplace. Too chewed up and mangled for her to even identity what it was. Her grandad's heart? His liver?

A crashing sound like broken glass got her back to her feet. It sounded like it came from the front of the house.

Then there was a shrill, girlish scream.

Maeve.

Becca skidded across the bloody kitchen floor as she jumped over Paul's body and ran to her friend's aid. But it was too late.

The driver's side window had been smashed in and there were a pair of legs hanging out of the broken window. From the porch, Becca could see some sort of altercation happening in the front of the car. She saw a flash of Maeve's blonde hair and the wood of her bat jerking around awkwardly before blood jetted across the windshield.

Becca dropped down to the floor and crawled her way into her grandad's bedroom. She shuffled her way across the room and shut herself into her grandad's wardrobe.

Her pulse pounded in her ears so hard it was deafening. She covered her mouth with both hands to calm her panicked breathing. She could still smell the blood. The smell was so strong she could taste it like it painted the back of her throat.

What is happening?

What is happening?

Maeve's dead.

Maeve's dead.

Grandad's dead

What's happening?

Her grandad's dress shoes stabbed into her back. His cardigans scratched her face. She slapped them away irritably then sobbed more and curled her fingers into the clothes. They smelled like him. Like dust and cherry blossoms.

But she couldn't hide in the wardrobe forever. The house wasn't safe. If a vampire had come in and killed Paul and her grandad, that meant it was free to come back and kill her. Was that vampire Gabriel?

Her heart stuttered and bile rose in her throat again.

She had invited Gabriel into the house.

Had he killed her grandad?

No, he wouldn't.

But he said he would never bite her and he did.

Had Maeve been right all along?

And now she was dead.

Tears streamed down her face and she had to lodge the sleeve of a cardigan in her mouth to stop her raking sobs from drawing attention to her.

There was blood all over the house. And two dead bodies. She couldn't stay here. But she couldn't get in the car because… because…

She couldn't use the car.

She needed another car.

The couple at number 23 were dead. They wouldn't need their car. Was it still stealing if the owners were dead?

Carefully, Becca stood and creaked open the wardrobe door. She paused, listening. She must have been in there for a good hour. Was the vampire still lurking outside?

Was *Gabriel* still lurking outside? Or was it the vampire she had seen in the carpark?

She thought back to the legs dangling out the window but then shook her head when the memory of Maeve's blood attacked her.

Don't think about that now. Just think about surviving.

Her road wasn't too far from her grandad's. It had been the reason she had moved into it. An easy fifteen-minute walk.

An easy five- minute run?

There was only one was to find out.

As she passed her car, she couldn't stop herself from looking through the broken window. A wounded cry leapt from her mouth at the sight of Maeve in the passenger seat. Her forehead was against the dashboard like she was sleeping; her big fur coat covered her body like a blanket but it was sticky and matted. In that position, her wounds weren't visible, but the interior of the car was coated in her blood. It trickled off the dashboard and ran in streaks down the windows.

"Maeve?" Becca whimpered. Was there any chance she could be alive?

There was no answer. No stir. Tears pressed hard against the backs of Becca's eyes. She had to keep moving. Choking back a sob, she forced herself to leave her friend there, alone, like forgotten roadkill.

Her low heels clattered far too loudly against the pavement as she ran so fast her lungs felt like blocks of ice. Her skirt was hiked so far up it was practically a belt. The air ripped against the back of the throat and her thighs burned. But she kept running. And running. And running. Fear and adrenaline were an unruly combination.

By the time she reached the Pattinson's house, her heart was thumping like a war drum. She barged through their back gate and then grinded to a halt at the sight of the huge dark stain on their neatly trimmed lawn. She bent double, hands gripping her middle. For a moment she thought she was going to throw up again but her throat had been scratched raw by the wind that her body refused to bring anything up.

There was no time. There was no time to stand there staring at the way the Patterson's blood had soaked into their grass. She needed to get away. Their spare key was slotted inside a fake rock under the bush by the back door. It had been entrusted to Becca so she could water the plants when they visited their grandchildren.

Her hand was oddly steady now as she slotted the key into the lock and shouldered her way into the house. Their car keys were handily draped over a display hook marked '*keys*'.

She unlocked the car and got into the stolen vehicle. When the world was going mad, morality meant nothing. And with that thought, she started the engine and drove off into the night, completely unaware of where the hell she was heading.

Chapter 27

"Gabriel?" Ezra slammed open Gabriel's bedroom door to find the room empty. Just like the rest of

the house. After Gabriel's phone continued to ring out, Ezra had run up and down the high street

looking for him before heading home with the hope he'd gone back.

"Where the fuck are you?" Ezra hissed, his hands turning to fists by his sides. His anger was a

coating. A papier-mâché suit of armour over his gut-wrenching grief. With every step he took, he

could feel that empty space inside him where his bond to Lillian had been. It tore open wider and

wider like an open wound as time continued to tick on. Lillian had been his only progeny. She had

been the only one he had Turned since Silas had commanded him to kill his other progeny back in

1926. Ezra had been a bad teacher then and she'd gone rogue.

Ezra's nails dug into his palms. Losing Lillian to the hands of someone else didn't make it

hurt any less. Mostly because he knew deep down that, it may have been the crazy vampire that had punched her heart out of her chest, but Ezra was to blame for Lillian's death. If he hadn't commanded her to stop, she wouldn't have been defenceless to the attack.

Ezra's whole body lurched as a broken sob escaped him. He crouched down, his head in his hands, and wept. Lillian's bloody goop still covered him from head to toe, making him look like the murderer he was.

Gabriel, where are you? You can't be gone.

You just can't.

He rubbed his eyes and slapped his bloody tears away before straightening. His gaze hit the broken table leg he had propped up in the corner of the room. After what had happened to Lillian, it seemed only logical to not go running about the village unarmed.

He picked up the table leg and felt the weight of it. His insides cringed at the memory of the sound of it tearing through the strange, crazy vampire. So, he hadn't been the only one. At the time, Ezra had put the legs around the house as a precaution. A *'just in case'*. He hadn't actually thought he would feel the need to protect himself in the quaint, lazy village of Hicklesbury.

But times had changed. And he was still trying to figure out *what* had actually changed.

As he headed down the street, the table leg swinging loosely in his grip, he made a mental list of where Gabriel could be then whacked his forehead with his palm with sudden realisation. *Becca's. Of course, he's gone to see Becca.*

But he was wrong. Having never been invited into the house, all Ezra could do was hope someone answered. But after frantically knocking several times, he paused and tuned into his senses. He searched the house with his nose. There was no trace of humanity in the house. He was sure of it. For the last month, his ability to sniff out human blood had somehow become enhanced.

The last month.

He had been feeling a change within him.

The diet.

It was their diet that had changed.

They were no longer drinking human blood so their desire for it had only grown stronger.

Their hunger had somehow mutated.

Mutated into something uncontrollable.

It had taken over Lillian first because she was young. But Ezra had felt the effects. He had been drinking a lot more than usual. And the fizziness behind his eyes? That was new. Or, at least, it was happening *way* too often for his liking.

So, if Lillian had been consumed by it and Ezra was feeling the change, what did that mean for Gabriel? He was younger than Ezra.

The need to find Gabriel had just become a lot more urgent.

Ezra turned on his heels and headed back down the path. He caught sight of twitching curtains in the windows of the neighbouring houses.

He hadn't been able to figure out why Gabriel would run away after Lillian's death. It was so out of character. He wouldn't have left Ezra to grieve alone. He would be by his side like a silent, comforting statue.

But that was the point. Gabriel was acting out of character because Gabriel wasn't Gabriel anymore.

It was the early hours of the morning when Ezra finally found Gabriel. But the sight of him wasn't pretty.

He was in a precinct- a small, pedestrianised area just on the outskirts of a council estate. His dark, glistening shape was huddled over a body of a man sprawled out across the flagged stones. The horrific sucking and tearing sound of blood and flesh attacked Ezra's ears and he cringed, falling back behind the wall to a nearby grocery shop.

The light of the streetlamp reflected off the huge black puddle of blood. The stench of it was thick, like a blanket cast over the horror scene.

Three other butchered bodies littered the flagstones. Each of them dismembered and violated in their own special way.

Gabriel's hands dug and scrounged – pulling open the body at his feet and ripping out entrails. He was covered head to toe in blood. The lower half of his face and neck was caked in it, like a gruesome beard.

Ezra swallowed hard, wondering what the hell to do.

This was his friend.

This was his *best friend.*

He had to save him.

He just didn't have any fucking idea how to.

Luckily, there seemed to be no one else around. It turned out the curfew had been necessary after all. Ezra's gut twisted. *Stay inside. Stay away from the monsters lurking in the dark.*

But Ezra couldn't stay away, because this was no monster to him. Gabriel was still in there somewhere. He had to believe that. He'd already lost Lillian; he couldn't lose Gabriel, too.

Fighting back his better judgment to run away, Ezra stepped out into the open. He automatically went to raise his hands to show that he wasn't there to harm him, but then remembered the weapon he was wielding. He looked down at the table leg and his insides grew cold as he tightened his grip.

He vampire-sprinted across the precinct, weapon raised and ready to strike Gabriel over the head, but Gabriel reacted impossibly fast. He spun to his feet and slammed his whole weight into Ezra. Ezra flew through the air. He collided against the metal shutters of a shop and dropped to the ground. If he had been human, he'd have definitely suffered some broken bones and internal bleeding.

Ezra rolled onto his side, his chest aching and head spinning. But he had no time to nurse his wounds because Gabriel was gaining on him. This was the first time he had gotten a good look at him, and the sight made him falter.

Gabriel's eyes were feral and black. The veins under them coiled like angry, purple snakes. His hands were by his sides, fingers outstretching and curled like talons as blood dripped from the tips.

He was almost unrecognisable. So much so that tears pressed against the backs of Ezra's eyes as he stumbled to his feet.

Then he realised he was unarmed. The table leg had flown from his grip. Frantically, he searched the area as Gabriel kept marching towards him. Not vampire-sprinting. No, he was studying Ezra as he closed the distance between them. As if he was toying with him. Wanting this fight to be drawn out and bloody.

The table leg was by a bin on the opposite side of the precinct. Ezra vampire-sprinted over and collected it in a blur but as soon as it was back in his hands, he was knocked to the ground once more with a backhand across the face. He felt his lips split and jaw break as he slammed onto the concrete. His body convulsed and he spat up blood.

Over him, Gabriel hissed and snarled. The same feral sounds Lillian had made.

"Please," Ezra managed to croak. He found Gabriel's eyes and openly sobbed. They were so black and evil and wrong. Tears ran down Ezra's cheeks. "Please, Gabriel. It's me. It's Ezra. I'm your friend."

Gabriel stomped on his chest and Ezra heard his ribs crack. Pain bloomed, making his vision blacken around the edges. He threw up more blood and with every jerk of his broken body; he felt his ribs rake against his insides like shrapnel.

Then Gabriel was on him, knees either side of his chest. He grabbed Ezra's hair and yanked his head to the side, exposing his throat. Blood dripped from his face and fangs and splattered onto Ezra's face and neck. It landed on his busted lip and trickled down his throat.

Human blood.

Ezra's fangs sprang free as his caged hunger stirred. The tingle behind his eyes cracked like electricity. He suddenly felt revived. Gabriel's fangs sank into his neck and Ezra cried out with pain and fury as he rammed the broken table leg into Gabriel's gut.

His friend juddered above him and careened backwards, his fangs tearing from Ezra's throat. Ezra kept his bloodied grip on the table leg, flew to his feet and swung it like a baseball bat, connecting with Gabriel's skull. His friend dropped to the ground and Ezra struck him again for good measure as he bled out onto the flagstones.

Ezra lay in the dimness of his kitchen, his dying friend strewn across his lap. He stroked Gabriel's hair idly while staring up at the ceiling, willing his tears to drip back into his skull. He had slung Gabriel's body over his shoulder and vampire-sprinted his way back home –all while his own bones were still knitting themselves back together.

Gabriel was still unconscious, but he wouldn't be for long. Ezra had staked him again and kept the table leg wedged in this time. It ran straight through his middle and poked out his back. It tapped against the kitchen counter when he moved. Ezra had stripped him of his jacket in a childlike attempt to make him more comfortable. The table leg was most likely just scraping against his heart by the way he had angled it. It had been enough to subdue him and get him home. That's all Ezra had thought of. *Just get him home.* He couldn't think beyond that. Couldn't plan beyond that. Because he had no idea what to do.

Ezra inspected the ugly wound around the table leg. Gabriel's partly exposed torso was completely red with the mix of human and vampire blood. It felt tacky to the touch. The scent was cloying. Ezra's fangs remained unsheathed. He couldn't even try to pop them back into his gums. His hunger wouldn't let him. It was baiting him. It wanted him to run out of the house and start tearing people apart. But he wouldn't let it take control. He needed to focus. He needed to save Gabriel. *Somehow.*

Gabriel stirred on his lap. His head dropped back against Ezra's shoulder. His eyes flickered open and the blackness shrank away to reveal his soft brown irises the colour of autumn leaves. He blinked up at Ezra, confusion pinching his features. He tried to get up but groaned, fangs clamping on his lower lip. He looked down at the stake poking out of his torn up, bloody t-shirt.

"Ezra…" he hissed. He was mad. "What the *fuck?*"

"I had to. Lillian's already dead." Ezra's tears finally fell. "I'm not losing you to."

"You *stabbed* me?"

"I had to. You were out of control."

It was then that Gabriel seemed to notice the blood on his hands and under his nails. Shock loosened his features. He ran his tongue over his bloody fangs.

"What's going on…" his voice trailed off. He suddenly sounded so small, "Lillian." He tried to push himself off Ezra but slipped and whacked his elbow against the kitchen tiles. "I remember… She was different. She was… she attacked me."

"And you attacked me."

He blinked up at Ezra. The confusion and stark horror shining in his eyes made Ezra feel sick.

Gabriel looked down at his hands. They were shaking. "I hurt someone, didn't I?"

Ezra's jaw clenched. "You were out of control," he repeated.

"Is Becca okay?" There was a fragility in Gabriel's voice. A wetness to it.

"I don't know. I went to her house and she was gone. Her housemate, too."

Gabriel brought his shaking hands to his mouth. Ezra thought maybe he was smelling the blood to check if it was Becca's. But then he wrapped both hands around the protruding table leg. "Help me get this fucking thing out."

"I don't know if that's a good idea."

"Then, what the hell am I supposed to do? Lie here with this thing in me for the rest of my life?" he snapped.

He had a point. Usually Ezra was the smart one. He was the one who always took charge. He was the one who always knew the right thing to do, even if it did tend to land on deaf ears. But this? He was making things up as he went along.

Ezra grabbed the table leg, his hands over Gabriel's, and they both pulled. Gabriel cried out in pain. It was a guttural sound that came from the deep recesses of his being. Then he started to pant like a wild dog. Ezra heard his teeth gnash and his insides turned to ice when he felt Gabriel's body start to vibrate. And then there were the noises again. The noises he was making back at the precinct. Hissing. Snarling.

Gabriel started thrashing against him, swinging them both from side to side wildly on the floor. Ezra could no longer see his face but he was sure his eyes had turned black again.

He jerked his head to the side and sank his fangs into Ezra's bicep, the bite so deep Ezra felt the scrape of fangs against his bone.

"Gabriel, *no*," Ezra begged in a rushed whisper, now trying to tear himself free.

217

The table leg was halfway out. It was ripping through Gabriel's insides with a sickeningly wet sucking sound. As Gabriel fought, twisting and turning, the wound was getting bigger and messier. Blood poured down his stomach and over Ezra's lap. But the pain wasn't stopping him. No. The pain was making him angrier. It was making him feral.

Gabriel ripped his fangs free only to sink them back into Ezra's arm at a lower point. Tears welled in Ezra's eyes at the state of his mangled flesh. Gabriel tore at him, whipping and jerking his head like a dog with a toy.

Ezra's fangs sank into his lower lip with the strain of trying to contain him. But it was no use. Once he got free, he was going to kill again.

Ezra had to stop him.

I'm sorry. I'm sorry. There's no other way.

A cry of agony peeled out of Ezra as he repositioned the tip of the table leg still inside Gabriel and thrust it upwards towards his heart. A small yelp escaped his friend before the bloody explosion hit Ezra like a freight train, the force slamming his head back against the kitchen cabinet. Ezra was, yet again, painted by the remains of one of the few people he held dear.

Ezra's body wilted and he coughed up bits from his mouth. The bloody mess of Gabriel's death covered him entirely. Thick, warm, stew-like clumps sat on his lap and piled between his thighs. In amongst the mess of pulpy insides were the tattered leftovers of Gabriel's clothes. Ezra pulled out a strip of his t-shirt and wrapped the slick, dark material around his shaking hand.

He was in a daze. So overcome with emotions that they all seemed to cancel each other out, leaving him numb and cold. He felt as if there was a protective film around his mind as he sat there, his eyes scanning over the massacre.

Chapter 28

Ezra must have been sitting on the kitchen floor for hours. The disgusting mess that had once been his dear friend had gone cold like old meat. But he hadn't moved. Why should he? Where would he go? The world seemed to be ending and his need for self-preservation was waning. He wasn't angry anymore. He was just… tired.

The front door clattered open and the bloody, broken table leg was clutched in his bloody hands in an instant. Was it more pyscho vamps? Here to finish him off now? He bared his fangs. Well, he wasn't going to make it easy for them. No. He was going to enjoy slaughtering those fuckers.

Okay, maybe he was still angry.

Footsteps clicked leisurely across the hallway laminate and Ezra sighed with relief, dropping the table leg onto the floor with a squelch at the sight of his Maker.

Silas surveyed the bloody mess. He was dressed immaculately as always. His hands were slotted casually into the pockets of his trousers. "Who's that?" he asked, using a slight tip of his head to gesture to the entrails and tattered clothing.

A lump suddenly lodged in Ezra's throat but he managed to choke out, "*Gabriel.*"

Silas frowned and he bowed his head solemnly. "You were in a lot of pain."

Tears pressed against the back of Ezra's eyes. Silas must have felt his suffering. Maybe he had accidently sent him a Cry for Help like Lillian had when she had killed Ben.

Silas crossed over the tiles, marring his polished shoes with Gabriel's remains. He stopped by Ezra's side and Ezra dropped against him, his bloody fingers knotting into the stiff material of his trouser leg. Silas's rough hand stroked his matted hair in silence while his progeny cried.

"I didn't know what else to do," Ezra sobbed. "He was out of control. They all are." His body convulsed as all of his emotions came rushing out of him, tumbling over each other like crashing waves in a storm. "It's the diet isn't it? The animal blood? It's messed us up."

"It appears so," said Silas, the deep timbre of his voice oddly soothing. A life raft cast out into tumultuous waters. Ezra clung to it desperately. "It's happening everywhere. It must be why more of our kind have ventured around here, seeking whatever they can. Our hunger is coming back with vengeance. It's taking down all of us, one by one."

Using his Maker's trousers like a tissue, Ezra rubbed his face and looked up at him. Silas' impossibly blue eyes gazed down at him with a softness he'd never witnessed before.

"Is it going to get to us?" Ezra asked, the questioning lilt in his voice making him sound like a fearful child asking his father if the monster under the bed was really gone.

The muscles in Silas' jaw flexed. "At some point. We're older. It'll take longer. But it would be foolish for us to think we're above this. We need to take what is happening as a warning for what is in store for us."

Ezra dropped back against the kitchen cabinet, releasing his knotted grip in Silas' trousers. He gazed down at the bloody mess. The strip of Gabriel's shirt was still woven around the fingers of his other hand like a collection of rings. "What do we do?"

"We need to go somewhere secluded- with a low human population – and barricade ourselves. Separately. We can't risk us changing and killing each other."

Ezra thought about the plan. About entombing himself like Dracula. His lips uplifted and a hollow huff of a laugh escaped him. Gabriel would have loved that reference.

"So, we'd just waste away in there?" Ezra asked hollowly. Without blood, they would both go into hibernation; living corpses waiting to be released from their eternal slumber.

"It's better than wreaking havoc and taking innocent lives, isn't it?"

Ezra looked around the room, at the blood spray arching up the fridge. The clumpy goop congealed on the cabinet door handles and hardened on the dining chairs. The living room beyond the wall, shut off from visitors due to the musky, old blood smell and the sticky furniture. The bricks on the outside still stained with red painted thrown by the angry mob.

This house wasn't a home anymore. It was a place of pain and despair.

Then he looked down at himself and his whole body sagged. Gabriel's blood covered his hands like red gloves. As he stared down at them, all he could think about was all the other times his hands looked like this. All the times he'd killed. All the lives he had cruelly ripped away when following the wicked guidance of the man beside him. But despite how many blood siblings he had destroyed in the past, and his own offspring, the thought had never crossed his mind that Gabriel would follow suit.

Gabriel had been different. Yes, he had made mistakes but he was good. He had integrity. He had morals – even if they had been a little murky.

Ezra rubbed the pads of his fingers together, feeling the slimy texture of the blood.

Gabriel would be his final kill.

Stiffly, Ezra nodded, accepting the road ahead. Silas held out his hand. Ezra grabbed it and his Maker hoisted him up to his feet. Meaty clumps tumbled off him and plopped to the ground, joining the rest of the mess. A dull ache throbbed in Ezra's bones as he stretched, his joints creaking after being in the same position for far too long.

They stood facing one another. Silas appraised his progeny and flicked a bit of goop off his shoulder. Ezra's arm wounds had healed, but the memory of his friend trying to rip him apart tightened his features and sat heavily on his chest.

"Get yourself cleaned up," said Silas, gesturing upstairs. "I'll do what I can with this mess."

Ezra nodded obediently and headed for the shower, his fist curled tightly around the strip of fabric, desperate not to lose it.

It was 3am and Becca was still driving. Hicklesbury had been left behind a long time ago, along with her best friend, and her grandad. Tears welled in her eyes and she shook her head to rid them. There were more cars on the road than usual. Most likely driven by people with a similar plan as her. The plan simply being 'get away.' She wondered if any of the other drivers had a destination, or were they just as frantic and lost as she was.

But as Becca headed onto the motorway, she found herself following a route she hadn't taken in over five years. The last time she had seen her parents, it had been at Christmas. She had put on a brave face and tried her best to play along with the chitter chatter and feigned interest in her auntie's second marriage. But her mum had been quick to steer the conversation towards where Becca had moved to, and *why*, while they ate turkey and stuffing.

Her mum's mouth had that pinched uppity shape to it which only happened when she was discouraging her daughter's life choices in a fun and pleasant tone so to come across as charming and not at all inappropriate. She had talked about how Becca was insulting her father by insisting on keeping Julian in the family, after her mother had done a splendid job of cutting him out. It was as if all that hard work had been for nothing.

But Becca didn't see it that way. She didn't think that people's pasts had to define them. She had caught a glimpse of a small, proud smile on her dad's face when she had spoken up against her mum. He didn't join in the discussion, but Becca knew that he understood her; he just didn't wish to get on the wrong side of Kathy, which she couldn't blame him for.

Soon, Becca was off the motorway and back on smaller, quieter roads as she headed towards her quaint, childhood home. Empty fields gave way to empty pubs and shuttered cottages.

Her heart began to hammer and her hands were clammy against the steering wheel as she started familiarising herself with the place.

She drove past the bus stop where Charlie Matthews tried to kiss her when she was twelve. She'd ended up freaking out and tried to run all the way home, only for her to call her dad when she had gotten lost and he had spent an hour driving around the town trying to find her.

The streets were desolate, and she hoped with every fibre of her being that what was happening in Hicklesbury was an isolated situation. She didn't really understand how it could be. She didn't really understand *what* the situation was. But she just needed to remain positive.

She turned a corner and slammed her foot on the break, her heart leaping to her throat at the sight of two black figures in the middle of the road. There were streetlamps dotted about but only bright enough to give everything a weird sepia quality. She squinted, trying to make out the figures.

One was taller than the other. They both moved closer, the shorter one staying a few paces behind.

Panic set in as they veered to come up to her window. She slammed her foot on the gas but she was shaking so much, her foot jerked and the car juddered, and stalled.

The taller of the two figures was male. She could now see him clearly as he stood by her wing mirror. He had long, dark, shoulder length hair. He had a bohemian quality to him. His clothes too baggy and relaxed, his hair ruffled and unkept but in a way that seemed purposeful.

He leaned down and his pale face filled the window. Becca bit down a fearful whimper. The stranger's thin lips formed a sad sort of smile and he rapped his knuckle against the glass. She locked eyes with him and her whole body loosened.

Two soft, blue orbs gazed at her. A warmth spread across her heart as he studied her face. He was a beautiful man, with high cheekbones and skin the colour of ivory. His eyebrow quirked up in a helpless motion and he pointed downwards.

"Open your window." His voice was as decadent as dark chocolate. Rich and smooth and wistful.

She obeyed, her fingers pressing down the button before her mind even registered what she was doing. It was as if her brain had turned to mush. All she cared about was what this beautiful stranger wanted her to do.

The window rolled down silently and a hiss came from behind the stranger. A young, red-haired girl appeared from his back, fangs out and eyes as black as the night.

"*Stay back, Evie,*" snapped the man. His voice was different that time. It reverberated through the air and hung there with purpose.

The girl receded, disappearing from view.

"I need you to do something for me and my companion here," the man said to Becca, his voice returning to its succulent tone.

Becca felt her head nod and a single word tumbled from her lips, "Anything."

The beautiful stranger smiled, but it didn't quite reach his eyes. There was a flash of pain there. It was only for a second, and Becca forgot it instantly.

"I need you to take us to an address I'm going to give to you. You're going to take us down into the basement and tie us up with these." It was then that Becca noticed he had a bag slung over his narrow shoulder. The backpack dropped to the ground with a heavily clang. He bent down and she heard him unzip the bag and then growl in pain. Her hand flew to the door handle to go and aid him but he reappeared at the window. Thick leather gloves now covered his pale hands, and in them was a knot of thick, shiny chain. It draped across the sleeve of his corduroy shirt and pooled by his feet.

"You're going to wrap us both up in this, okay?"

Becca nodded.

"We don't want to hurt you. This is for your protection."

Becca nodded.

"Okay. We're going to get in the back of your car now."

Becca let them. He took the seat directly behind her, the bag lodged between his long legs, and the red-head slid in beside him. Her eyes were no longer black but she kept her gaze on her lap;

subdued. The man watched her, his eyebrows pinched with unease. He placed a hand on her lap, no longer gloved.

"We're going to make it," he said in a hushed tone. "This will work."

The girl nodded and looked out the window, but her hand blindly found his and squeezed.

"She'll be our only kill. One sacrifice to save hundreds," he spoke softly.

A spike of fear shot through Becca. Were they talking about her? As if pulled from a reverie, she regained control of her mind and went to grab the door handle. Something blurry flashed before her and she heard the click of the door lock. Her heart thudded and her eyes flickered up to the rear-view mirror. The man was sitting behind her like he hadn't even moved but the lock had been pushed down. His eyes latched onto her reflection. That warm sensation cast over her again. Entranced by his soothing gaze, she couldn't look away.

He watched her, like a wolf inspecting a fawn. A wetness swelled in her eyes, her real emotions seeping through her fake calm. "Once you've tied us up, I'm going to give you a date, it'll be in a few months' time, and you are going to come back and release us, okay?"

She nodded, letting a tear slip free. It rolled down her cheek and dropped onto her lap.

"Say you will."

"I will," she said affirmatively, her voice alien to her own ears. And just like that, Becca's fate was sealed.

Printed in Great Britain
by Amazon